Winter
Nights

BOOK YOUR PLACE ON OUR WEBSITE AND MAKE THE READING CONNECTION!

We've created a customized website just for our very special readers, where you can get the inside scoop on everything that's going on with Zebra, Pinnacle and Kensington books.

When you come online, you'll have the exciting opportunity to:

- View covers of upcoming books
- Read sample chapters
- Learn about our future publishing schedule (listed by publication month *and author*)
- Find out when your favorite authors will be visiting a city near you
- Search for and order backlist books from our online catalog
- Check out author bios and background information
- Send e-mail to your favorite authors
- Meet the Kensington staff online
- Join us in weekly chats with authors, readers and other guests
- Get writing guidelines
- AND MUCH MORE!

**Visit our website at
http://www.kensingtonbooks.com**

Winter

Nights

BY

FRANCIS RAY

SHIRLEY HAILSTOCK

DONNA HILL

BET Publications, LLC
www.msbet.com
www.arabesquebooks.com

ARABESQUE BOOKS are published by

BET Publications, LLC
c/o BET BOOKS
One BET Plaza
1900 W Place NE
Washington, D.C. 20018-1211

First Hardcover Printing: December, 1998
First BET Printing: November, 1999
10 9 8 7 6 5 4 3 2

Printed in the United States of America

Contents

Until Christmas

BY
FRANCIS RAY

Dear Readers,

I love Christmas. I love the sights, the sounds, the foods, even the hectic shopping and frantic search for just the right gift. It's a special time with friends and family, a time when wishes come true and miracles happen.

My earliest Christmas memory is of the kitchen filled with mouthwatering aromas, my sisters and brother laughing and kidding around, Mama baking candy cane cookies, and Daddy watching us with a proud, indulgent smile on his face. Now, I have a family of my own and the collection of wonderful memories continues.

For me, Christmas will always be a family time. In writing *Until Christmas*, I wanted to portray the same type of strong, loving father I was privileged to grow up with. My father was an honest, hardworking man who constantly put his wife and children before his own comfort and pleasure. We never doubted his love, his support, his understanding, his ability to keep us safe and happy. I strongly believe that for every good man, there is that one unique woman who will make his life complete. My father had my mother, for Ethan Rawlings there is Samantha Clark.

During this holiday season and in the months to come, I wish you and yours a wonderful life filled with unconditional love and boundless miracles. Always be receptive to both and thankful when it happens.

Happy Holidays,
Francis Ray

Chapter One

"**P**rincipal Rawlings, Miss Clark is here to see you," Mrs. Lewis, his secretary, informed him on the phone.

"Send her in," Ethan Rawlings said.

A cursory glance around his office told him it wasn't too bad. The manuals were gone from the small sofa. The top of his mahogany desk was visible. He didn't want his potentially new housekeeper to bail before he had a chance to hire her.

Heaven knew, he and the boys needed someone dependable and competent after the last two. Their present housekeeper constantly complained about her bad back and hadn't smiled since she accepted the job six weeks ago.

But from Samantha Clark's outstanding references, and their two brief telephone conversations, she was healthy, dependable, and there was a cheeriness in her voice that often bubbled into laughter. The law of averages deemed he and his sons were due for a break.

At the brief knock on his office door, he stood. Straightening his tie, he circled his desk. "Come in."

Mrs. Lewis opened the door, then stepped aside for Samantha Clark. Ethan stopped in midstride. All he could think of was, *housekeepers didn't look like her.*

He noticed her eyes first. The color of expensive cognac with enough kick to knock a man on his back if he wasn't careful. And exactly where he wanted to be if she were standing over him. The lashes were lush; the eyebrows bold. Surprisingly the nose was dainty, and a man might breathe easier until he saw the lush, wicked mouth.

Her mocha-hued face was framed by a wealth of wavy black curls that brushed the black velvet collar of her bold houndstooth check jacket. The French cuffs of her white blouse looked casual and at the same time classy and elegant with the long black skirt. She moved with a fluid, supple grace.

She was temptation with a capital T.

"Dr. Rawlings, or do I call you Principal Rawlings?" Samantha asked, a smile deepening the unforeseen dimples in her smooth oval face.

All Ethan could think of was that his sons had dimples when they were babies, and everyone always said they were cute. Samantha's were lethal.

"You should hear some of the things the students call him behind his back," Mrs. Lewis interjected playfully.

Ethan flashed his secretary a look of thanks and saw her mouth twitch knowingly. He didn't mind. Since he had started in July, and it was now the first week in November, she'd yet to betray a confidence. No boss in their right mind would keep a secretary who couldn't keep her own counsel. Just like no widowed single father and newly appointed high school principal would hire Samantha Clark for his housekeeper.

"Ethan would be fine," he finally said and shook the small, delicate hand extended toward him. "Please have a seat."

"Thank you."

"I'll close the door on my way out."

"Mrs. Lewis?"

His secretary turned with the doorknob in her hand, an eyebrow raised in query.

Ethan knew that look. It had bolstered him through a conference with more than one irate parent or upset teacher or indignant student. One of the best decisions since returning to Oakville to take the position as principal was to keep Deloris Lewis on as his secretary.

"Please hold all calls."

"Yes, sir." The door closed.

Ethan started for his high-back chair. What was the matter with him? As a matter of routine he handled hormone-driven, rule-testing students every day in his school of 575 teenagers. He could handle Samantha Clark.

Her perfume caught him as he passed. Something exotic and fragrant that made a man want to wallow in it, and the woman wearing it.

Tugging his tie loose, he retook his seat and shifted some papers on his desk before lifting his gaze. Those light brown eyes stared wearily back at him.

"You're younger than I expected."

She laughed, a soft musical sound that sent a punch directly to his solar plexus. "You never asked my age when we talked on the phone, and I took it that it didn't matter."

"How old are you?"

"Twenty-seven."

"You don't look as old as some of my students."

"That's because they're trying to look older, whereas I know that old age is edging up on me each day."

"Old age?"

"Thirty," she answered with a sigh.

Ethan smiled at the disgruntled expression on her face, which made her look barely old enough to be of legal drinking age. "I'm thirty-seven."

She waved her hand dismissively. "Men don't age, they

become seasoned. Only women grow older. For that reason half the women I know won't admit their age."

He chuckled, knowing she was right. His own mother had stopped "aging" at sixty and refused to have more than one candle on her recent birthday cake.

Samantha relaxed back into the burgundy armchair. "So what else would you like to know?"

Ethan was the one to sigh this time. Leaning forward, he placed his arms atop the desk. "I'm still trying to get past how young you are. My sons need someone mature to take care of them."

"You've checked out my references, I'm sure. Before I was hostess of the Oak Tree Inn, I was an accountant for a large manufacturing firm in Denver for four years." She shook her head. "I didn't like the snow or the backbiting office atmosphere, so I searched the Internet until I found something I did like."

"Being the hostess of a bed-and-breakfast inn in a small town?" he questioned.

"Occasionally during the summer when I was growing up, my four younger sisters and I would spend the summer with our grandmother. They hated it, but I loved the slow-paced living in the small town, the friendliness of the people."

She leaned forward.

"I guess I'm like my grandmother, who was a nurturer. The more people she had to care for and fuss over, the happier she was." Samantha's lips curved into a smile at the warm memory. "Housekeeping and cooking for others is not a chore for me when it's appreciated. It's something I love, and since I'm single, it's the next best thing to having my own family."

The walkie-talkie on his desk started to make static noises. "Excuse me." Ethan's long-fingered hand closed around the instrument. "Principal Rawlings."

An out of breath male voice said, "We have a code one emergency in the boys' locker room."

"I'm on my way," he answered, already standing. "Please excuse me. We'll have to finish this later."

Samantha watched him move quickly out the door. She followed, noticing his athletic build and long graceful strides. He paused only long enough to repeat the message to his secretary, then he was moving again.

"He certainly moves fast," she idly commented.

"And looks good while he's doing it," said Mrs. Lewis.

Surprised by the comment, Samantha glanced around at the attractive, auburn-haired woman, who appeared to be in her early forties. Humor sparkled in her brown eyes. "I may be happily married, but I can appreciate a good-looking man."

"You won't get an argument from me." Samantha's gaze went back to Ethan and watched him disappear down a hallway. He had a hard lean body that the well-cut pin-striped suit he wore accentuated perfectly. He also had a mouth that was pure sin.

She shivered. Ethan Rawlings wasn't what she expected either. And she couldn't be happier.

When thirty-seven minutes had passed and Ethan hadn't returned, Samantha wasn't sure what she should do. He had had to reschedule two previous appointments already. She needed to know today if she had the job.

There weren't many choices in a farming town of twenty-three thousand. Oakville, Texas, had become her home, and she intended to stay. Call it pride or whatever, but she wanted a job before it was too widely circulated that the new owners of the Oak Tree Inn hadn't wanted to keep her. They hadn't even given her the courtesy of letting her interview for the position. That hurt. A lot.

She had two interviews scheduled for Monday, but working at Super K as an evening shift manager or at the First National Bank in accounts receivable didn't appeal to her. Unless she were starving. Since she received her severance check from the B&B, she hadn't reached that point. And she didn't intend to.

She had some savings, but she didn't want to start dipping into it. Once she started, it would be gone before she knew it and she'd have to take any job no matter how unhappy it made her. She needed the housekeeping job.

"Does he usually bring students back to his office when there is a problem?" she asked his secretary.

"Not if he can help it," Mrs. Lewis answered. "He knows most students and parents equate going to the principal's office as something undesirable and have their defenses already up. He could be anywhere on campus where he and the students involved can talk quietly and blow off steam."

Samantha had heard a lot of glowing comments about the hometown boy returning as a man to be the first black principal of the town's only high school. His outstanding reputation was one of the reasons she considered being his housekeeper. Single women couldn't be too careful. "Sounds like he cares."

"He does. The school board picked a winner when they hired Principal Rawlings."

"Now if I can just get him to hire me," Samantha said, a note of worry in her voice.

"With your reputation at the Oak Tree Inn for pampering the guests and your fantastic cooking, I'd hire you myself if I had the money. One thing for sure, Principal Rawlings will do what's best for his sons." The secretary picked up a pen and began scribbling on a white notepad.

"School will be out in less than thirty minutes and getting out of here to the highway will be maddening. Why don't you go on out to his place, meet the boys, and I'll try to get him out of here on time for once." Tearing off the sheet, she handed it to Samantha. "Since today is Friday, I might get lucky."

"Thanks." Samantha looked at the address in surprise. "I've heard about Duck Creek."

"There are only twelve homes in the subdivision. Each one is gorgeous and sits on an acre or half-acre lot. There are two families of ducks out there, and the creek runs through the back of each lot."

"It sounds perfect for a family," Samantha said. One day she hoped to have such a place for her own family.

"Ethan does all right by his boys." The telephone had the secretary moving in that direction. "Don't let all the street names ending in creek, throw you. There's a guard on duty at the entrance, and he'll point you in the right direction. You'll love the place and the boys."

Samantha slowly cruised by the Rawlings home for the second time and turned into the paved driveway. Despite the guard's instructions, she had bypassed it the first time. She didn't consider that her fault.

The ranch-style house sat at least a hundred and fifty feet from the two-lane road. Reading the house numbers was impossible from that distance. Since the cluster mailboxes were located in the front of the subdivision, and there were no curb numbers, you had to go by landmarks. She hadn't seen the flagpole until she had passed the house.

What a house it was, white brick with lemon-yellow trim on the eaves and shutters. Lush green ornamental shrubbery hugged the perimeter with dramatic impact on each side of the front. Grass so green it looked artificial continued around the back of the house before gently sloping toward the creek. And not a duck in sight.

Two immense oaks stood guard in front as they apparently had since long before the house had been built. English ivy covered the base of one tree and was sneaking up the trunk of the other.

Parking her car by the walkway leading to the front door, Samantha got out of her Volkswagen Beetle. Idly she wondered if Dr. Raw—Ethan knew what a headache the ivy could be later on. It was pretty as long as—

"Look out!"

Samantha quickly turned at the frantic sound, saw a white blur hurtling toward her face, and instinctively lifted and cupped her hands. A softball smacked in the center. Hard.

"You caught it!"

"Wow! What a great catch."

"Do you live near here?"

"Do you have any children who can catch like you?"

Her heart out of her throat, her lungs functioning normally again, she glanced down to see two boys staring worshipfully up at her—then did a double take.

Apparently used to the reaction, the one with the bat cheerfully said, "We're twins."

"Yeah, twins," added the one carrying a catcher's mitt.

Samantha couldn't help looking at each young boy again. They were as alike as the proverbial two peas in a pod: black hair, thick-lashed black eyes, robust cheeks. They were dressed in jeans that had seen better days and tennis shoes that had seen worse. Only their blue and white NFL jerseys looked reasonably new. Each had a different number.

"I think this belongs to you," she said, handing the ball to the twin wearing the catcher's mitt with number eighteen on his jersey.

He tucked his head a second, then took the ball. "I'm sorry I didn't catch the ball. I didn't know you were there."

She was charmed. She lifted her hand to place it on his head, then stuck it in the pocket of her skirt instead. He'd probably gag and lose all respect for her if she did that. "No harm done. You're a gentleman for apologizing. Not many people do that these days."

"Dad says the same thing," announced number twelve.

"Are you Principal Rawlings' sons?"

"We sure are. I'm Alan, the oldest." Tucking the bat between his elbow and side, he presented his grimy hand. Samantha took it without hesitation.

"I'm Alex, and he's only five minutes older." Another grubby handshake.

Samantha smiled at them, remembering the good-natured bantering she had carried on with her four younger sisters while she was growing up. "I'm Samantha Clark."

Their eyes lit up again. They glanced at each other, then back at her. Alan spoke first. "You're the new lady."

"If by that you mean the new housekeeper, I'm not sure," she answered honestly. "There was some sort of emergency, and your father had to leave. The secretary suggested I come out here to meet you and wait."

"Way cool," Alan said happily, then frowned. "You can cook, can't you?"

"You name it and I can cook it."

"How do you feel about barking dogs?" Alex asked.

"Very liberal. I like dogs."

Alan folded his arms as if he were about to give her the final test. "Gerbils?"

Samantha took the question as seriously as it was given. "In general or are we talking about a particular gerbil?"

"Pete has gotten out only once," Alex said, his gaze anxious. "I didn't close the cage and he got out. Mrs. Owens, the housekeeper, freaked and started running through the house. We had just brought **in Max**, our German shepherd, and he thought it was a game and he started after her." The brothers shared another look.

"Boy, was Dad mad."

"I'm sure he didn't stay upset at you for long," Samantha said, although she felt Ethan had overreacted a bit. Accidents happened.

"Not at us," Alan clarified. "When we finally caught Max, Mrs. Owens was so mad she took off and left us by ourselves."

"We tried to tell Dad it was no big deal since we're eight and in the third grade." Alex looked indignant. "He thinks we're still babies."

Samantha couldn't help it. She placed a hand on each of their shoulders. "Parents worry because they love you. Always remember that."

"Who are you?"

Samantha glanced around at the sharp tone to see a rotund woman wearing a stiffly starched cotton print dress. Peeking from beneath the ankle-length hem were light brown support hose and thick-soled white shoes.

"I'm sorry. I should have come inside to meet you." Removing her hands from the boys' shoulders, she stepped forward. "I'm Samantha Clark. I've come to interview for the position of housekeeper."

"Praise be." The woman disappeared into the house only to come out seconds later, moving at a fast clip. "Stew meat is cooking. The house keys are on the kitchen table."

"Wait!" Samantha cried. The woman kept on going around the side of the house. "Where's she going?"

"Out of our lives, I hope," Alan said.

"The garage," Alex interpreted, folding his arms.

An older-model Chevrolet Impala came barreling around the house. Instinctively Samantha grabbed the boys and stepped back.

The faded, dented automobile stopped abruptly. "Tell

Principal Rawlings I stayed until I was relieved and to mail my check. I'm tired of caring for creatures and trying to keep up with those two. Way tired.''

Samantha watched helplessly as the Chevy disappeared. What was she going to tell Ethan?

Chapter Two

With the boys at her elbows, she phoned the high school. Principal Rawlings wasn't in. Calmly she related the abrupt departure of the housekeeper to his secretary. Beneath her cool exterior Samantha was livid. The woman hadn't known a thing about her, and she had left two small children in her care.

If Ethan had been mad the first time, he would be boiling now. The only problem was, Samantha thought some of it might spill over on her.

"Of course I'll stay with Alan and Alex. Good-bye, Mrs. Lewis." Hanging up, she turned to the twins, thankful they didn't seem the least bit disturbed that they had been left in the care of a stranger.

"Why don't we see what's cooking?" Samantha suggested.

"Whatever it is, it won't taste good," Alan said, his arms folded around his bat.

"The kitchen is this way," Alex said, tentatively taking her hand, his black eyes studying her.

She squeezed it. "I won't leave until your father comes. That's a promise."

"He's going to be steamed again." Alan trailed behind them through the den and into the kitchen. "She's the third one since we moved from Philadelphia in June."

Samantha heard the worry in his voice and curved her arm around his shoulder. "None of that is your fault, and your father knows that. He . . . my goodness. Why is everything on the counters?"

"Mrs. Dawkins had a bad back and she couldn't stoop or reach high, so she kept everything on the countertop." Alex leaned against the island counter. "Drove Dad crazy, but we couldn't find anyone else."

"You've found someone now." Samantha opened the light oak cabinet and began putting things back. "Would you boys like a lemon cake or apple pie for dessert?"

Alan straightened. "None of the other ladies could cook good stuff. We had to go to Grandma's."

With a smile, Samantha took the can of asparagus from Alex. She had already decided he was the quiet one. "I told you, you name it and I can cook it. But I could use some help putting these things back."

Alex picked up a saucepan, opened a lower cabinet, and stuck it in the first empty space. Alan did the same with a bowl. Samantha had a pretty good idea what their room looked like.

"House rule. Wash your hands when you come back inside from playing."

"They aren't that dirty." This from the outspoken Alan.

"House rule. No dirt. Now move. I'd hate not to have time to cook dessert."

Alex moved first with Alan on his heels. Midway across the den, Alex stopped and looked back at her, uncertainty and fear clear in his black eyes that were so like his father's.

She conceded her heart to him. "I'll be here when you get back. You'll learn I never break a promise."

"You think Dad will keep you?" he asked, still troubled.

"I hope so, Alex, I sincerely hope so."

Ethan was livid. He slowed down in his Jeep Cherokee just enough to make the sharp curve on his street. He had specifically told Mrs. Dawkins she was never to leave the boys at the house unless he was there. Alan wouldn't mind, but Alex tended to be shy and sensitive and took things more to heart. If his children were upset, there'd be hell to pay.

Ethan wheeled into the driveway and came to an abrupt halt. Alex was chasing Samantha with a softball in his hand. Both were laughing while Alan rooted them on. His youngest caught her a foot shy of Alan.

"You're out! You're out!"

Stepping on the gas, he pulled to a stop beside the jaunty red Volkswagen with its top down and got out. It didn't miss his attention that his sons stood easily by Samantha's side. Neither had cared for the other women. They always did have good taste.

"Hi, Dad."

"Hi, Dad."

"Hello, boys. You all right?"

"Yes, sir," Alex answered. "Sam took good care of us."

"Sam." Ethan look at Samantha. It certainly hadn't taken her long to break through his youngest son's shyness. "I'm sorry about what happened, Samantha. Mrs. Dawkins will hear from me."

"After the initial shock, everything was all right." Samantha glanced down at the boys, glad for a moment to compose herself. Ethan Rawlings was a forceful and handsome man. "We managed to cook and have time to play."

"She's great, Dad. She can catch, likes gerbils, and unlike Mrs. Owens, she didn't get mad when Max chased her. Not even when he tore her skirt," Alex said in an excited rush.

"What?" Ethan shouted, his gaze running over her again.

"We were playing in the back while the stew was cooking, and Max got into the act and caught her skirt." Alan explained, not liking being left out of the conversation. "She fixed it with some masking tape. You can't even tell. That's why we're playing in the front."

Ethan rubbed his hand over his face. What worse could happen? He didn't have to worry about not hiring her, she was probably more than ready to leave. Although he knew it was for the best, he didn't have to be happy about it. "I'll replace the skirt of course."

"Thank you," she said. "I better get back to the kitchen. The cake is probably cool enough to ice. Any volunteers to help?"

"Me."

"Me."

"I thought so." Their hands easily slipped into hers. "Dinner will be ready in twenty minutes. And your parents are coming."

"My parents?"

"When I couldn't reach you, I thought the boys might want to be reassured by someone they trusted. Since they had mentioned their grandparents, I called." She smiled. "We've talked with them twice."

"Thank you."

"My pleasure. Now if you'll excuse me, we have a cake to ice."

His parents liked her immediately. She was vivacious and beautiful, but more than that, she genuinely appeared concerned for Alan and Alex. When she said she had cooked a huge pot of beef stew, his parents readily decided to stay for dinner. After asking if they wanted anything and receiving a negative reply, she had gone back to the kitchen, his sons following closely.

Betty Rawlings, sixtyish, slender, and six months into retirement from the Oakville School District after thirty-five years as an honors English teacher, watched them leave with shrewd eyes. "You finally got lucky with a house-keeper."

Ethan rubbed the back of his neck. "I know the boys have attached themselves to her like magnets, but I can't hire her."

"What?" His mother whirled on him. Even as a grown man, the annoyance in her black eyes made him uneasy. Growing up, he and his younger brothers had known that, unlike their softhearted father, their mother wasn't a push-over. You definitely didn't want to get on her bad side.

She ruled their home with unconditional love and a wooden spoon she called Justice. "Why would you do an idiotic thing like that? Do you know who you have in your kitchen?"

"A very attractive young woman, and I'm a single father and the new principal of the high school," Ethan repeated the same reason to her he kept repeating to himself.

"Poo." Betty waved his words aside. "Samantha has a reputation for being a gracious hostess and an excellent cook. Townspeople have gone to the Oak Tree Inn just to taste her cuisine and be pampered." She glanced toward the laughter coming from the kitchen. "Sounds like she's making Alan and Alex feel special already."

Ethan folded his arms. "They'd be that way with anyone after Mrs. Dawkins."

"I seem to remember they didn't like the other two, either, or the couple of women you had in Philadelphia," commented Richard Rawlings, his father, sixty-nine, stout, and recently retired after forty-one years as a mail carrier.

He might be softhearted, but he had always stood firmly behind his wife's decisions.

"They weren't beautiful," Ethan grumbled.

"Now I see the real problem." His mother tilted her head of black hair streaked with gray to one side, a smile on her lips.

Ethan's arms came swiftly to his sides. "Oh, no you don't. You know how gossip gets started in a small town. I don't want that for the boys or myself."

"Stop worrying then," his mother advised him. "Some of the wealthiest people in the state have stayed at the Oak Tree Inn, and it's because of Samantha Clark."

Ethan didn't doubt his mother was up on the latest happenings in town, but there remained one irrefutable fact. "If she were so fantastic, the new owners would have kept her on."

"Their loss is your and the twins' gain," Betty said with calm assurance.

Richard Rawlings sniffed the air. "Something tells me you're going to gain a great deal."

After two bowls of beef stew, three corn bread muffins, and a huge slice of lemon cake, Ethan was willing to concede his father might have been right. His mother was a pretty good cook, but he had to admit, if he'd tasted better, he didn't remember.

From all the sighs and slumping back in their chairs, everyone at the dining-room table agreed with him. And to his surprise, no green peas and carrots were littered around his sons' plates.

"Would anyone care for more lemon cake or coffee perhaps?" Samantha asked, glancing around the dining-room table.

Richard shook his full head of gray hair. "Maybe a wheel-barrow to roll me to the car."

"Make that two," Betty added.

Samantha dimpled a smile. "I'm glad you enjoyed the meal."

"I scraped and chopped the carrots."

"I peeled and chopped the potatoes."

She sent both boys sitting on either side of her a warm look. "I'd never forget my helpers. I couldn't have cooked the meal without you. Thanks for making me feel welcome."

"We want you to stay forever, isn't that right, Dad?"

All eyes turned to Ethan, but the ones he felt the most were Samantha's, golden-bronzed and filled with endless possibilities . . . none of which a single father should be thinking of with his children and parents watching him.

"A young woman like Samantha might find it dull and tedious caring for us after the excitement of the inn," he ventured carefully, not glancing at his mother. "I hadn't thought of that."

Alex frowned. "We can be exciting."

"Yeah," piped up Alan.

"Today had more excitement for me than anything at the inn," Samantha said. "Believe me, I'm looking forward to caring for three people instead of upwards of twelve. It'll give me a little more time to work on a special project I've wanted to begin for a long time."

"If you have something else in mind, I won't hold you back." Even as he said the words, he regretted having to say them.

"I haven't. The special project is writing down my grandmother's recipes for a cookbook. I told you whenever you wanted or needed me, I'd be available—and I meant it."

For some reason, the softly spoken words and steady gaze sent another punch to his midsection. She had him as mixed up as he'd ever been. She definitely had to go. "If everyone will excuse us, I need to talk to Samantha in private." He stood. "We can use my study."

Realizing she was about to be fired before she was hired, Samantha slowly pushed to her feet. "Of course."

Alan and Alex jumped up, each taking her hand. They knew when their father frowned and had wrinkles between his eyebrows, he was unhappy about something. They stepped closer to Samantha.

"She likes animals."

"She knows how to bake cookies and cupcakes, and the Thanksgiving party is coming up."

"She doesn't have a problem with her back."

"She laughs a lot."

"She—"

Ethan held up his hand as Alex opened his mouth again. He studied the worried expression of his sons, then the woman standing between them. Although they were holding her hand, he somehow knew she was the one offering reassurance.

In his memory they had never taken to anyone so quickly. Leaving their friends in Philadelphia hadn't been easy for them. Nor was his erratic schedule. More than anything he wanted stability and love in their lives. That desire was the main reason he'd left a higher-paying job and moved back to Oakville. He wasn't about to ruin that for them because he had the hots for Samantha.

"Ethan."

Slowly he met his mother's gaze, then followed her slight nod toward his sons, their expressions now full of hope. It hadn't taken them long to learn that whenever Grandma said something, he listened. Rightly so.

He had never made a mistake by following her advice. However, this time she didn't have all the facts. Yet they both wanted what was best for Alan and Alex.

Considering that, there was only one choice to make. "We'll give it a try until Christmas."

Alan and Alex started yelling. She bent to hug them. "Thanks, fellows. You're quite a team."

"That's what Dad always says."

She regarded Ethan over their shoulders. "Thank you."

"I want to do what's best for my sons." His tone was brisk.

"You can trust me to take care of them."

But could he trust himself? "We'll see."

"You made the right decision, Ethan." His father's chair scooted across the carpeted floor. "Come on, Betty. We better get home if we're going to get an early start in the morning."

"Where are you going?" Samantha asked, glad to shift the focus of the conversation away from her.

"On a genealogical research trip," he answered.

"My aunt did ours. It was fascinating." Samantha's interest was piqued. "Where is your first stop?"

"Shreveport, Louisiana," Richard answered. "We planned this trip in the fall and obtained special passes so the tours and other facilities wouldn't be so crowded."

Mrs. Rawlings sent Ethan an exasperated glare. "Of course if we had known Ethan was moving back or would have so much trouble finding a competent housekeeper, we wouldn't have thought of going."

Ethan was used to the censure and basked in the love behind his mother's comment. "You're never going to forgive me for not telling you, but I didn't want to get your hopes up and the job not come through."

"I'll forgive you only because I love you and hope your brothers will come home, too, once they see how nicely things have worked out for you." Mrs. Rawlings glanced warmly at Samantha. "You have Samantha to help you take care of Alan and Alex. Now I won't worry while we're gone."

"We'll be fine," Ethan assured her. "Enjoy your retirement. Go, have fun, and we'll see you at Christmas."

"Yeah, I hope you find a pirate in our family." Alan made a fencing motion with his hand.

Alex countered the attack. "With his own ship and treasure chest."

"So do I," Mrs. Rawlings said to the boys, then turned back to Samantha. "The only meal Ethan takes time to eat properly on weekdays is dinner with the boys. He hates oatmeal and loves grits."

"He'll eat breakfast."

Ethan opened his mouth to tell Samantha he'd eat when he got good and ready, then saw his mother's pleased expression. He contented himself with a scowl.

Giving Samantha's hand a squeeze, Betty bent and gave each grandson a tight hug. "I love you."

"I love you, Grandma."

"I love you, Grandma."

"How about my hug?" asked their grandfather.

They readily went into his open arms. "Good-bye, Grandpa."

Afterwards everyone piled to the front door. Darkness had fallen. Ethan frowned. Once you left the perimeter of his house the heavily wooded area was jet black. He glanced at the small Volkswagen with the top down.

"Mom, Dad, wait. Samantha can follow you out."

"Sure, Ethan." Opening the truck door for his wife, Richard went around to the other side and got in. The motor came to life, the lights came on.

Wide-eyed, Samantha stared up at her new employer. "I haven't finished the dishes."

"The boys and I aren't helpless. We can meet tomorrow around ten and discuss their schedule."

Samantha accepted her dismissal. He hadn't wanted to hire her and apparently had enough of her for one night. The thought hurt more than she wanted to admit. "I'll get my jacket."

"I'll get it." Alex took off with Alan behind him.

"Get in and put the top up."

Inside the car she started the motor. "There's no need. I'll be home in ten minutes and put it up then."

"Here it is, Sam," Alex said, breathing hard.

"Thank you. I'll see you guys in the morning."

"Bye."

"Bye."

Ethan's hand clamped down on the window frame in the door. "The top."

She activated the control. It wasn't worth arguing about in front of the children.

"Lock your doors."

His additional command brought her head up. Next he'd tell her to call when she reached home. If she didn't know better, she might think the stern-faced man staring down at her was worried. Impossible. Putting the car into gear, she backed out of the driveway.

Ethan watched Samantha's Volkswagen follow his parents until they were out of sight. She moved like sin, smelled like heaven, and made him crazy just thinking about what her red lips tasted like. He was nuts to try this.

Turning, he followed his sons back into the house, listening to their excited voices about Sam and shook his head. The things you did for love.

Chapter Three

Ethan wasn't looking forward to the conversation with Samantha, and the scowl on his face when he answered the front door showed his displeasure. It didn't seem possible, but she looked even more tempting in the bright sunlight.

Today she wasn't wearing a jacket. She should have been. The red turtleneck sweater fit her generous breasts too well and made his hands itch to close around them.

Thoroughly ashamed of himself, he pulled his wayward gaze upward and groaned. Eyes as sultry and as beckoning as hers should be outlawed. She had a way of looking at a man that made him forget all his good intentions.

If he could form a coherent sentence he was lucky. "I should have my head examined," he muttered.

Sooty eyelashes lifted. "I beg your pardon?"

His hand gripped the brass doorknob. "Nothing. Good morning, Samantha. Come on in."

The frown on her face cleared. "Good morning, Ethan." In the foyer, she glanced behind him. "Where are the boys?"

"Out playing with Max." He closed the door. "Don't worry. Every few minutes they've come back inside to see if you've arrived."

She smiled. "They're great kids."

"They like you too."

Her head tilted. "You sound surprised."

"They've never taken to other people easily, especially Alex."

"I've never considered myself 'other people.'"

He couldn't have agreed with her more. "No, I don't imagine you have. The study is this way."

Trying not to sigh, Samantha followed. Ethan might be casually dressed today in a jacquard crew sweater, pleated pants, and suede shoes, but he remained the uptight man he was yesterday in his gray striped suit and silk tie.

How two adorable, friendly boys could have such a grumpy father was beyond her. How her attraction was growing each time she saw him was also a mystery. She usually went for the uncomplicated type. Ethan was worse than Rubik's Cube. "Your parents get off all right?"

"Yes, Dad called before they left. Thanks for asking." Waving her to an upholstered chair inside his study, he picked up a blue pocket folder from his desk. "This is the boys' schedule. They're in a lot of extracurricular activities and are on the Pop Warner's football team, which has games on Saturdays."

Samantha accepted the folder and studied the neat computerized page. "They're busy."

"Students who are in extracurricular activities usually don't have time to get into trouble. They also excel more academically and socially than their counterparts." Ethan stared down at her. "Alan and Alex have always been on the 'A' honor roll."

"If they slipped to a 'B' or 'C'?" She didn't believe

in driving children too hard to meet their parents' rigid standards. She was an average student, and she had made out fine.

Folding his arms across his broad chest, he leaned back against his desk. "I'd try to find out why. I don't push them to excel, but they know I expect their best. Any other questions?"

"No, I'm sorry." She should have known better.

"Don't be. I hired you because you care." Unfolding his arms, he went around the desk and took his seat. "We're on the bus route, but because of the distance, students in this area are picked up an hour before school, which starts at eight. Most of the parents take their children or carpool."

"I should hope so. I'll take them."

His black eyes narrowed a fraction. "Some people in small cars like to drive fast. I hope you aren't one of them."

Samantha flushed. She did have a heavy foot. "Not with Alan and Alex."

"Thank you." He leaned forward. "As you can see, part of your duties will be to take them to and from their activities, including Saturdays if I have a meeting or something. That shouldn't be too often. I try hard to spend as much time with them as possible on weekends."

He extended his long-fingered hand toward the folder. "The names of their coaches, music teacher, Boy Scout troop leader, and advisors are there along with phone numbers and meeting places. I expect you to start Monday morning at six-fifty. I leave at seven. When I get home in the afternoon, you're off duty."

He didn't want her around.

The unexpected stab of disappointment only allowed her to nod. He must dislike being in the same room with her. She had foolishly thought they would eat dinner together as they had last night. Alan and Alex along with his parents had insisted she join them. She hadn't realized Ethan had objected.

"For the next two Friday nights, I might not be home until around twelve. The tenth is the coronation of the homecoming queen, the seventeenth is the homecoming game. I know it means driving home late, but at the present I can't think of another alternative." Heavy eyebrows lifted. "Do you have any problems or questions thus far?"

With your attitude, she was tempted to say. If he wanted to be formal, that was fine with her. "Not with their schedule, but we haven't discussed a household account."

His shoulders jerked back abruptly. "This isn't a bed-and-breakfast."

"I'm aware of that, but the kitchen needs to be restocked, and I'll need cleaning supplies."

"Mrs. Dawkins always gave me or my mother a list."

"That's probably why you're almost out of everything and have dust thick enough to plant seeds on the furniture." Closing the folder, she placed it in her lap. "I can give you a list, but it would be quite extensive and there are certain brands I favor."

His skepticism remained. "We don't need fancy food."

Samantha kept her composure. Barely. "I don't consider hot chocolate or hot cereal on a cold day, fancy. You have neither. I was actually glad your parents didn't ask for coffee, because there's not enough for a single cup. After I baked the cake, there was very little flour or sugar or eggs left and no fresh fruits or vegetables. Shall I go on, or would you care to check for yourself?"

Black eyes flared. "I wasn't inferring that you weren't being honest."

"I wasn't inferring that you had," she returned with equal heat.

Across the desk they stared like silent adversaries. Samantha had never been one to hold back. "Is it just my age, or is there some other reason why you don't like me?"

Shock widened his eyes. "What?"

"Don't even try and deny it. You scowl every time you look my way," she told him with a mixture of sorrow and regret in her voice. She shouldn't care, but she did and she had never played games with herself.

"You're mistaken." Ethan stood. "Make a list of what you need, and I'll pick them up this afternoon."

She lifted a brow. One day she was going to get an answer to her question. "Have you ever tried to go grocery shopping on a Saturday afternoon?"

"No."

"Figures. I'll do it this morning, and you can reimburse me."

Ethan knew he had hurt her somehow, regretted that he had done so and tried to make up for his behavior. "There's no need. I keep some cash on hand. How much do you think you'll need?"

"A hundred should be enough for now."

"I should hope so." Opening a locked desk drawer, he removed the money, then relocked the drawer. "Remember, educators don't make that much."

"I'll remember." Standing, she took the money and put it into her purse. "Housekeepers make even less."

"Point taken." Leaning back in his chair, he studied her closely. He didn't understand her at all. "You have a master's in accounting, you could be making three times the money someplace else."

She had heard it many times before. Mainly from her parents and four sisters, who were all high achievers. "It may sound corny, but I'd rather be happy. You can wear only one outfit, one pair of shoes at a time. The only thing I regret is that it's taking me longer to save up for my own home."

He picked up a black pen on his desk. "The Floyds certainly gave you a glowing reference."

Her stiff shoulders relaxed at the mention of her former employers. "Working for them was fantastic. I hated it just as much as they did when they decided to sell, but they wanted to do some traveling before they were too old to enjoy themselves."

"How did you feel about not being asked to stay?" He flipped the pen end over end, but his gaze never left hers.

Betrayed. Her chin lifted. "The Andersons have a right to run the inn the way they want."

"That's very magnanimous of you, considering you lost your job." A thought struck. "The severance pay couldn't have been that great."

"It's enough," she said emphatically.

The sudden suspicion that it wasn't didn't sit well with Ethan. "Do you need an advance on your paycheck?"

"No, but thank you for asking."

A brief knock sounded on the door. "Looks like they've discovered your arrival. Come in."

Grinning broadly, Alan and Alex charged into the study, propelling themselves at Sam. They had the outdoorsy, doggy smell of children who had been playing outside. Her arms closed firmly around them.

"Hi, Sam."

"Hi, Sam."

"Good morning." She glanced from Alan to Alex, noting the tiny differences in their facial expressions that set them apart. "You two must have been having fun."

"We were teaching Max to fetch the stick, but he hasn't got it yet," Alan said, his disappointment obvious.

"Don't give up on him."

"We won't," Alex said. "It sure took you a long time to get here."

"It's five minutes past ten," commented Alan.

Her forefinger playfully touched each cute nose. "I'm here now."

"But we have to go to the game and then to a stup—" Alex glanced at his father. "Stupendous birthday party at four."

Samantha kept her face straight with an effort. Nice save. "I'll see you bright and early Monday morning to fix your breakfast, then take you to school."

Ethan came to his feet. "Now that you've seen Samantha, you need to take a bath and put on your uniforms."

"We'll just get dirty again. My hands are clean," Alex said, holding them up and turning them back to front.

"Sam said house rule, clean hands." Alan glanced toward Samantha for help and confirmation.

"Well, I'm making a new house rule. Clean bodies with clean hands and baths, unlike last night, that take longer than a hot minute." He stepped around his desk. "Now say good-bye to Samantha and hit the bathtubs, and I want to see more than an inch of water in them."

Their shoulders slumped. "Yes, sir," they said in unison.

"I'd like to see you in your uniforms," Samantha said, trying to raise their spirits. "I'll be in the kitchen going over a list of things you and your father need."

Their eyes brightened. "Things like you need to bake cookies?" Alex asked.

"Definitely things you need to bake cookies."

"Dad, I bet you're happy about that. Now you won't have to worry if the bakery sells out again." Alan nodded his head emphatically. "Mrs. Bennett will be so happy we're bringing homemade cookies this time, like she always asks."

"Sam knows how to make them in all kind of shapes like turkeys and trees, and I bet they taste good," Alex added. "Not that you didn't try, Dad, but yours were a little hard."

"I didn't think they were so bad," Ethan defended.

"While they were hot," his eldest confirmed. "Cold, they were hard and flat."

"Billy Peters said they'd make good skimmers." Alex's lower lip jutted out. "I started to deck him, but you said we had to be tolerant of others. It sure was hard watching him stuff his mouth with the bakery cookies you brought over later."

"I'm proud of your restraint." Ethan's gaze met each child's. "I'm also proud of mine. I don't intend to tell you again to go get in the tub."

Identical black eyes widened. The door closed abruptly behind pounding feet.

Samantha's lips twitched. They certainly could move when they had to. "I probably shouldn't ask, but what are skimmers?"

"Flat rocks that are thrown underhand across the water with the objective of making them skim or skip as many times as possible."

"Have you ever tried?"

"Not since I was a kid myself."

"I guess you know you have two very special boys."

"I know. They're the best and most important part of me."

Samantha stood. The animosity was gone from Ethan's face, from his eyes. She didn't want to chance it coming back. "I better get to the kitchen and double check my list."

"I'll be in here if you need me."

Clutching the folder to her chest with one arm, she closed the door to the study. Perhaps she had misjudged Ethan's hostile reaction to her. He made her heart beat like a trip-hammer and her body tingle, yet he hardly looked at her. Annoyance coupled with a big dose of disappointment was probably causing her to overreact.

In the kitchen she placed the folder on the island and took out a pen and pencil from her bag. It was her own fault that she liked everything about Ethan Rawlings, except his grumpiness of course, and she knew he tolerated her for his sons' sake.

At least he cared enough for them to let her stay. It was her own foolish heart that couldn't stop wishing he cared just a little bit about her.

Chapter Four

Monday morning. As usual the weekend passed much too quickly for Ethan.

Saturday had been hectic with Samantha, then after the boys' football game they had rushed home so they could bathe again and change for their classmates' birthday party. They reacted to another bath like it was punishment.

Stepping under the hot blast of water in the shower, Ethan recalled one of the divorced mothers at church Sunday trying to pick him up. She'd been too obvious and too needy.

Instead of being sexy, as she probably thought in the out of place, low-cut, tight-fitting red dress, she'd looked desperate. Instead of being aroused, he'd felt sorry for her. He supposed he'd have to get used to being a prime target for single women.

Except one.

Toweling dry, he thought of Samantha and the note she'd left Saturday after bringing back the groceries. The boys were disappointed they'd missed her.

He wasn't sure how he felt about Samantha. The sexual

urges of his body didn't count. No, that wasn't true. They counted *against* her. He'd taken one look at his ex-wife Carol, on stage as the fiery *Carmen* and wanted her. They'd had a flaming affair before they were married a month later at the courthouse. Carol didn't have time to take off or plan a formal wedding—she had been busy rehearsing the lead in another play.

Becoming a star on Broadway was her driving ambition. Foolishly he had thought there was room for him on her way to the top. He'd learned differently when she'd gotten pregnant. Birth control pills caused her to gain weight, so she had started using the diaphragm. One night she'd forgotten. The confirmation of her pregnancy had sent her into a rage. Their marriage went downhill from there.

Alan and Alex were less than a week old when she returned to the theater. Three weeks later she left them at a neighbor's with a hastily written note saying she wasn't cut out for motherhood. Like a fool he had tracked her down to the theater. He had begged her to come home for the sake of Alan and Alex.

He'd never forget her reply as she put on her makeup in preparation for going onstage that night as Katharina in *The Taming of the Shrew.* "I have no children. I made sure the doctor fixed it so I never will."

Without another word he'd gone home and picked up the twins from the neighbor. Both were screaming their lungs out. Oddly it helped. Time on his hands would have allowed him to feel sorry for himself. He'd filed for divorce and never looked back. She didn't even bother to come to court. Two years later she was killed in a car-train accident.

He didn't want mindless hot passion that burned everything in its wake, leaving only ashes and bitterness. He much preferred a slow-burning flame. That way there was no chance for things to get out of control.

Buttoning the cuffs of his white shirt, he pulled on his olive two-button suit jacket, then checked his watch. Six-thirty. He'd check on the boys again and then make some coffee. Samantha should be arriving in twenty minutes. He hoped she was punctu— Coffee. He smelled coffee.

Samantha.

He found her in the kitchen, looking outrageously tempting in a mauve-colored silk blouse and miniskirt. The least she could do was cover up. "You're early. The boys aren't due to be up for another thirty minutes."

"Good morning, Ethan." The toaster popped up a blueberry bagel, and she placed it on a small yellow plate beside a steaming bowl of grits. "Maybe you'll feel better after you've eaten."

He shoved his hand over his head. "I'm sorry. Good morning. You just surprised me, that's all. The other women were more likely late than on time."

Coffee carafe in hand, she stared at him. "I thought we already decided I wasn't like other women."

"I'm beginning to see how much."

Twin dimples winked. "Was that a compliment?"

"I'm not sure," he answered truthfully.

She sighed. "Sit down and eat before it gets cold. I tried to gauge the time by the shower."

Ethan sat before his legs gave out. The thought of her thinking about him in the shower, however innocent, went straight to the place it shouldn't. "You're dressed up for housecleaning."

"I thought I'd go inside with the boys and meet the principal and their teacher so they'll recognize me. If it's all right with you."

"It's fine." He'd had to ask the other housekeepers. He pushed the bagel aside. "I'll just have coffee."

She pushed the yellow plate back. "You'll eat your grits and bagel." She poured his coffee. "I promised your mother. You wouldn't want me to tell her I failed, would you?"

Conceding defeat, Ethan said grace, then sprinkled

brown sugar over his hot cereal. "Mother called last night. She was glowing about the apricot bread and peach preserves you took over late Friday night. That was very kind of you."

"I'm a kind person." She replaced the coffee carafe and came back to the table and took a seat. "Most people seem to realize that except you."

Ethan set his spoon aside. "I told you Saturday, you're mistaken."

"Hogwash. Now spit it out so we can clear the air. Children pick up when there is something going on, and neither of us want that for Alan or Alex." She gave him a long, level look. "I'd leave if I thought my being here would cause them to be less happy or secure than the day I met them."

The sincerity in her words touched him. He wasn't a man to back away from a confrontation, but he wasn't ready for this. "I have nothing against you personally."

"I thought you were more honest than this."

Incensed, he stood and pushed his chair under the table. "Just take care of my sons."

She didn't appear the least bothered. "I get your message. Now you get mine. Either sit back down and eat, or your mother told me to dispense a little wooden Justice to you."

"She what!?"

From beneath a dish towel on the table, she pulled a wooden spoon and waved it from side to side.

"You wouldn't dare."

"Don't tempt me."

"Why not—you certainly tempt me," he said tersely.

Very, very slowly Samantha lowered the spoon. "What did you say?"

"Nothing." Ethan pulled out the chair and began eating his breakfast, cursing himself for his loose tongue. He didn't look back up until his cereal bowl and coffee cup were empty. And then wished he hadn't.

Samantha's red lips were slightly parted, the pulse erratic in her throat, her eyes dark and beckoning. Desire in a woman's face could be beautiful or frightening, depending on the perspective of the person looking at her. The depths to which Samantha had invaded his mind became apparent when he couldn't decide which.

The one thing he was sure about was it wasn't going to happen. He wasn't a hit-and-run kind of guy, and if Samantha had that kind of reputation around town, his mother wouldn't have wanted her around her grandchildren. Since neither of them were into one-nighters, he felt even more assured of himself.

"Ethan."

His name rolled over her lips like a lover's plea, sending white-hot embers of desire through his body. The swiftness of his hunger staggered him.

He wanted her with a fierceness unmatched by any other need. He wanted to plunder that wicked mouth of hers, plunder the lush body in all the soft places hidden to him. He wanted to hear her voice break when he—

Ruthlessly he controlled his rampaging thought and the hunger clawing though him. Never again was he going to let that kind of passion harm his children or him. Carol had set him on fire, and in the end she had burnt him and his children.

"Thanks for breakfast. Good-bye." He left without waiting for a reply. His emotions were under control, but he wasn't willing to test them if she called his name in that same needy voice again.

Watching Ethan's stiff-backed departure, Samantha's hand tightened on the wooden spoon. Her entire body felt tight, hot, and needy. Whatever had happened between her and Ethan had been like nothing else she had experienced in her life. She had wanted before, but never with such uncontrolled hunger.

If he had touched her, she would have willingly let him do anything to her he desired—because it would have been her desire as well.

Eyes closing briefly, she drew in a shaky breath. She wasn't sure if she was thankful or disappointed he hadn't made the move. She was attracted to him, but frankly hadn't taken it very much further. Affairs weren't her style.

"Sam!"

"Sam!"

Thrusting Ethan from her mind, she smiled and opened her arms for Alan and Alex. With them, she didn't have to worry. She had already given her love.

Long after Samantha had returned from taking Alan and Alex to school, she couldn't get a handle on her emotions. Ethan was certainly single, straight, and stable. But he was also weary and, from his angry outburst, not the least bit happy about his attraction to her. That left her with a problem.

She wasn't a woman of the nineties who could go after the man she wanted—certainly not in the face of such obvious hostility. She had more pride and sense than that. Taking a load of whites from the washer, she loaded them into the dryer and set the timer. She had her answer.

Ethan was going to be her employer and nothing more. Her time would be spent compiling the special recipes her grandmother had asked her to pass down to the next generation, not worrying about Ethan.

Ethan's reserved manner that afternoon when he came home for dinner proved she had made the right decision. After asking her how things went with the boys, he turned his attention to Alan and Alex. She might as well have been a piece of furniture.

When he went to his bedroom to change clothes, she said good-bye to the boys and went home. The table was set, dinner ready. She didn't want to be around a man who obviously despised wanting her.

Tuesday evening Samantha opened the door to her apartment to a ringing phone. Placing the plastic-covered dry cleaning over the back of the floral sofa, she picked up the phone from the end table. "Hello."

"I have two children who won't eat their dinner."

Samantha recognized Ethan's deep, annoyed voice and took that as normal. Alan and Alex not eating was not. "Are they sick? Did you take their temperatures? They were laughing and playing when I left."

"That's the problem. This is the second day you've sneaked out of here when I went to change. Why?"

"I did not sneak. During our interview Saturday you told me to leave." No matter how she tried to get around it, his words hurt.

"I did no such thing," he thundered back.

"You most certainly did," Samantha told him. "You said once you were home, I was off duty."

He came back instantly. "I didn't mean you had to leave. It meant you didn't have to wait on us during dinner or bother with cleaning up the kitchen afterward. I expected—the boys expected you to eat dinner with us. You did Friday night."

Biting her lips, she sat down on the arm of the sofa. "Your parents and the twins insisted."

"That hasn't changed."

She rubbed her forehead with her fingertips. By trying to keep herself from being hurt, she had upset Alan and Alex. "May I please speak with them?"

"Boys. Samantha wants to talk to you."

"Hello, Sam. We want you to come back and eat with us."

"Hi, Sam. You gotta come back."

From their words overlaying the other, she realized they were sharing the receiver. "No, fellows, I'm not. I know you meant well, but not eating will make things worse. How do you think your father feels knowing you won't eat with him when he plans his entire day to have that special time with you?"

"I didn't think of that." This from Alan.

"Me neither," Alex said.

"That's what happens when we think only of what we want."

"You mean we were selfish," ventured Alex.

"Yes, just like I've been selfish sometimes in my life. The thing you have to do is recognize what you've done wrong and try to correct matters." She was talking to herself as well as the twins. "Your father loves you more than anything. He hired me because he thought I'd take good care of you. How do you think he feels after my being on the job full-time for two days, and neither one of you will eat dinner?"

"Mad," Alan answered softly.

"Very mad," whispered Alex.

Samantha just bet he was, but he was also dealing with more complex emotions. "That's because when grown-ups are hurt, they don't always know how to express what they feel. He's disappointed you don't want to eat with him and confused about what to do about it."

"We just wanted you to eat with us."

"It was nice having you."

"That's the same thing your daddy wanted. For you to eat with him," she told them.

"I'm sorry."

"Me too."

Samantha heard the crack in their voices and wished

she were there to give them a comforting hug. "I know, but he needs to know. Grown-ups need reassurance sometimes too. I bet he would like a hug about now. I'll hold." She heard the usual drumbeat of small feet across the floor, and then their return.

"You mad at us?" Alex wanted to know as soon as he spoke again.

"No. I admit to being a little disappointed, but at the same time very flattered that you care that much about me. But you have to remember, I may be there only until Christmas." Her hand flexed on the phone before she continued. She didn't want to leave them, but it wasn't her choice. "I'm only the housekeeper. I'll be gone from your lives one day. Your father will be there always."

"I want you to stay," Alex insisted.

A hard lump formed in her throat. "I want to stay, but life doesn't always work out the way we want. Now go eat dinner. I put a lot of effort and love into those stuffed pork chops."

"I'll eat a whole lot."

"Not as much as I will."

Smiling despite her sadness, she said, "Please put your father back on."

"Bye," they said together

"Bye, Alan. Bye, Alex. I'll see you in the morning."

"Hello."

His voice sounded only slightly mollified. She plunged ahead anyway. "You shouldn't have any more problems with them tonight or in the future. It's because I'm new and can play with them. They'll soon tire of me."

"You really think so?"

"If they did I'd hate it like hell," she said tightly "But their caring for me doesn't mean they love you any less."

"I never had a rival before."

"You don't have one now."

"Sam— Alan. Alex. That's enough food on your plates."

"I better let you go."

"Sam—"

"Good-bye, Ethan." Hanging up the phone, she curled up on the sofa. There was no sense fooling herself anymore. She didn't want an affair with Ethan because she wanted the whole thing, marriage and happily ever after with Alan and Alex. She had done the unthinkable, fallen in love with a man who wouldn't let himself return her love.

Like she told the twins, life didn't always work out the way you wanted.

Ethan held the phone, a frown wrinkling his forehead. Samantha's voice had sounded thick, choked as if she were about to cry. Something twisted in his gut at the thought.

If she had been leaving shortly after his arrival home, it had been because of what happened Monday morning. His fault. His mixed signals were probably confusing the hell out of her. He owed her an apology and an explanation. He hit the disconnect button, then began dialing her number.

"I fixed your plate, Dad."

"I filled your glass with tea."

In the midst of dialing, Ethan glanced up and saw the remorse on Alan and Alex's faces. Whatever Samantha had said had certainly gotten them back on track. And she was crying.

He replaced the receiver, took his seat, then said grace. The boys had to come first. He forked the first bite of the three stuffed pork chops piled on his plate. His appetite was gone, but he had to eat for their sakes. "Samantha's a good cook."

"She sure is." Alex swallowed his third bite.

"She said we might bake cookies while you're at the homecoming dance Friday night." Alan's face became thoughtful. "I hope she won't change her mind."

"She won't." Certainty rang in Ethan's voice. "She's a friend to both of you, no matter what."

"She said she'd be gone someday, but you'd be with us always." Alex looked sad. "I wish she could stay, but I'm glad you won't leave us."

"We won't be selfish again," Alan promised.

Ethan's chest felt tight. He loved his sons and seeing the love and trust in their young faces always made him feel blessed. Although he didn't like the idea of sharing them, it was his problem. He wasn't about to let it be their problem.

"I love you, no matter what. Never forget that." He took another bite. "How about after we take care of the kitchen, and I check your homework, we'll play a video game."

His announcement was met with loud approval. Video games were reserved for the weekends. He'd enjoy the boys' enthusiasm a lot more if he knew Samantha was all right.

Chapter Five

The next morning Ethan met Samantha at the front door. His eyes searched her surprised face. The puffiness beneath her eyes and the wariness in them made him all the more sure of what he had to do. "Good morning, Samantha."

Her tongue darted across her lower lip. "Good morning, Ethan."

"Come on in."

Her gaze skittered to him, then away as she stepped past him into the house. One hand gripped the strap of the oversized bag slung over her shoulder.

"Let me have your jacket, and I'll hang it up," he offered, his hand held out.

"Thank you." Pulling off her fringed lamb suede jacket, she handed it to him.

"Coffee is ready. Why don't you go pour yourself a cup."

She hesitated, then turned and walked away. Ethan hung up the jacket and quickly followed. He had thirty minutes.

She stood with the kitchen island between them, the

wariness once again in her light brown eyes. "What do you want for breakfast?"

"I've eaten." He smiled as she glanced around the spotless kitchen. "I cleaned up afterward."

Obviously confused, she shook her head. "I don't understand. You haven't smiled at me or been cordial since we first met in your office. Why today?"

"Because I thought I heard tears in your voice last night."

Her head came up. "I was upset about Alan and Alex."

He let her explanation slide. This was his day of confession, not hers. "I'd like to talk to you before the boys get up. Do you mind sitting down?"

"Are you going to fire me?" she asked in an unsteady voice.

"I said until Christmas and I haven't changed my mind." He pulled out one of the oak chairs at the round pedestal kitchen table.

She took the seat. He was bolstered that her back was straight, her hands resting easily on the table. She had backbone. "Can I get you some coffee?"

She shook her head again. "Just tell me."

"This isn't going to be easy for me because no one except my family knows the story that I'm about to tell you, and some of the worst parts they don't even know."

"Alan and Alex aren't sick, are they?" she asked, her hand gripping his arm in sheer terror.

"No." His hand covered hers naturally in reassurance. It felt delicate and at the same time strong. "This is about me and my first wife, Carol."

"Oh." Pulling her hand back, she placed it in her lap.

He took the seat beside her. "I'll make this short because it was and still isn't pretty. I met her when I went to the theater to see a live performance of *Carmen*. She had the lead." He gave a short bark of rough laughter. "Now that

I think about it, her casting was perfect. She had a high energy level and sparkled on and off stage."

He picked up the wooden salt shaker. "She was beautiful and very sensual. It was lust at first sight. From then on we were together every night. We married a month later. Three months later she was pregnant with the boys."

His face harshened and so did his voice. "She didn't want them or me. She left when they were twenty-seven days old, and she left running back to the theater, her first and only love. She never came back or tried to contact me about them. Alan and Alex know only that their mother was an actress and singer, and that she died when they were two. That's all they'll ever know."

"Oh, Ethan."

He glanced up to see tears shining in Samantha's eyes. "We survived, but I learned a hard lesson. Lust and uncontrolled passion don't last."

"What are you trying to say?" Samantha asked, afraid she already knew the answer.

"I look at you and I want you anyway . . . and every way. But it can never happen."

Despite his words, a hot surge of desire swept through her. "Don't I have any say in the matter?"

"No." The harshness returned to his face. "Whatever this is that's between us wouldn't last beyond a few hot tussles on the sheets." She winced and he ruthlessly continued. "I have the boys to think of and my responsibility as a principal. Nothing can jeopardize that."

"I see." She couldn't decide if he was being selfish or noble or a little of both. There was certainly no sense in being outraged by his assumption that she'd let him make love to her—they both knew she would in a hot second.

"I hope you do. I don't want the boys caught in the middle or you to be hurt either." His hands clenched on the shaker. "I don't want to see tears in your eyes and have to live with knowing I put them there."

"You don't think this hurts?"

"Not as much as when the affair ended. And it would end."

Samantha saw the determined look on Ethan's face and realized his mind was made up. He truly believed the hogwash he had just spouted to her. The fact that he had revealed intimate and painful details about his life to back up his claim made her care for him more, not less. He was trying to protect her, protect the twins, protect himself.

Until he relegated Carol to his past, he'd always have his guard up against Samantha. She had until Christmas to see that he changed his mind.

Glancing at her watch, she stood. "It's almost seven. Both of us better get moving."

His gaze narrowed, he came to his feet. "You're all right with this?"

"No, but I can live with it if you can."

Ethan didn't know what he expected, but her calm acceptance wasn't it. Certainly not her dare. "I'll go wake the boys and say good-bye."

"Why don't we do it together?" she lightly suggested. She'd show him there was no place she'd rather be than with him and the twins.

"We never woke them up together before."

She smiled and walked past him. "I know, but this will show them that everything is all right between us."

As Samantha had expected, Alan and Alex were ecstatic. She hugged them tight. They had missed out on so much growing up without a mother: hugs, kissed scraped knees, storybook time just for them. Ethan had done a wonderful job, but he couldn't do it all.

She wanted so much to be there to help. She wanted forever. Ethan wanted until Christmas. Her plan was simple: treasure each day without regrets and an abundance of love. After sending the boys off to take their baths, she followed Ethan through the utility room to the garage in back of the house.

"I'll try to be home on time for dinner," Ethan told her at the door.

She smiled, her hand on the door frame. "Whenever. We'll be waiting."

The softly spoken promise had his body humming. Around her he was in an almost constant state of arousal. Uncomfortable and dangerous.

Whirling around, he went to his Cherokee and backed out. The garage door closed on Samantha standing in the door. He wished he could close the door on his wanting her as easily.

After dropping off the boys at school, Samantha went by her apartment to pick up a few things. She loved scented candles and potpourri and kept a supply in her linen closet. She thought Ethan and the boys deserved something nice.

Back at the house she placed the potpourri in the crystal bowl she had thought to bring with her in the living room. The three-wick candle went in the den on the brick hearth. Nodding her approval at the flickering flames, she went to the kitchen to marinate the tenderloins for dinner.

Ethan opened the back door to the sound of music— piano to be exact. From the occasional missed note, he knew it to be Alan. He didn't have as much patience as Alex and hated the daily practicing. The only reason he stuck it out was that it was conditional to his playing sports. The smoothness of the next piece confirmed Ethan's supposition.

Pushing open the door leading from the utility room to the kitchen, he was struck by two things at once: the beautifully set table, complete with linen and fresh flowers, and the scent of vanilla. He and the boys hadn't eaten at a table like this at home since . . . he couldn't remember if they ever had.

His mother liked to do buffets on the holidays because he and his brothers tended to arrive at different times since they were coming from different parts of the country. The only occasion they came early for was Christmas. Then with all the catching up since the last time they were face to face, a formal dinner was impossible.

As for Ethan, if he and the boys had napkins and flatware on the table he considered it a triumph. Samantha apparently didn't share his philosophy.

"You're home."

Ethan glanced up and was caught by the warmth in her eyes. "Yes."

Alan and Alex came around her to their father. "We helped set the table and everything."

"Sam said we didn't have to dress up or anything," Alan said. He detested shirts and ties. Sundays were a struggle.

Laughing, she placed a hand on Alan's shoulder. "If you can't enjoy yourself, what's the point?"

Alex took his father's briefcase. "Hurry up, Dad. I'll put this in your study. I'm hungry."

His gaze caught Samantha's. Since there were four place settings, she wasn't going anyplace. "Give me five minutes."

"I'll put the ice in the glasses."

Ethan spied the candle on the way to his bedroom. Nice. It wouldn't hurt for the boys to be exposed to some of the softer things in life, to be pampered a little bit. As long as he didn't think about wanting a little pampering himself from Samantha, he was all right.

The tenderloin was succulent and delicious, his salad crisp, the homemade vinaigrette had just enough sweetness. Alan and Alex took turns explaining how they had baked their wedge fries. Ethan listened while he devoured his giant baked potato.

There was only one bad moment when Alan knocked over the ketchup bottle, reaching for a dinner roll. The unscrewed top came off, and the thick red liquid shot across the table. His son's eyes were huge when he turned to Samantha.

Calmly she picked up the bottle. "No harm done. The tablecloth is washable, and I've dealt with enough stains at the inn to know how to get it out." Standing, she returned with a wet cloth and blotted up the spillage, then retook her seat.

Ethan looked at Alan's rapt expression. Samantha had just elevated herself to sainthood. Ethan wasn't sure he wouldn't have made some comment about being careful. Samantha seemed to take it as the natural course of dinner with two eight-year-olds. She was a remarkable, caring woman. The touches, the hugs, the reassurances all appeared to come naturally to her.

"Alan, you were telling us about the class Thanksgiving party," Samantha encouraged smoothly.

"I volunteered us for the homemade cookies right off. Heather Jacobs tried to get her name on the list, but when the teacher asked who was baking the cookies, and I told her you were, the teacher asked Heather to bring brownies. I told the class we're going to bake some samples while Dad was at the coronation dance for the homecoming game." He stopped suddenly and cast a worried glance at Samantha. "We are still going to bake the cookies, aren't we?"

"Absolutely. We'll start on them as soon as your father leaves."

A frown marred Ethan's face. The more he had thought about it lately, the more it worried him. "It'll be late when I get back. There are a couple of long stretches of winding, pitch black road before you get back into town."

"I've traveled it, remember? I'll be fine going home."

She smiled impishly. "I'll lock my doors and keep the top up."

Since the temperature was predicted to be in the mid-fifties for the next few days, he didn't doubt she'd keep the top up. Still. "Do you have a cell phone?"

"No."

"You'll take mine."

There was no questioning the authority in his voice. "I suppose you want me to call when I get home?"

"Absolutely. Isn't that right, boys?"

"Absolutely."

"Absolutely."

Warmth radiated through her. "Absolutely."

It was going to be one of those days.

Ethan knew it before the first bell sounded and he had to break up a shouting match between two football players who wanted different girls to be crowned Miss Homecoming Queen that night. The day went downhill from there.

He didn't sit down for longer than five minutes until after lunch. He, the assistant principals, and the counselors were in the halls and classrooms. He considered announcing that any infractions would cause expulsion from all homecoming activities. He didn't.

One thing he had learned as a principal for three years in his old job was that the truth didn't always come out—and teachers, unlike parents, didn't always have eyes in the back of their heads. He didn't want to unnecessarily punish anyone. So he kept moving, kept the administrative staff moving.

Sometime around a quarter to two, he called Samantha. "I won't be home for dinner."

"Is everything all right?"

He propped his hip on an uncluttered corner of his desk. He wasn't surprised by the concern in her voice, but he was surprised by how much it soothed his jagged nerves. "The students are restless. I think I better stay while they finish decorating the cafeteria after school. When you pick up the boys, can you bring my clothes? They're already laid out."

"Have you eaten?"

He laughed. No surprise this time. "No time and the last lunch period is over."

"Can't you call the cafeteria manager and have them make something?"

Ethan freely admitted it was nice having a woman like Samantha worry about him. "I don't want special privileges. I won't starve. There's some peanut butter and crackers around here someplace, compliments of my mother."

"Oh, Ethan."

"It can't compare to your cooking, but I won't starve. I'll see you and the boys later this afternoon. Good-bye."

"Good-bye, Ethan. Take care."

Hanging up, Ethan bent to rummage in his desk for the peanut butter and crackers. A call on the walkie-talkie had him hurrying out the door instead, thoughts of eating relegated to the back of his mind. His students needed him.

Chapter Six

Samantha felt herself become the center of attention as she and the twins entered the cafeteria. She sensed it was because of the foil-covered pan in her hands. Despite what Ethan thought, she didn't think too many people would get upset if they were romantically involved. As long as he wasn't involved in amoral or criminal activities, his life once he left the high school campus was his own.

He climbed off a ladder where he had been helping attach blue and white streamers and crossed over to them. Her breath trembled over her lips. Ethan was a fantastic specimen of manhood. With his jacket off, his tie gone, the sleeves of his white shirt rolled up to his forearm, he looked positively scrumptious. In a word, yummy.

"We brought you dinner," Alan said, holding a plastic grocery bag that contained paper plates, plastic forks, and napkins.

"And dessert." Alex held up a plastic cake carrier.

"And you have the main course, I imagine," Ethan said mildly.

A wicked, but oh so delicious thought of Ethan nibbling

on her from head to toe raced though her mind. "Your mother said to make sure you ate."

He crossed his arms. "Although it smells delicious, I don't think at my hungriest, I could eat all of whatever you're carrying."

"We're going to help you," Secretary Lewis said, coming over. "Hi, Samantha, Alan, Alex."

"Hello," they returned.

Ethan unfolded his arms and stared down at his secretary. "So that's why you opted to stay?"

"You betcha." The older woman took the container from Samantha. "When Samantha called and wanted to know if it was all right to bring food and how many to prepare for, I decided then I was going to stay."

"You didn't have to go to the trouble or expense." Shaking his head, he gave his attention back to Samantha.

"Chicken enchilada casserole is easy and inexpensive, but very filling. Besides, I didn't want you to miss eating with Alan and Alex."

Was there ever a woman beside his mother who cared so much about them? "Me either," Ethan said.

Seeing his youngest son's attention wandering to the different decorations of crepe paper and balloons, he took the cake out of his hands. "Come on, and I'll introduce all of you to everyone and then we can eat."

The food was almost inhaled. She had to laugh on seeing Michael, a burly football player, picking up the last crumbs of the three-layer chocolate cake from the platter. The student smiled back.

"We should have gotten Miss Clark to cater the banquet for us."

A loud roar of approval went up.

"Thank you for the compliment, but taking care of Principal Rawlings, Alan, and Alex is enough. Speaking of which, we have to get home and start baking cookies."

"Any chance you'll bring some back?" Michael asked hopefully.

Everyone laughed.

"It seems as if the party has started early."

Everyone at the table turned and focused on the portly, gray-haired man in a dark, three-piece suit. Samantha heard more than one teacher groan.

"Superintendent Hodge, this is a surprise." Ethan stood and shook hands with the man.

"A pleasant one, I hope." The elderly, white-haired man's mouth curved, but just barely.

"Always. We were just taking a break," Ethan explained, hating that he had to do so. He was on probation, and they both knew his contract could be yanked at the end of the year or he could be demoted.

"I hope today went well." Superintendent Hodge's blue eyes were shrewd. "Last year there were three suspensions and a few upset parents because none of the football players in the altercation were suspended."

"No suspensions. No major problems." Ethan rocked back on his heels, more sure of himself. Hodge was a stickler, but he was fair. "That's why we're taking a break to eat. There wasn't a chance to today because we stayed on the move with the students."

"Did the students also miss their meals?" he inquired mildly.

"No, but my housekeeper didn't think it fair to feed the faculty and not the students." Ethan knew what was coming and saw no way around it.

"Your housekeeper?" Hodge questioned, glancing around the familiar group of adult faces.

"That would be me, Mr. Hodge," Samantha said, standing and facing the superintendent.

His eyes rounded, his teeth bared in a face-splitting grin. "Samantha Clark. I can't believe it."

She chuckled. "Believe it." She extended her hand. "How have you been doing, sir?"

"Much better now that I've seen you." He pumped her hand. "Still feeding and taking care of people, huh?"

"It's what I do best."

Smiling, Superintendent Hodge turned to Ethan. "Housekeeper, huh? You got yourself the best cook in the county. Did you know that?"

Ethan, who had never seen the superintendent so animated, could barely think of an answer. The man was known as a perpetual grouch. "You two know each other?"

"You bet we do. For the past year my wife and I have had standing reservations every two months at the Oak Tree Inn." Stepping around Ethan, the superintendent gazed longingly at the cleanly scraped pan. His shoulders slumped. "What did you cook?"

"Chicken enchilada casserole."

"And I haven't eaten dinner yet."

He looked so mournful with his double chin hanging down, Samantha said, "If I hadn't promised the boys we'd make cookies when we got back, I'd make you some."

He perked up. "Cookies for what boys?"

"Principal Rawlings's sons, Alan and Alex." She motioned them from their seats next to the football players. They came without hesitation and, when their father introduced them, they were polite and well mannered. She couldn't have been prouder of them.

"So you're going to be baking cookies?" the superintendent asked.

"Yes, sir. We're going to see which kind we like best for the Thanksgiving party," Alan explained.

"We're bringing cookies for the whole class," Alex added. "Sam can cook anything."

"You don't have to convince me, young man." His attention shifted to Samantha. "I don't suppose you might bake some extra?"

She smiled indulgently. "I think that can be arranged. Where can I bring them tomorrow?"

"I wouldn't want to put you to that much trouble. You can send them Monday to school with Ethan."

"I'll also send along something for your lunch that you can just pop into the microwave," she told him.

He caught her hands again. "The new owners of the Oak Tree Inn lost a treasure when they didn't keep you on. Lost my business too."

"Thank you." His words of praise made her feel better. She had been tossed out like an old shoe. "Please say hello to Mrs. Hodge for me, and I'll make sure I send enough for both of you."

"A treasure." He looked at Ethan. "You seem to be settling in nicely. Hearing good things. Very good things. Good-bye." Hands in his pockets, he strolled away whistling.

At twelve-thirty that night, stuffed from eating too many decorated cookies, Samantha lay on the sofa in the den, waiting for Ethan to get home from the dance. The TV was on, but it was more to keep her awake than entertainment.

Like the twins, a full day and a full stomach were lulling her to sleep. Unlike them, she couldn't give in to it until Ethan was home. He had called to check on them for the second time an hour ago.

He still wouldn't tell her why everyone looked at her so strangely once Superintendent Hodge had left. She didn't hold out much hope for obtaining her answer. Ethan didn't have loose lips, but he certainly had beautiful ones.

Sighing, she closed her eyes and pulled the light quilt over her head. She'd fantasized more than one night in her bed about the taste, the texture of his hot, insatiable mouth gliding over her body with a relentlessness that set them both afire.

He'd take his time. She figured Ethan was a thorough, generous man. He'd want her to feel as much as he did. He'd start maybe at her forehead, work his way downward, paying special attention to her lower lip, the arch of her neck, the slope of her shoulder.

All the time his mouth would be driving her crazy, those fantastic, blunt-tipped fingers would work their magic on her sensitive skin, caressing and kneading and arousing. Her breath hitched as she imagined his finger and thumb plucking at her nipple. His laughter was rough with triumph and hunger as he bent his head and gently closed his teeth over the aching point.

White hot heat spiraled outward from the center of her body. She groaned.

"Samantha, are you all right?"

All she had time to do was draw in a startled breath of embarrassment before the cover was snatched away. Ethan's face filled her vision. He was kneeling by the sofa. Her only consolation was that his wide shoulders sufficiently blocked the light from the TV set and left her face in the shadows.

"What's the matter? You were moaning."

"I-I must have fallen asleep and had a bad dream."

His head tilted to one side as he studied her. "It didn't sound like a bad dream to me."

She flushed and tried to stand, forgetting in her haste she had tucked the quilt around her legs. With a cry of dismay, she tumbled on top of him. Her hands splayed on his chest, she stared down into his dark eyes. The heat of their bodies and breaths mingled.

She couldn't move, didn't want to move unless it were closer. Her fantasy made her bold. She felt him everywhere. The broad chest, the concave stomach, the strong thighs, the masculine bulge against her stomach.

For a long moment Ethan submitted to his humanness and just enjoyed the fragrant softness of Samantha's body flush against his. He'd tried to think **of he**r only as the housekeeper, but occasionally fantasies of her just snuck up on him.

This was the real thing, more potent, and almost impossible to ignore. He estimated it would take him all of fifteen seconds to be sheathed inside her velvet warmth, loving her.

His hands on her upper forearms trembled. Shutting his eyes, he fought for control.

"Ethan?"

There it was again, the need in her shaky voice that made him get inexplicably harder, but he hoped not crazier.

"Get off slowly. Carefully," he managed though gritted teeth.

Unsure if she were hurting him in a very sensitive area, she tried to lift the lower half of her body, forgot the quilt again, and succeeded only in rocking against his hard erection. Breath hissed through his teeth.

"I'm sor—"

His hot mouth cut her off, plundering her mouth. It took Samantha all of a second to join in the kiss. It was better, hotter than her fantasy. She wasn't prepared for the urgent mating of their tongues, the surge of pleasure.

She tried to move one leg to edge closer and once again was caught by the cover. She made a frustrated sound, twisting restlessly against Ethan.

"Stop that. My control isn't limitless. I'm hanging by my fingernails here," he told her, his voice ragged and harsh.

"Why do you get to make the decision about us making love?" she asked, not sure where she had gotten the courage to ask such a bold question.

"Because my sons are down the hall."

Distress widened her eyes. "I forgot."

"Stop struggling and come back here." She felt too

good in his arms to give up just yet. After a long pause he said, "I did too."

She played with a pearl button on his white pleated shirt. "That doesn't make us uncaring."

"What it makes us is horny."

His callous words incensed her. She rolled away. Somehow she managed to extract herself from the quilt and grab her purse from the chair. When she did, Ethan stood in front of her.

"Where are you going?"

"Why, I'm taking my horny self home." She pushed against him to move him aside. He didn't budge. Annoyed, she gritted her teeth, stepped around him, and got her coat from the hall closet.

"Samantha, come back here. Be reasonable."

"I don't want to be reasonable." Opening the front door, she stalked to her car.

Ethan was right behind her. "Slow down. Come back inside and let's talk."

Unlocking her car, she got in. "Believe me, you don't want to hear the things that are running through my mind."

He grabbed the car door. "Settle down. I don't want you driving angry."

"In four seconds I'm going to lean on my horn until it wakes up the boys. Unless you want to explain to them why, I suggest you take your hands off my car."

"Sama—"

"One."

"Be—"

"Two."

"Ple—"

"Three."

"Sto—"

"Four." Her hand hit the horn. Ethan released her door. Slamming it closed, she spun out of the driveway, wishing she knew how to burn rubber, wishing Ethan hadn't taken a chunk out of her heart.

Arriving at her apartment, she tossed her things aside and paced the floor in front of the sofa. Who did he think he was to throw her affection back in her face, to treat it as if it were nothing?

The phone rang on the end table. She shot the instrument a hostile glare. After the twelfth ring she knew he wasn't going to give up.

"Yes."

"Are you all right?"

"No." Despite the worry in his voice, she slammed down the phone. A childish act, but it made her feel better.

The ring came again. She unplugged it from the base. How dare he insult her as if she were a rabbit in heat or something. Her eyes smarted with unshed tears, but she refused to let them fall.

Her mother had repeatedly told her five daughters that after the tears had run their course, they still had to face whatever it was they were crying about—and what was worse, they now had to do it with red, irritated eyes, a runny nose, and a killer of a headache.

No, Ethan wasn't going to make her cry. The unappreciative jerk.

Just her luck that she had to fall in love with a guy who tried to dismiss combustible physical attraction instead of enjoying the obvious benefits. She might not be experienced, but she knew what they shared might be as scary as hell, but it was also uniquely wonderful.

Ethan needed to be taught a lesson about letting his mouth get ahead of his brain. And she was just the woman to do it.

Chapter Seven

Ethan had a miserable weekend. Every time one of his sons mentioned Samantha's name, he remembered the fiasco of Saturday morning. Few things in his life he regretted more than his crude handling of the aftermath of their passionate encounter.

Long before his alarm went off Monday morning, he had showered and dressed. Any attempt at sleep had been futile. Every time he closed his eyes, he'd see the passion go out of Samantha's eyes, see pain take its place. There had been other emotions too: anger, embarrassment, anguish, before she had driven away and he had to live with the fact that he had caused each one.

Rubbing his forehead, Ethan stared through the gauzy curtains in the living room, watching for her car. She had come to him with tenderness and fire, in return he had devastated her.

He admitted he meant what he had said about them being horny in principle, but the words had come out all wrong. He'd tried calling all weekend, but her line stayed busy. It hadn't taken him long to decide she had taken the phone off the hook.

This morning she'd have to talk to him. She might hate his guts, but she adored his sons. She'd come. Knowing that truth, his behavior Saturday morning was ever harder to accept.

He owed her an apology. He was the one who kissed her. What had happened wasn't her fault. He planned on telling her the second she stepped though the door.

Her red Volkswagen Beetle turned into his driveway. His heart rate increased. His palms felt moist. He hadn't been this nervous when he had interviewed for the principal's position.

She'd be ticked, but she'd get over it in time. If she knew how he had lain awake until daybreak Saturday morning, wanting her and worrying about her, it might go a long way toward her forgiving him, but that was his secret. He'd crossed the line once. He wasn't about to give her any reason to believe that it might happen again.

The front door opened before he had a chance to move. Carrying a large canvas tote, she entered in a swirl of lavender. From head to toe she was covered by a long, hooded cape. Removing her wrap, she hung it up in the hall closet.

She wore a fuzzy angora lavender sweater with a low scooped neckline that hung off her smooth shoulders. Her long legs were enclosed in tight black velour leggings. On her feet were low-heeled black boots.

Seductive and stylish. And despite his best effort, he found himself thinking he'd enjoy nothing better than slowly removing every article of clothing until she was deliciously naked and quivering with need.

Closing the closet door, she started out of the foyer with the tote in her hand. Suddenly she halted and turned in his direction. Their gazes met. Her eyes widened, and he braced himself for her attack.

"Oh, Ethan, good morning. I didn't see you standing there."

She was smiling, not spewing malicious words or hurling accusations. "What?"

Dimples flashed flirtatiously in her mocha-colored face. Laughter bubbled from her arched throat as she neared and gazed up at him. "You must still be tired from staying up late Friday night. A good breakfast will fix you up."

Mutely he stared after her retreating figure. Humming floated back to him from the kitchen. His brows bunched. Humming? Where was the venom of the incensed woman? She acted as if Saturday morning had never happened.

The reason hit him. She was hiding her anger. He couldn't allow that. They needed to discuss what had happened, know that the mistake wasn't going to be repeated, then move on.

He found her putting a fresh filter in the coffee machine. "There is no need to pretend. I know what you're trying to do."

Relief swept across her expressive features. "I knew you'd understand. With any other man it might be impossible after what happened Saturday morning." She shook her head. "I mean, talk about fireworks. The thing is you didn't go off like a Roman candle."

Ethan's mouth gaped.

Turning on the machine, she turned her back to him, bent over and opened the light oak cabinet beneath the counter, and removed a quart saucepan. "I must admit, I was upset at first, but then I decided you were right. Horny is no reason to have sex."

Ethan licked his lips, wishing the sweater were longer and the leggings didn't cup her hips so well. "I-I didn't exactly mean horny."

Laughter tickled down his spine. She added several ingredients into the water and milk mixture. "Ethan." She seemed to purr the word and added grits. "Don't go noble and try to spare me. Things got out of hand, and you called them to a halt."

Covering the pot, she walked to him, close enough for him to inhale her fragrance, close enough for him to feel the imprint of her body, close enough for him to wish he had kept his mouth shut. "You won't ever have to worry about me squirming on top of you, thrusting my tongue in your mouth, running my hands over your body, wanting you to do the same to me."

Ethan's breath hitched at her vivid imagery. His unruly body responded before he could help himself. He took an embarrassed step backward.

Samantha didn't appear to notice. She was already moving back to the stove. "What do you want with your grits?"

"A-Anything," he managed. His mouth was bone dry.

"You're sure?" She glanced around, tugging the sweater up over her shoulder only for it to slide back down the moment she released the material. "I want to please you."

Ethan had to get out of there. He had been kidding himself to think he could stop wanting her. "I'll be in the study."

Samantha listened to Ethan's hasty departure and slumped against the counter. This wasn't going to work. Teasing Ethan was wrong. He had hurt her, but she was calm enough now to realize he hadn't meant it deliberately. He could have called them horny after they had made love.

Bringing him to his knees with desire wasn't as important now as bringing him to his senses. He had to realize that they could share something special if he'd just give them a chance. She had to do it honestly. Without giving herself time to back down, she went to the study door and knocked.

"Come in."

Taking a deep breath, she entered. There was no easy way, so she just spit it out. "I'm sorry about what just happened in the kitchen. Rejection hurts, and I wanted to hurt you back in a way that you'd understand."

Behind his desk Ethan's face remained remote. "You wanted to put the screws to me by making me want you again."

Her hands clenched. "Exactly. Only I ended up putting the screws to myself as well."

"Is that why you're here now?"

"No." She shook her head. "I don't like lies and subterfuge."

He braced his arms on his desk. "Neither do I. Thank you for coming." She turned to go, but his words stopped her. "By the way, your plan worked very well."

She whirled back around, her eyes bright with amazement. "It did?"

"You know it did," he said, but there was no animosity in his deep voice.

She bit her lip and remained quiet.

"I have an apology to make as well. I didn't mean to infer you were sexually indiscriminate. I was trying to say and putting it very badly, that this attraction between us overrides every other consideration. We see, we want."

She took a step closer. "What do you think we should do about it?"

Ethan steeled himself against the desire he saw flaring in her eyes. "Nothing. We go on and make sure there is not a repeat of Saturday morning."

"You really think we can do that?"

"Yes." He had to if he wanted to survive.

Dark brows lifted. "Then you're not as smart as all those degrees on the walls of your office at the high school say you are."

The door closed, and Ethan slumped back in his seat. On that they agreed. He had been insane to hire Samantha. Until Christmas. Surely he could last that long.

* * *

The rest of the day didn't get any better for Ethan. Superintendent Hodge arrived in his office immediately after morning announcements. For the next thirty minutes, he had crunched on his cookies, sipped coffee heavily laden with cream and sugar that Mrs. Lewis had brought him, and talked about Samantha.

During those weekends at the Oak Tree Inn, he and his wife had come to appreciate her intelligence, wit, and culinary skills. He didn't endear himself to Ethan when he stated if he had known she was available, he would have snapped her up. He went on to say if things didn't work out he would consider it a personal favor to be notified first.

With his tin of cookies perched on top of the plastic container of seasoned baked chicken breasts and wild rice, he finally sauntered happily from the office. Ethan came out later to see Mrs. Lewis sneak a cookie coated with powdered sugar from beneath a napkin on her desk.

"Hodge offered you a cookie?" he asked, surprised. He'd offered Ethan one, but it had been halfhearted at best. He'd declined.

Puzzlement widened her eyes. "Samantha just dropped these off." She indicated a large canister tied with an orange and gold bow behind her. "They're for those of us who were at the cafeteria, decorating."

"Oh."

"Here. Have one." She opened the tin top to reveal a colorful array of shapes and sizes covered in everything from powdered sugar to nuts and gumdrops.

"No, thanks." He went back to his office, feeling oddly left out. He'd seen the boys munching on the cookies all weekend, but hadn't eaten one despite their insistence that he do so. Somehow he hadn't felt right about eating her cookies until they had straightened things out between them. Now that they had, he wasn't going to get a cookie anyway.

Samantha, in her usual caring manner, had done something nice for everyone except him. What worried him most was how much it bothered him. As the day progressed, he thought of her more and more. By the time he started home, he was determined to put things back in their proper perspective. Samantha was not going to get to him.

When he arrived, Samantha, Alan, and Alex were in the backyard trying to teach Max to catch a Frisbee since he had mastered fetching a stick. Ethan hadn't meant to join in, but Samantha had tossed the Frisbee to him, and he had caught it automatically.

Without missing a beat, she had turned to Max and said, "See how it's done?" Max barked, then all three of them told him to throw the Frisbee. He had. When they all went inside thirty minutes later, Max came with them, the Frisbee hanging triumphantly from his sharp teeth.

The next day he came home to her planting daffodil bulbs by the front steps. The boys would like them when they shot up around Easter. Wednesday after dinner, nothing would do, but they had to go to the nursery for a pumpkin and decorative colored corn to set on the porch for Thanksgiving. They had a lively discussion before settling on a monster pumpkin they had to take to the Cherokee in a shopping cart, then used Alan's wagon to get it to the porch.

Thursday he was treated to a surprise Christmas piano recital by Alan and Alex. Samantha snapped pictures and his sons hammed it up, eager for their night to shine in December. Later they walked her out to her car as had become their habit. The three of them watched until her car taillights disappeared.

"I wish Sam stayed here all the time," Alex said.

"Me, too. Was our real mother like her?" Alan inquired.

Caught off-guard by the question, it took Ethan a long

time to answer. They hadn't asked about their mother in a couple of years. "Your mother was beautiful too."

"That's not what I meant." Alan stared up at his father in the foyer. "Did she read us stories and play with us, hug us the way Sam does? I don't remember."

"Me neither."

Ethan felt like someone was squeezing his heart as he stared down into the faces of his sons. He cursed Carol as he had a thousand times, drew a deep breath, and thanked her for Alan and Alex. "Yes, she did. All the time."

Alan nodded. "Do you think she would be hurt because we like Sam?"

"Or think we're selfish?"

His throat tight, Ethan placed a hand on each of their shoulders. "No, sons, I don't. No one can have too much love. She'd be very pleased you have someone like Samantha."

"Night, Dad."

"Night, Dad."

"Good night, Alan, Alex." Ethan watched them go to their room. They had grown up without the love and affection of a female figure daily in their lives. It was natural for them to revel in the love and attention Samantha gave them. It was natural for them to succumb.

He was stronger.

The outdoor football stadium was packed Friday night for the biggest event of the football season: homecoming. The Oakville Mustangs were pitted against their old rival, the Corsicana Tigers. There was as much activity off the field as on, Ethan thought.

Because he was involved with the homecoming activities on the field, Samantha had brought and stayed with Alan and Alex. Those who didn't know who his housekeeper was, knew by the time Alan and Alex were through. They introduced her to everyone, and she in turn introduced them to her acquaintances.

To his surprise, he didn't pick up any undercurrents of disapproval. Word had already gotten around about her bringing food for the students as well as the faculty. Her act of kindness was retold again and again. Superintendent Hodge and his wife certainly showed their support. For a quarter of the game, she and the boys sat with them.

What was so strange to Ethan was that they didn't spend much time with him. Despite his best efforts he missed her laughter, her smile, her tender concern.

He wanted her. He was tired of fighting the truth, but if he yielded to his desire what would be the consequences? Thanksgiving was less than a week away. All he had to do was stick it out until Christmas.

Ethan made sure he used the linen tablecloth and napkins, the good silverware, and the best glasses they had. He was determined that their Thanksgiving dinner be a success. He might as well have saved himself the effort.

It wasn't as if he and the boys weren't used to spending the Thanksgiving holiday by themselves, choosing instead to go to his parents' home for the longer Christmas holidays. He'd usually order a turkey or ham dinner with all the trimmings. They'd stuff themselves without worrying about calories, watch the football games on TV, and afterward Alan and Alex would seriously get down to hinting about what they wanted for Christmas.

This year, despite Samantha repeatedly telling him she wanted to cook their dinner, he had gotten it into his head to cook dinner himself. It was time to start putting some distance between them. He'd show her and the boys that they could get along very well without her in their lives.

His plan failed. The ham was salty, the yams overcooked. Their dinner was eaten in relative silence. All of them kept sneaking glances at the empty chair directly in front of him.

Samantha's chair. Even on weekends no one sat there.

Alex picked at his green beans. "Alan, you think Sam's finished with her rounds?"

"Rounds?" Ethan queried.

"She's taking food to some senior citizens of her church," Alan explained. "I bet it tastes good too." He jumped, then bent down to rub his leg, frowning at his brother across from him.

"Not that this doesn't." Alex glared at his brother and brought a tiny sliver of ham to his mouth.

"Don't eat that."

Alex quickly lowered his fork with a look of relief on his face. If it hadn't been for Ethan's libido, they could be eating a wonderful meal. "I'm sorry dinner turned out so bad. Guess I should have let Samantha cook."

"Why didn't you?"

Ethan leaned back in his chair. "That's a good question, Alex. When I come up with a good answer, I'll let you know."

The twins traded worried glances. "Dad, maybe you shouldn't eat any more either."

They loved him. It was there, staring back at him in their trusting faces, and he had condemned them to a miserable Thanksgiving.

"Let's get the kitchen cleaned up and go find someplace to eat."

"We could go over to Sam's house," Alex said. "She invited us, remember?"

"Can't we can get along one day without Samantha?"

"Yes, sir." His head dropped.

Ethan put his hand on his son's head. "Sorry, Alex. I shouldn't have yelled."

His head lifted. "That's okay, Dad. I know you worried

about the dinner not turning out so good, but Sam said cooking is a flair and not everyone can do it."

"The green beans weren't so bad," Alan said.

Ethan smiled. "I bet even Max won't eat them."

"I bet he will." Picking up his plate, Alan ran for the back door. His brother followed.

After cutting off a wedge of ham, Ethan went after them. At least the dog would have a good dinner.

Chapter Eight

Samantha couldn't stay away from their house. She couldn't eat for thinking Ethan, Alan, and Alex weren't enjoying a good meal. Ethan had assured her he had everything covered. She wasn't so sure. She had snuck a peek inside the paper sack he had brought home Wednesday night and saw the picnic ham. They could be good, if you knew how to cook and baste them—otherwise it was like eating pure salt, she thought.

Rubbing her hands on her taupe wool skirt, she rang the doorbell. After waiting a short time, she rang again. Nothing. Disappointed, she shoved her hands deep into the pockets of her jacket and walked back to her car, head down.

Her hand was on the car's door handle when she heard the excited bark of Max and the laughter of Alan and Alex. A smile blossoming on her lips, she hurried around the side of the house and let herself inside the cedar fence. All three of the Rawlings were staring down at Max while he gulped from his food dish.

"Is something wrong with Max?"

Max's head came up. Ethan, Alan, and Alex turned in unison. "Sam," the boys yelled and ran toward her. Max was faster.

Laughing, she swept up the flared hem of her skirt and lifted it away from some very sharp teeth. "No, you don't." Max whined. Still smiling, she patted him on the head and received a forgiving bark.

"Hello, guys," she greeted when they reached her.

"I'm glad you came."

"I missed you."

With her free hand, she playfully rubbed their heads. "Likewise."

Ethan ran an appreciative look over her long legs bared from her knees downward. "Hello. What brings you out this way?"

Her smile slipped a bit. "I was just out driving and thought I'd stop by."

Heavy eyebrows lifted. "We're kind of out of the way for that."

Her chin lifted. "I wanted to make sure you all had eaten properly."

The boys looked at their father. He appreciated their loyalty, and yielded to the beseeching look in their eyes. "Max enjoyed it more than we did."

Alan giggled. "I told Dad he'd eat the green beans."

"Dad gave him some ham too," Alex added.

"He's the only one who could eat it," Ethan said, oddly not embarrassed by the admission. "You just caught us. We were going to go find someplace to eat."

Samantha glared at him. "You eat anyplace else after I invited you and wooden Justice is going to tap dance a tune all over your stubborn head."

Ethan chuckled. "How could I turn down such a charming invitation?"

"You're really coming?" she asked over the boys' excited shouts, hardly able to believe it.

"As soon as we get the kitchen cleaned up."

"We'll go get started." Alex took off, Alan behind him.

"I can help," she offered.

"We'll do it and then follow." Ethan reached out and brushed a strand of hair away from her exquisite face. "I hope you prepared a lot. Breakfast was a long, unsatisfied time ago."

She let out an unsteady breath. He'd touched her. Was he changing his mind about them? "You won't be disappointed."

"Finally, I'm starting to believe that."

Hands clasped as they stood around Samantha's small kitchen table, Ethan gave thanks, then set to carving the golden-brown turkey. While he did, Samantha dished up corn bread, dressing, giblet gravy, candied yams covered with baked marshmallows, and broccoli and rice casserole. The dinner rolls were freshly made as was the chess pie and pineapple cake.

This time there was no hesitation on anyone's part as they ate dinner, laughed and talked. Ethan glanced at his sons and came to a decision. The table setting was lovely, the food great, but it had nothing to do with Alan and Alex's easy laughter ringing in the small apartment. It was the woman who brightened their day just by being.

Instead of watching football as was their custom after dinner, they played a black history board game. Ethan and Alex won, but Samantha and Alan were close seconds. No one seemed inclined to call it a night, but by ten-fifteen, Ethan could see the boys tiring.

He got their jackets. "Thanks, Samantha. I can't remember a better Thanksgiving."

"Me neither." She helped Alan with his uncooperative and heavy arms. "You're going to get your tree tomorrow?"

Alex's droopy eyelids snapped upward. "I hope we get a real one this time."

"You've never had a real tree?" Samantha asked, her gaze going from Ethan to Alex.

"An artificial one just seemed easier," Ethan confessed, wondering why he felt as if he had let his children down in some way.

She stared into Ethan's eyes. "There's a tree farm about thirty miles from here. I usually go and pick one out for the inn. This year I was going to pick one for myself."

"Can I go?" Alex asked.

"Go where?" Alan said, and yawned.

"To a tree farm to pick out a real Christmas tree," his younger brother told him.

Sleepiness vanished in an instant. "Great! When do we go?"

Samantha bit her lip. "I didn't mean—"

"Yes, you did," Ethan said, cutting her off, but there was no censure in his voice. "What time do we pick you up?"

She wasn't going to play coy. "Nine-thirty and I'll fix breakfast."

"No. We'll get something on the way. You've done enough cooking." He straightened Alan's slipping cap. "Come on, guys. We better get to bed if we're going to be tromping all over God's creation trying to get a tree."

"It'll be fun," Samantha said.

"That remains to be seen," Ethan told her, guiding Alan and Alex toward the door.

They ate breakfast at Callie's Restaurant. Ethan could only shake his head and smile at the exuberance of Alan and Alex. They told everyone from the waitress to people in the buffet line where they were going. He stopped smiling when he realized if things did get hot and heavy between him and Samantha, they'd be just as forthcoming about the information.

"Everything all right?"

Ethan paused in opening the Cherokee's passenger

door. Samantha stared up at him with concern in her beautiful brown eyes. Resisting their pull was becoming more difficult with each passing day.

"Ethan?"

"Everything is fine. Let's go get our trees." He closed the door and went around to the driver's side. Buckling his seat belt, he drove away. Why was he worried about what Alan and Alex would say about Samantha and himself? Nothing was going to happen.

They found a perfect tree for Ethan and his sons. Samantha couldn't make up her mind and came away empty-handed. Ethan suspected the reason. The nine-foot, fat spruce the boys decided on took up the entire roof of his utility vehicle and then some. Driving home, he promised himself she'd get a tree.

She was as excited as Alan and Alex to see the tree in the den. She suggested the placement instead of the living room so they could enjoy it nightly, and they wouldn't forget to turn off the lights.

"What theme do you think you should have?" she asked.

"Theme?" Ethan walked up to stand beside her. "We just throw on decorations."

"Lots of tinsel," Alex told her.

Samantha turned. "Aren't there any special ornaments you put on the tree each year?"

"We use the blue and green balls every year," Alan said.

Samantha simply continued to stare at Ethan. Once again he felt as if he had failed his children by not having a special Christmas tradition. "Not especially. I think their grandmother might have sent them something for their first Christmas."

Interest lit her eyes. "Where are they?"

"I'm not sure. With the rest of the decorations I suppose." He didn't like the way she was now glaring at him.

"If you'd show me where, I'd like to see if I could find them."

"Now?"

"Yes, now." Samantha placed her hands on her hips.

Ethan had been around his determined mother enough to know when not to argue. Besides, he was beginning to feel rather bad that he hadn't kept up with the ornaments better. "They're in the attic. I'll show you."

An hour later Alan and Alex placed their hand-painted, gold, ebony-hued cherubs, and two huge gold ornaments decorated with ribbon and pearl beads dated with the year of their birth on the tree. As Samantha thought, they were fascinated with the finds. When she suggested they build the tree and house decorations around the cherubs using gold and white, they readily agreed.

"What do you think, Ethan?" She wanted his approval as well.

"I think I better get some more money out of the cash box," he said with a smile.

"Nonsense." She walked over and picked up the large plastic bag of tree cuttings she and the boys had gathered for free at the tree farm. "I work best on a budget."

Sunday night the fir tree sparkled like a golden snow queen dressed in her golden bows, golden glass ball ornaments, and cherubs. Around the room soft white candles of different sizes and shapes glowed as they sat amid greenery. Over the fireplace a large wreath hung with an elegant gold ribbon trim, bow, and gold beads.

Samantha turned off the lights and watched Ethan, Alan, and Alex's expressions. Wonder and joy shone back at her. The hours spent sewing and using the glue gun, scouring the discount stores for bargains, had paid off.

Ethan turned to her. "It's beautiful. I don't know how to thank you."

"You already have." She sent him a shaky smile. "It's in your face, all of your faces."

Without thought, he reached for her hand. She didn't hesitate. Alan leaned against Samantha; Alex against Ethan. Loving arms circled the boys' shoulders and pulled them closer. For a long time they just stared at the tree and basked in being together.

As the days zipped by toward Christmas, Ethan wondered how they had ever gotten along without Samantha. There wasn't anything she couldn't do, and she did it all with a smile. The beautifully decorated house was only one example.

The boys wanted to make something for their piano and classroom teachers, their football coach, and their troop leader for their Christmas presents. For the women she helped make pecan divinity, which they wrapped in pretty but inexpensive crystal bowls, then covered with a red plastic wrap, bow, and a sprig of holly. The men received chocolate fudge in decorated red and gold boxes with matching ribbons.

For Ethan's office door they made a rustic wreath by covering a twig wreath with blue ribbon trimmed in gold and adding little gold boxes. The homemade red and green jellies for his candy dish were gone within a day once word got out.

His secretary told everyone upfront she was taking her candy home, so don't ask. More than one faculty and staff member hinted they'd like a wreath or homemade candy. Ethan always told them he'd get the instructions or the recipe. Samantha had enough to do taking care of them, which she did extremely well.

Samantha didn't just pamper the boys, she pampered

him as well. Fresh sheets and large fluffy bath towels, which she picked up on sale, hot breakfasts, a clean house—and every afternoon she met him with a smile, a fantastic meal, and happy children. He should have been ecstatically happy and he was, until Samantha left each night.

A strange silence seemed to settle over the house that not even the splendor of the Christmas decorations helped ease. Because each flickering candle, each handmade stocking hanging on the mantel with everyone's name, including Pete and Max's, was a constant reminder that she wasn't there.

Lying in his bed at night, Ethan realized he missed her more with each passing day. He'd think of her beside him, not just for the loving, but to hear her laugh, see her smile, to give back to her what she so selflessly gave to him and his boys and those who touched their lives.

Someone needed to pamper Samantha. The thought solidified in his mind. That someone was going to be him.

Chapter Nine

Ethan was having difficulty carrying out his plan, and he wasn't pleased about it. Two nights in a row after dinner, Samantha kissed and hugged the boys and hurried out of the house. He'd tried to pin her down to set a day to go pick out her tree, but she kept insisting hers didn't matter as long as Alan and Alex had theirs.

By the fourth night of watching her hastily leave, he was more than a little piqued that she kept hurrying home. In the three weeks since Thanksgiving, she had stayed around after dinner to read to the boys, help them with their homework, or just relax with all of them.

Ethan had had enough. He gave her enough time to get home, then called from his bedroom. His irritation increased when there was no answer. He stopped trying after ten. He wasn't piqued any longer, he was jealous. Samantha wasn't just rushing home, she was rushing to meet some man.

The next morning he met her at the front door. "I called you last night until ten, and you weren't home."

Samantha blinked at the brusque voice and unyielding

face. She had thought the old Ethan was gone forever. Then another thought struck. "Are the boys all right?"

"Why does it always have to be the boys?" he snapped. "I wanted you for me."

"Oh, Ethan," she said, unable to believe he was finally going to admit he cared about her.

"Were you on a date?"

His attitude might have ticked her off if she didn't already love him so much. She hung up her coat in the closet and went to the kitchen.

"I asked if you were on a date?"

He looked ready to blow. Samantha wished she could bask in his jealousy. She couldn't. He had to know how she felt about him. "You're the only man I want to date, Ethan. I don't believe in substitutions."

His head snapped back. Surprise was written all over his face, but he wasn't going to back down. "You shouldn't be out late at night."

"Yes, Mother," she teased.

He glowered at her. "This is not funny."

That she agreed with. It wasn't funny loving a man, wanting with every breath to have him love you in return— and he was fighting it tooth and nail. "If you must know, I was at the music center helping them get ready for the piano recital tomorrow afternoon."

"Why?"

"They sent out a notice for volunteers and apparently didn't get much response." She opened the refrigerator and took out a package of turkey bacon. "I thought I'd help. After the gifts Alan and Alex made for Mrs. Johnson, she was very glad to get my help."

He frowned. "I don't remember getting any letter."

She busied herself placing the bacon in the skillet. "She needed only one person from each family. And if you say I'm not family, I'll brain you with this skillet."

He couldn't help himself. He caught her around the

waist, turning her to him. "I'd be a fool and a liar to say that."

"Thank you." The words trembled over her lips.

His hand brushed the hair back from her face. "How many other mothers are helping?"

Samantha's breath caught at the wording of his question. "Four."

"What!" He snatched his hand down and stared back at her. "I know there are fifty-odd children who will have their recital sometime during Saturday. What about the rest of them?"

She made a helpless gesture. "I don't know. Maybe they work."

"And you don't? You work harder than two women, taking care of us and this house. You could use the extra time to work on the cookbook." Suspicion narrowed his gaze. "What else did Mrs. Johnson ask you to do?"

Samantha moistened her lips. Ethan wasn't going to like her answer by the way he was glaring at her. "Just to bring something for the parents to snack on."

She was right. "No. I forbid it."

"Eth—"

"No. You're not going to work like a pack mule. Let some of the other mothers do something." Reaching under the cabinet, he pulled out a phone book. "Call the bakery and order four dozen cookies. If Mrs. Johnson has a problem with that, tell her to call me."

"I don't mind."

His hands circled her arms. "You should. People take advantage of you because you're so giving. That's going to stop."

She stared up into his fierce eyes. "Not everyone."

"Yeah. Who?"

"You," she answered tenderly.

His grip tightened for a second, then he leaned his

forehead against hers. "I want to, probably more than anyone."

"I'd let you too."

He groaned. "Oh, Samantha."

"Maybe if we kiss we'll both feel better."

"You really believe that?"

"No, but I'm willing to say anything to get you to kiss me again. I'm tired of aching."

"Kissing will only make it worse."

"Let's see," she said, pulling him under the kitchen door frame where she'd hung a ball of mistletoe.

Her chin tilted upward. On tiptoes, she brushed her lips gently across his. With a guttural curse, he pulled her into his arms, kissing her with all the pent-up need and frustration he had endured since their last kiss. It was a long time before he lifted his head.

Samantha laid her head against his chest. "I-I think you were right about the aching part, but do you want to kiss me again just to make sure we did it right?"

Laughing, he hugged her to him. "How did we ever think we were happy without you?"

Samantha felt him stiffen at the admission and tightened her hold. "Don't do this to me again. Please."

Tension eased out of his body. "I wish things were different."

"They are, Ethan. You just can't see it yet." This time it was Samantha who pulled away.

Alan and Alex's Christmas piano recital Saturday afternoon was a tremendous success. It probably helped that school was out for the winter break. Loud applause sounded from the crowd when they finished their duet of "Minuet in G" by Bach, a piece that was one level above their age. Ethan had the camcorder rolling while Samantha snapped pictures.

Afterward everyone was shown to the reception area. Ethan glanced at the familiar festive green and red ribbons the boys had used on some of their gifts, the red damask stockings at each corner of the table that were identical to the ones hanging on their mantel, the assorted cookies covered in powdered sugar, nuts, and gumdrops, and turned to Samantha, a reprimand on his lips.

Before he could speak, Mrs. Johnson was asking for everyone's attention. "Thank you all for coming, and a special thanks to my parent volunteers, and especially Samantha Clark, the Rawlingses' housekeeper, for so generously helping with the decorations and providing us with these wonderful goodies."

Everyone in the room applauded. Samantha was smiling, but it seemed forced. It was more than Ethan could tolerate. How dare Mrs. Johnson relegate her to housekeeper when she had worked so hard to help make the day a success for all the children and parents.

He started across the room, but a small hand on his arm stopped him. "It doesn't matter. As long as Alan and Alex are happy."

"It does matter."

"Your reputation matters more." Her fingers flexed on his arm, then slid away as she turned to greet one of the parents.

At the moment he didn't give a flaming leap about his reputation. He started for Mrs. Johnson again and was stopped by an old high school friend who had a daughter in the recital. By the time he finally reached Mrs. Johnson, his anger had cooled considerably. He realized why.

To the general public, Samantha might be their housekeeper, but to them she was everything. While there was nothing wrong with being a housekeeper, he and the boys just didn't think of her that way anymore and neither did she. They were a family, even if no one else recognized the fact.

The powerful realization scared and comforted him. The question was, what was he going to do about it? He'd told her she was hired until Christmas. Four short days away. Sometime before then he had to make a decision that was going to affect the rest of his and his sons' lives.

Chapter Ten

The weatherman forecasted snow for Monday, the twenty-third of December. He had missed it by a country mile.

Ethan stared at the bright sunlight streaming through the curtains in his study and shook his head. Sunday afternoon Samantha, Alan, and Alex's conversation on the phone had centered around the best way to build and dress a snowman. Thank goodness, she was used to the unpredictability of Texas weather and had cautioned them into not being too letdown if it didn't snow.

This morning when they woke up, their disappointment was due more to Samantha not coming over than not seeing snow. She had sounded just as down as the boys looked when she called. All three had seen and played in snow before, they just had never done it together. More to the point, it didn't give a logical reason for her to visit.

Restless, Ethan pushed up from his desk. She shouldn't need a logical reason to come to his house. It should be enough that they missed her and the house wasn't the same without her.

Last night he found himself sitting in the den with the lights off, just staring at the radiant Christmas tree she had gifted them with. Her love and caring thoughtfulness permeated the house. She did so much for others and expected nothing in return, not even a simple thank you.

A rare woman in today's world. And he would lose her if he made the wrong decision. *Until Christmas.* He rubbed the back of his neck. The answer to his dilemma eluded him. Samantha could be his lover or his housekeeper. Never both. He wasn't too sure how she would react to giving up taking care of Alan and Alex. Just the thought had him searching for another answer. They belonged together. They had connected immediately, and the bond continued to grow stronger each passing day. For the past hour Alan and Alex had—

Ethan's thoughts halted. Tilting his head, he listened. *Too quiet.* Eight-year-olds weren't this quiet unless they were into something. The question was, what?

The door to their room was closed. Since these days it wasn't because it looked like a bomb had exploded in their closet, there had to be another reason.

He rapped on the door. "Alan. Alex. Can I come in?"

The door opened abruptly. Alex grabbed him by the hand and pulled him across the room to their desk. "Come see what you think. We made Sam a stocking."

"Doesn't it look cool?" Alan stated proudly, holding up the stocking.

The red damask stocking in no way resembled the neatly stitched ones hanging from the mantel with fringes and organdy trim, each name in elegant gold thread. But it was the name on the stocking that made the air stall in Ethan's lungs.

"Sam told us not to use the glue gun she left in the kitchen without you or her there, so we had to improvise since we wanted to do it by ourselves." Grinning broadly, Alex glanced from the stocking to his father. "We used the staple gun, then used the red Magic Marker to cover the staples."

"We tried to sew the name on, but it looked kind of messy." Frowning, Alan stuck a couple of fingers into his mouth. "I pricked my finger, but I didn't get any blood on it. Her name glued on with gold glitter looked almost as good."

Ethan couldn't say a word. Not one.

The boys traded worried glances. This wasn't the reaction they expected. Their father didn't have any wrinkles in his forehead, so he wasn't mad. But what was the matter with him?

Unsure, Alan lowered the stocking. "You don't think she'll like it?"

"We don't have any more red material to make another one." Alex appeared as anxious as his brother. "We gotta make it right for her."

With trembling hands Ethan took the stocking, then ran his fingertips over the gold glitter. The answer he had searched for stared boldly back at him. Instead of the fear he expected, he felt at peace for the first time in weeks.

He was smiling by the time his head lifted. "You make me proud. I always knew you fellows had good taste."

Twin frowns quickly turned into wide smiles. "You think she'll like it?" Alan asked.

"She won't mind about the glitter?" Alex wanted to know.

Ethan's smile widened. "She'll cry like a baby, and tears from a woman means she loves it."

"When can we give it to her?"

"Can we call her now?"

"Not just yet. First, I have a couple of things I need to take care of, and I need your help." Ethan's arms curved around the boy's shoulders. "And if things work out the way I think they will, this is going to be the best Christmas this family has ever had."

* * *

Samantha was restless. She missed Ethan, Alan, and Alex. She had thought they might invite her over Christmas Eve and had stayed home all day waiting for the phone to ring. Numerous calls came—from family, from friends—but not from the one she most wanted to hear from. Since it was near midnight, he wasn't likely to call now. She finally had time to work on the cookbook, but her enthusiasm was gone.

Trying to keep from crying, she concentrated on wrapping Ethan's present. A sensible, friendly sweater. She had wanted to be daring and give him some sexy underwear with a little note asking him to model it for her. Too bold. Too obvious. But the image of Ethan in only skimpy underwear and a smile was difficult to put out of her mind as she tied the red bow on the gold foil box, then placed it on the table with the rest of the gifts she had wrapped.

Although she had promised herself a tree this year, she just hadn't felt like getting one. Some things were better shared. Especially during this time of year.

The sharp bite of loneliness was never felt more strongly than now when her loved ones across the country were gathering together. Her independent, fun-loving sisters had gone skiing with a group of friends. Her outgoing parents had flown to New York.

They all had someplace special to go, someone special to be with. She was spending Christmas Eve in her apartment by herself and not even a cup of spiked eggnog to keep her company. She might need something to fortify her after tomorrow. *Until Christmas.*

It was only a short time away to find out if Ethan had come to a decision about letting her stay as his housekeeper.

Her arms circled her waist. She wanted so much more. That was what had upset her at the boys' recital. She didn't mind being called a housekeeper—it was a respectable position. She just wanted to be called wife and mother more.

In the season of miracles, was it so selfish to wish for one tiny miracle, to wish for Ethan's love, to wish he'd give them a chance to be a family. . . . She'd shown him her love in countless ways, but he still refused to give them a chance.

Tomorrow was Christmas. Time was running out for her.

The ringing of her doorbell caused her to frown. Cautiously she checked the peephole. Ethan, Alan, and Alex stood in the doorway. Quickly she opened the door. As usual the boys gave her an exuberant welcome, a tight hug, and excited conversation.

"We came to get you to show you the lights we put up."

"It's way cool."

Ethan chuckled. "Hello, Samantha. Guess you can tell they're excited."

She wondered if the warmth was really in Ethan's voice and face or if she just wanted it to be there. "Come on in," she invited, trying not to be disappointed that they hadn't asked her to help. "I didn't know you were going to do any more decorating."

Ethan winked at his sons. "Me neither until yesterday."

"We're starting a family tradition," Alan said.

"We wanted you to be the first to see it." Alex grabbed her hand. "Hurry up and get your coat."

Samantha felt her spirits plummet lower. They had begun a family tradition that didn't include her, then she looked at the wide grins on Alan and Alex's faces and chastised herself for her selfishness. Their happiness was all that mattered.

"While I'm getting my coat, could you please put those gifts on the table in the shopping bag beneath them?" She smiled down at the twins. "I think you might find your names on one or two." Actually there were several.

"We got you something, too, but you have to see the lights first," Alex told her.

"You won't even have to wait long to open it."

Berating herself even more for her selfish thoughts earlier, Samantha hurried to get her coat.

If Samantha expected to see the lights when she arrived, she was doomed to disappointment. Instead, Ethan drove the Cherokee into the garage, and they all went inside. He stoked the fire, then motioned her to the sofa in the den. Seated, Alan handed her a cup of steaming cider and Alex a gingerbread man. She lifted inquiring eyes to Ethan.

"Stringing up lights is tough," he said, taking a seat beside her. "I thought we'd rest for a few minutes, then I wanted to read a story."

"It's going to be another tradition," Alex informed her.

"So are the candles." Alan cut out the lights, then began lighting the candles. Alex helped.

"Aren't you going to eat your gingerbread?" Ethan asked.

Unsure of what was going on, but feeling better that they were including her as part of a family tradition, she took a bite. "This is good."

"Mother made it. They started back early because of the prediction of snow," Ethan explained, picking up a gold-leafed book, but he didn't open the pages until Alan and Alex perched on the hassock in front of them.

"The title of this story is 'Until Christmas.' I'm sure you'll recognize the author." His voice mellowed. "Once upon a time a beautiful lady from a land of snow and ice went to a far-away town to bring love and happiness to a grumpy father and his two wise sons."

"Ethan."

"Fellows, maybe you better take the cider and the gingerbread."

Samantha gladly relinquished the things. Her hands, her entire body were shaking.

"The boys were wise because they knew from their first meeting the beautiful and kind lady was special. The father wasn't so sure. He wanted the lady gone from their lives and agreed to let her stay only until Christmas."

"Ethan . . ." Samantha sniffed, then took the tissue Alan handed her to wipe the tears from her eyes. She didn't want to miss seeing a thing.

"But a wonderful and magical thing happened while the lady cared for the family. The father saw her unselfishness, her devotion to his sons, and most of all the boundless love she possessed and how happy she made them all."

Ethan took her hand in his, his eyes gazing tenderly into hers. "He fell in love and the day before she was to leave, he asked the lady to marry him."

Samantha was leaning toward Ethan, who was leaning toward her when she heard, "Not yet. You gotta see the lights first."

Too dazed with happiness to protest, she allowed herself to be pulled out the front door and halfway across the front yard. Ethan pushed a control in his hand and lights came on.

Tears streamed down Samantha's cheeks. Spelled out in white lights was *Keeper of my heart, will you marry me?*

"Yes," trembled across her lips.

Ethan pulled her into his arms to the loud yells of Alan and Alex. "Each Christmas thereafter the man continued to express his love in lights for the beautiful lady for all the world to see. The end."

"And they lived happily ever after," Samantha managed just before his mouth closed on hers.

"Now can we hang it up, Dad?"

"You said we could."

Ethan reluctantly lifted his head. They'd be in bed soon.

Besides, they had showed him the way. "Come on, there's another tradition waiting inside for you."

Inside, Alan and Alex ran straight to the hearth where the stocking hanger was already waiting. Alan guided the top of the red damask stocking while Alex held the bottom. Like the others it had a name.

Mom.

Samantha started crying again. Alan and Alex looked at their father. He smiled and curved his arm around her shoulder, hugged her to him with one arm, then held out the other for his sons to join them.

The clock on the mantel struck twelve. Christmas. They were a family.

Epilogue

"Stop giggling or you're going to wake the children."

"Then you stop."

"I can't. You taste too good. Especially this spot right here."

"Oh, Ethan."

"And this one here?"

"Oh, Ethan."

"Sam."

"I can't wait."

"I can't either."

A loud knock sounded on the door. "Mom. Dad. It's time."

Another knock. "We wanna start celebrating."

A dog barked.

"Me twu."

Ethan lifted his head from a very intriguing part of his wife's anatomy and gazed into her eyes. "Our daughter is up also."

Samantha smiled. "What do you bet our sons woke their baby sister up?"

"Mom? Dad? Adrian looks like she might start crying."

"Yeah. She's got that wrinkle in her forehead just like Dad does, and you know what that means."

"She's two years old today. It's time she started learning about the Rawlings' Christmas tradition."

"It's almost midnight on Christmas Eve. Dad has to read *Until Christmas.* This year we better keep the book away from Adrian or she'll chew on it like the cookbook Mom made for her."

"After Dad finishes reading we can go outside to see what he wrote in lights. But, Mom, I really think you should have made Adrian's stocking over this year. Dad tried but the letters are crooked."

Ethan and Samantha smiled at each other and began getting dressed. From experience they knew the children would be asleep within an hour and then they could get back to a little tradition of their own.

Kwanzaa Angel

BY

SHIRLEY HAILSTOCK

To the Township of Cranbury, New Jersey

Dear Reader,

Holiday memories are the warmest ones we have. Bringing them to mind is something we share annually with family and friends as we gather for our personal celebrations. The principles of Kwanzaa inspire us all to believe in ourselves and do what we can do to make this a better world. Erin and Raimi found each other during this wondrous period. Not only will they build a better life for themselves, but enhance all those who touch them.

The beautiful city of Cranbury, NJ, was used as their setting. It's a place I often amble through drinking in the rich history of the area and contemplating the setting sun by Brainerd Lake. Erin and Raimi get to live there, creating their memories for many Kwanzaas to come. I truly hope you enjoy visiting with them, glimpsing a part of their lives and knowing that they found each other and their true love.

I receive many letters from the women and men who read my books. Thank you for your generous comments and words of encouragement. I love reading your letters as much as I enjoy writing the books.

Sincerely yours,

Shirley Hailstock
Shirley Hailstock

Chapter One

"Can you help me?" Erin Scott felt the tug on her skirt and heard the little voice at the same time. She turned away from the stack of sweaters she'd folded and refolded at least seven times that day. The store was crowded with people taking advantage of the after-Christmas sales and people returning or exchanging yesterday's ill-fitted or unwanted gifts. Behind Erin stood a little girl about seven years old with long dark braids.

"My uncle said it was all right to ask a stranger for help as long as I went to the stranger and they did not come to me," her young voice explained. "He also said a lady would be better than a man."

Erin smiled as she stooped to the child's level. "Your uncle must be a very good parent," she told her.

"Oh, he's not a parent. He has only me. I'm his favorite niece." She said it with all the adultness a seven-year-old could muster. Erin stifled a laugh.

"Are you lost?" Although Erin smiled, the little girl didn't.

"No, ma'am." She shook her head from side to side.

The long braids, clipped with red barrettes, slapped at her face. She had bangs that flowed dark and engaging to her eyebrows and eyelashes that Erin wished were her own. "I know where I am."

"Then how can I help you?"

"It's my uncle. He's lost." She checked over her shoulder. "He was buying a gift and I looked around. Then he was gone."

Erin looked about the store. Everyone here was buying something. It was the day after Christmas, sale day, the largest shopping day of the year, equal to Black Friday. The store was so crowded Erin had left her office to join the sales staff. She admitted she loved doing it, but today had been so busy she hardly had time to look at any of the people she was serving, just their credit cards or checks.

"Don't worry, sweetheart. We'll find him. Now what's your name?"

"Alicia Marie Allen."

She spoke distinctly, like she'd learned her name in nursery school.

"Okay, Alicia Marie Allen, my name is Erin." She pointed to the small white name tag pinned to the lapel of her red suit with her first name printed in block letters.

"Can I call you Erin?"

Erin nodded.

"My uncle makes me call big people Ms. or Mrs."

Erin smiled broadly. She wanted to hug the child. "Well maybe in my case, he'll make an exception. Now what's your uncle's name?"

"Uncle Raimi."

Erin stiffened. She lost her balance, putting her hand on the floor to keep from falling. It couldn't be him, she told herself. "Uncle Raimi Allen?" Erin asked, grasping at a straw, knowing she was wrong even before the child's head moved from side to side. There was only one person she'd ever met named Raimi.

"Uncle Raimi Price," the child supplied as if on cue and with the same aplomb with which she'd given her own name.

Erin caught her gasp before it escaped. Raimi Price was in her store. What was he doing here? When had he returned to Cranbury, New Jersey, and why did no one mention he was in town?

The rumor mill here was as lively as it was in any small community. Cranbury was only a few miles square. She could walk it end to end in under an hour. Yet the grapevine had failed to get word to her that the man who'd dumped her at the senior prom was back and likely to cross paths with her at any moment.

The small hamlet in the center of the state was quiet and reserved with only a meager area they could call downtown. On any summer evening you could find people walking down the streets. At this time of year, they admired the holiday decorations and store scenes. Erin's store sat in the center of town, near the lake. When she'd bought the old warehouse building, people called her idea crazy, but today those same people shopped regularly here and spoke to her with a smile and a nod. Any one of them could have told her Raimi was back. Yet none of them had. Had they forgotten what happened to her? It was years ago. She was thirty-three now, no longer a sophomore, and no longer in love with Raimi Price.

What would Raimi's presence change? Would they remember what he'd done to her? Of course they would, she told herself. It was a hazard of living in a small town. Everyone knew everyone else and memories were long.

"Do you think we could look for him?" The little voice brought her back to her position on the floor.

"I'll—I'll get someone to find him," Erin stammered.

"There he is." Alicia's voice sounded excited, and she scampered off toward him. Erin wanted to turn away, but she was crouched on the floor. She stood up slowly, fear making her heart beat faster, waiting for that moment when he'd make eye contact with her, the moment he recognized who she was.

In one hand Raimi had a shopping bag with the store's logo on its side. With the grace of a large cat, he knelt to the floor and received the running child. Erin watched him hug her, then push her away, saying something reprimanding before pulling her against his chest and hugging her again. Finally, he stood, taking the child with him, holding her with only one arm. The other he used to pick up the shopping bag.

Erin hadn't seen Raimi Price since her last day of high school, sixteen years ago. He'd humiliated her so badly at the senior prom that she never wanted to see him again. Yet here he stood, looking directly at her. The crowd in the store seemed to recede as Alicia pointed toward her and Raimi came forward.

He hadn't changed much in seventeen years. As a seventeen-year-old he was the best-looking guy in school: tall, athletic, tight buns. At thirty-four any boyishness he had had long since vanished. The man approaching her was blindingly sexy. His skin was dark and rich like smooth silk. His hair was thick, closely cut, and he wore a small mustache. He still had that outdoor athletic look. Erin remembered thinking he reminded her of a Montana cowboy—rugged, strong, capable of anything—and how she'd wanted those strong arms banded about her body.

The weather outside was warm for December. She'd seen a lot of sweatshirts and jeans this afternoon. Raimi Price wore no coat. Gray wool slacks and a cable knit sweater outlined his body to the point that Erin wanted to run her hands over him, despite the amount of time between them and despite what she'd just been thinking about him. Looks this good should be against the law, but Raimi Price was a law unto himself.

Quickly she moved behind the service desk. Her mouth

went **dry**, and her heart started a tom-tom beat that was more than a little familiar. He approached her, standing Alicia on the floor next to him, but keeping hold of her hand. He set the shopping bag down and extended his hand to her.

"Thank you," he said. She allowed her fingers to be swallowed in his. "Alicia said you were helping her find me. It's so crowded we got separated. I can tell you, my heart nearly jumped out of my chest when I discovered her missing."

"I wasn't missing, Uncle Raimi," the high, sweet voice contradicted. "You got lost."

"Everything is fine now." Erin's voice was a whisper as she pulled her hand away from the warm grasp. She didn't know what to say. She didn't know just seeing him again could make her knees weak. She hated him. She'd hated him for sixteen years, but he appeared not to know who she was.

One part of her wanted to remind him of what he'd done, confront him with the details of their one and only date. The other part of her was grateful the event had no significance in his mind.

"I see you've been doing some after-Christmas shopping." Erin said the first thing that came to mind. It beat having him scrutinizing her like a lab rat.

"Kwanzaa," he said.

"Oh-h-h." Her mouth formed an O.

"Is there something wrong with that?"

"Of course not." She gave him her associate smile. "Happy holidays." Erin tried to walk away. The area had been completely crowded a moment ago. Now that she looked around to help another customer, everyone was being taken care of.

"What did that mean?" Raimi asked.

She turned back, knowing it was rude to ignore him. She met his eyes. They were brown like most black men's eyes, yet his had a depth to them that had turned her knees to water in high school and had the same effect on her at thirty-three.

"It's just that . . ." She hesitated.

"Go on."

"It doesn't seem in the spirit of Kwanzaa. Aren't you supposed to make gifts for Kwanzaa if you're going to give them?"

"I suppose you made every one of yours."

She had, but thought it prudent not to admit it. It would sound pretentious. "They aren't a requirement. You don't have to give gifts."

"I know that. Every family celebrates the holiday differently. My family gives gifts."

Erin could only smile. "I apologize." She looked down at Alicia, who hung tightly to Raimi's hand. "I hope you enjoy yourself." She smiled at the child. "Good-bye, Alicia."

"Happy Kwanzaa, Erin," the little girl said.

Erin looked up at Raimi one more time. They'd probably never see each other again. A pang went through her that she hadn't expected. "Mr. Price," was all she could manage.

Erin went to see to another customer. She felt Raimi's eyes on her back and wondered why he didn't leave. She refused to look over her shoulder. She wouldn't let him know he was having any effect on her. She pulled a picture frame off the shelf, and her clumsy fingers dropped it. It didn't break when it landed. She reached down to retrieve it and looked at the place where Raimi and Alicia stood. They'd moved. She saw him look over his shoulder and point toward her as he said something to Anne Marie, the department manager who ran the specialty gifts department. A second later he glanced toward her again. A frown marred his face. Then he and Alicia disappeared from sight.

Erin stood up and reached for an identical frame, which

she handed to the customer. Her gaze remained on the space where Raimi Price had stood.

Raimi poured shampoo into his hand and washed his hair for the second time. Why did she make him so angry? He'd enjoyed himself the last few days. Spending Christmas at the family's house had been his sister, Laurel's, idea. It had come at an opportune time. He'd thought of returning to his birthplace for more than a holiday period. He and Laurel had never sold the house after their parents died, and coming back to spend the holiday was more enjoyable than he'd imagined. There weren't any ghosts haunting them mostly due to Alicia's spirit. Having a kid around for Christmas made it happier, had him remembering his own past Christmases. The sight of Alicia's face yesterday when she'd seen all the ribboned boxes under the tree and the empty milk glass and cookie plate she'd left for Santa was priceless. And there was Laurel's announcement that they'd have another child by next Christmas. Raimi had been happy, but his brother-in-law looked as if she'd handed him fifty-yard-line tickets to the Super Bowl.

Raimi tried to concentrate on his family, but Erin Scott's face kept seeping into his memory. The two of them had exchanged only a few words, yet he'd reacted to her with more anger than she deserved—and he couldn't figure out why her words bothered him. She was right. Kwanzaa was a holiday that didn't require gifts, but if you chose to give them they should be something that was made and not bought. The spirit of Kwanzaa called for creativity, not commercialism, but he was a busy man. He ran a large corporation. He didn't have time to make things, and he'd never been good with his hands unless they were on a computer keyboard. His shop projects were always the worst in the class, but he could turn abstract designs in his head into computer models on his screen. That was how he'd gotten his first job out of college and what allowed him to work his way to the top. Erin Scott knew nothing about that.

He turned off the shower and toweled himself dry then entered his old bedroom. He'd occupied this room as a boy. His posters still hung on the walls as a reminder. Laurel had come early though. He could tell by the lack of dust and the absence of sheets covering the furniture. He heard Alicia's high-pitched laugh from downstairs somewhere as he pulled clothes from drawers and the closet and began to dress.

For a moment he forgot about Erin and remembered his niece. She always made him smile. It was too bad they were leaving tomorrow to go and visit his sister's in-laws. They'd spent Christmas here but would spend most of Kwanzaa with his brother in-law's family.

Raimi could return to New York. Except for manufacturing and support services, the offices were closed between Christmas and the New Year. There would be no one in the administrative offices. He had plenty of work he could get done. He wanted to inspect the land in Hopewell they were planning to buy. He hadn't seen it in years. In fact, he hadn't been back to Cranbury since his parents died in a car accident five years ago.

He thought about work. It usually consumed him but not today. Soon his mind was back on the beautiful brown eyes, lurking behind long black lashes. They haunted him, and he could think of no reason why they should.

Erin Scott seemed familiar. He couldn't say why, just as he didn't understand why her comment about Kwanzaa had struck him the wrong way. So he didn't make his gifts. Raimi dropped down in a chair and looked out the window. In the distance the sun was setting. He smiled at the sudden memory of him and his sister making Kwanzaa gifts around their dining-room table. They wanted to please their parents. One afternoon it was planned that their parents would spend the day away from the house so he and his sister could make the gifts. The two of them made a huge wreath for his mother. It had some kind of sugared fruits and vegetables his sister had made, dried flowers, pine-cones, and berries in it. It wasn't the most beautiful thing they'd ever done, but it was filled with the love they felt for their mother, and they knew she'd like it. Laurel tied a huge bow around it, and they both made a holiday card and signed it. Their mother had cried when she opened the box. She'd shown that wreath to everyone who came to the house. She'd told everyone who'd called about it.

Raimi tried to remember if she'd done the same thing for later presents he'd given her. He knew she appreciated them but couldn't quite remember the enthusiasm of those days before he'd begun to buy his presents.

"She's right," he said aloud. He should have made the gifts, but it was too late now. Alicia and Laurel were leaving tomorrow. They'd agreed to exchange their gifts tonight before the community gathering for the First Fruits Cere-mony. He'd bought his sister a sweater and his niece a doll. Today he'd finally decided on an autographed baseball for his brother-in-law.

Standing up, he slipped his feet in his shoes and grabbed his jacket. There might still be time for him to get materials to make something. He could at least try. Maybe he could find something to make that would meet the stringent approval of Ms. Erin Scott, the brown-eyed beautiful owner of Scott's.

And maybe something more . . .

Luck was with him, Raimi told himself. In truth, he knew this was his destination before he left the house. He'd told himself he was going to a craft store. He would ask the clerk to suggest something he could make for his niece. Something easy. She would be the easiest to please. His brother-in-law and sister would have to take what he bought them. He would give them a different gift at another time. But the car steered itself to Scott's and here he was.

The parking lot was still full, and he found a space around back. Parking, Raimi walked toward the back entrance. Before he reached the curb, Erin came out of the employee exit. She wore a long purple coat that seemed to flow around her. The hat on her head matched the coat and framed her face. Purple was definitely her color. It signified royalty, and she looked like a queen. For a moment he watched her. Her stride was easy. Her heels clicked on the pavement with an unhurried rhythm. She held her head high and her shoulders straight. All she carried was a purse slung over her shoulder. As she passed one of the streetlights illuminating the parking area, it flooded her face then plunged her into a silhouette. The thought that he knew her hit him. He recognized something about the way she walked but couldn't pull the memory into focus. He had no time to analyze the feeling. Erin stopped when she saw him. They stared at each other without speaking.

"I'm glad I ran into you," he said.

The sun had set. The lights in the parking lot and the entrance shone brightly. Christmas decorations were as elaborate on this side of the building as on the main entrance. Erin stood before them as if she were part of the display. Backlighting highlighted the fringe of hair sneaking out from under the hat. The mass of brown curls on the top tapered into a smooth short cut that ended in a blunt square across the back of her neck. It made her eyes huge and deep. They were shadowed now, but this morning they'd been large and brown. He remembered looking into them, being mesmerized by them. The pupils were light brown circles surrounding dark brown irises. They were so striking he couldn't tear his gaze away.

"I'm afraid I'm leaving, Mr. Price. The store will be—"

"We don't have to be so formal, do we?" He interrupted her. "My name's Raimi." Her body was as stiff as her words. He understood this morning had not put them on friendly terms, but he wanted to change that. "Let me apologize for this morning."

"No." She stopped him. "It was my fault. I was rude and I—."

"Apology accepted." He stepped closer to her. "I thought about what you said regarding Kwanzaa. You were right. I should have made the gifts, and I'm here to find something to make. I was hoping you'd help me."

"The store is open until nine, but I'm afraid I have to leave now. I'm sure you'll find someone inside who can help you. They're very competent people."

She started to walk away. Raimi could have done several things to stop her, but the only decision that asserted itself had him stepping in her path. She stopped just short of ramming into him. With them both on the same plane, she had to look up at him. He took a step back. He had to move away from those eyes before the compelling need that shot through him like a bolt of lightning made him move in close enough to see the tiny rings that defined the iris. Grabbing his thoughts, he stopped their wayward direction.

"Have you completed all your Kwanzaa projects?" The first thought that came into his head, other than kissing her, he voiced.

"I have one to finish," she said a bit tightly. "It's nearly done."

"Good." He smiled. "I'm sure I won't be able to complete anything tonight, but I'm going to give it a try."

"Go on inside. Someone will help you."

Again she tried to walk away. He didn't block her path but stopped her with a question. "Would you have a cup of coffee with me?"

She turned back but said nothing. Raimi wasn't used to

women taking time to think over going out with him. This one did. He held his breath. They had only just met. She didn't know him, and they stood in a parking lot effectively alone. Shoppers came and went while they stood there, but she could think he was an ax murderer.

"I assure you, I'm not a criminal, and I have no intention of becoming one. I'm simply inviting you to have coffee with me. This is the season for unity and friendship." He quoted a couple of the principles of Kwanzaa, hoping to sway her decision. "Have you had anything to eat?"

"I'd planned to eat at the Kwanzaa celebration tonight."

"That's got to be a couple of hours away." He checked his watch. "I'll bet you haven't eaten anything since breakfast."

The tiny smile that lifted the corners of her mouth told him he'd hit home.

"All right, Mr. . . . Raimi," she corrected herself. "I'll have coffee with you. There's a shop in the store."

Automatically he reached for her when she turned toward the building. His hand caught hers. She turned back, and both sets of eyes went to their joined hands. Quickly he dropped the contact. "Why don't we go to the diner." He wanted to take her someplace where she didn't know everyone in town. "I love coffee from the diner. It's always freshly brewed." He didn't want to be interrupted for the next hour or however long he had. Extending his hand toward the car he'd vacated only a few minutes ago, they fell in step together. He was careful not to let his hand touch hers again. The contact hadn't produced any shock in him, but he liked the way it felt, soft and slightly cold from the air.

Minutes later they were on Route 130 and pulling into the Americana Diner in East Windsor. The red-and-tan flagstone building gleamed under the streetlights. The parking lot was packed, but inside they found the back booth empty. Erin followed the waitress to it and ordered coffee.

Raimi took his coffee black and looked uncomfortable now that they were seated together.

"Which night does your family exchange Kwanzaa gifts?" Erin asked, opening a packet of sweetener and dumping it into her cup.

"When my parents were alive, we used to spread them over the seven nights. In the last few years, I haven't been around for the celebrations."

Erin wondered where he had been. She'd often thought of him. The town wouldn't let her forget him, and often she'd received unwanted reports on his progress at MIT. In the years after his parents died, she'd hadn't heard much about him, yet the annual spring sale on prom gowns always brought him to the forefront of her mind.

"My family usually exchanges gifts on both the third night, Ujima, and the sixth night, Kuumba. Ujima because it means collective work and responsibility—my parents thought that working hard deserved rewards—and Kuumba because it means creativity. On this night we got to show what we'd done." She laughed, remembering some of the crude gifts she and Asha had created as children.

Erin's family had always celebrated both Christmas and Kwanzaa. Christmas held the religious ceremony and the annual gift-giving tradition, while Kwanzaa reaffirmed their strength in each other, their homage to Mother Africa, and their knowledge that working both collectively and individually would help build a better community.

"Why are you laughing?" Raimi asked.

"You should have seen some of the awful things my sister and I made when we were young."

"You should have seen some of mine," he told her.

"Like what?" she asked.

Erin felt relaxed. She never would have believed she

could sit in the same booth with Raimi Price and not want to kick him under the table. She'd been smarting over his treatment of her for years, and now she felt all the hostility float away as he told her about crudely made pot holders, Popsicle-stick jewelry boxes, and seashell necklaces that didn't quite hold up to wear. Erin laughed and had more coffee. She told herself it could be because Raimi didn't know who she was. For the time being they had met only this morning, and they were getting to know each other. The fact that she could give him chapter and verse about his life was beside the current point. There was time for that later if need be. At this moment she hoped that would never come.

Time slipped by, and the waitress asking if she wanted another cup of coffee made her check her watch.

"Oh, no," she said. When the woman left, Erin said, "I've enjoyed this, but I have to get home and change."

Raimi quickly paid the bill and left a generous tip. Outside he helped her into the car and drove her back to the store's parking lot. She directed him to her car and, when he stopped, she was reluctant to leave.

She heard his seat belt snap open. Pulling her own off, she prepared to get out of the car. On impulse she turned to him. He was looking at her. The car suddenly seemed smaller. They were closer than she expected. Her throat went dry, and she forgot what she wanted to say.

"My grandmother was a storyteller," he said softly. Erin didn't know why he'd brought up his grandmother. She didn't care. She wanted only to spend a few more minutes with him before the fantasy she was sure had enveloped her faded or was broken. "She told me a story once about herself and my grandfather. It was before the first Kwanzaa celebration in 1966. She met my grandfather on December twenty-sixth, the day after Christmas. They met in the morning on the way to a sale and that night—"

Erin dropped her head to hide her smile. She knew he

was telling a story about the two of them and not his grandparents.

"That night," he continued. "When he returned her to her house after dinner and a long conversation, he told her he knew they had met only that morning, but he couldn't help himself."

She waited a moment. "Help himself what?"

Raimi raised his hand and slipped it around her neck. She trembled as he pulled her closer to him. She didn't resist.

"I want you to know," she whispered when his mouth hovered over hers and he could taste the coffee on her breath. "That I don't believe a word of that story, but it's one of the best lines I've ever heard."

"Every blessed word is the God's honest truth," he said and brushed his mouth against hers.

Erin thought all her wishes had been granted. This was how she'd envisioned the prom ending, with him standing on her doorstep, kissing her good night. She leaned into him. His mouth took hers with a passion. His tongue swept into her mouth and she welcomed the invasion, twining one arm about his neck. She breathed in the smell of him. It reminded her of cold winter winds and hot fires. Her entire body was burning. She'd never experienced anything so potent, so sexy, and so downright freeing as what Raimi was doing to her. And he was only kissing her. God, what would it be like if they weren't hampered by the car seats? She wanted to put her arms around him, align her body to his, and feel the bridled strength she'd always known was present.

Raimi pushed back first. Just as he'd begun the kiss, he ended it. Erin didn't have the strength to stop. She didn't want to stop. She wanted to stay in his arms. The thought caught her off guard, and she dropped her head. She couldn't look at him, didn't want him to see that she'd become that sophomore again, the one with the terrific crush on him.

The burst of cold air made her look up. Raimi opened the door and got out. She still couldn't move. He was coming around to help her out. Erin straightened her hat and checked the buttons on her coat. Everything was in place. She was the same as she'd been minutes ago, before Raimi told her the grandparent story, before he kissed her, and before she'd become the gawky kid who attended Cranbury High School, and long before her legs turned to liquid.

The door opened. Cold air rushed in and fanned her hot cheeks. Raimi offered her his hand. She swung her legs around and took his hand. Her own car was mere steps away. She went to it, fishing her keys from her pocket and pushing the security door lock on the key to unlock the door. Raimi didn't follow her. He watched her from a distance. Erin was thankful he didn't come. She didn't think she could stand being close to him without saying something or doing something that would betray her feelings.

"Good night," he said.

"Good night," she repeated. He returned to the driver's side of the car. "Raimi," her voice was small. "Kwanzaa."

"Yes?"

"My family is celebrating it tonight. Would . . ." She had to stop. Her throat was nearly closed. "Would you like to spend it with us?"

"I already have plans," he said.

Erin nodded, got in the car and closed the door. Of course he had plans. His sister and her family were here. She knew that. Why did she ask such a stupid question? Why did she feel like a sixteen-year-old who'd spent days getting up enough nerve to ask a boy to the dance, only to have him tell her he already had a date?

She put the car in gear and drove away. She needed to

rally her forces, she told herself. If there was any strength she had inside herself, and she felt completely depleted, this was the time to pull it out. Before arriving at her mother's house for the beginning of Kwanzaa, she had to act like the old Erin, the one who'd existed when she got out of bed this morning, and the morning before—not the one who'd evolved while Raimi Price told her stories about silly-looking Kwanzaa presents in the diner, not the one who'd been kissed in his car. She couldn't let anything show that indicated she'd changed. Yet she had. Asha, her all too intuitive sister, would surely notice a difference in her.

And after Raimi's kiss, the change was nothing less than a total metamorphosis.

Chapter Two

The township of Cranbury had long since opened a new high school, but the community Kwanzaa activities were being celebrated in the old high school. Erin had attended this school. Her classes had all been in this building. Her memories were here along with her name carved into the lab table of the third-floor chemistry room. She'd had some good times here and some of the worst ones too. She supposed every high school student could say that about their school. Thankfully, she'd resolved those problems. At least she hoped she had.

The gym seemed smaller than she remembered when she walked into it. Looking around, it was the same as it had been when she attended classes here. The jerseys for seven basketball championships hung from the ceiling, but they were nearly obliterated by the kente cloth and boldly colored tribal material that waved above their heads for the celebration. The room had been transformed. A podium and raised stage stood in front of rows of chairs set theater style. On one side of the podium stood a table with a huge kinara and seven candles. She could see the kikombe and symbolic vibunzi. She was sure the other symbols were also present. After the libation and lighting of the first candle, the chairs would be moved and a dance floor established. Erin already heard the music. Along the side were tables of food, representing a good harvest. Her mouth watered at the thought of eating. The cup of coffee she'd shared with Raimi hadn't quelled her hunger.

For him or for food . . .

Raimi. She hadn't been able to get him out of her mind since she'd seen him this morning. This was the last place they'd been together. She remembered hating this gym, hating everything about the school and the town. Raimi could leave. He graduated, went off to college.

Escaped.

She didn't have that choice. She had to stay here. She wasn't old enough to leave, and when she graduated her parents were ill. Both recovered, but by that time Erin had the idea for the store, and this seemed the best place to try it out.

She'd withstood the stares and looks of pity, even the sniggering of the other students—and now Raimi was back. What would they think when they found out he was here? It wouldn't take long. She was surprised the rumor mill hadn't already beat out the message like it would have been done in Mother Africa, on drums.

"Habari Gon Gani."

"Umoja." Erin immediately gave the first night of Kwanzaa's greeting as she was addressed. She turned to find Oliver Rendell. He'd been her rescuer way back when Raimi abandoned her almost in this exact spot. Oliver had driven her home, and never once had he derided her over the fact. Oliver was sixteen years older now. He'd been a slightly overweight teenager with a winning smile and heart of gold. Neither of those things had changed. His hair had just begun to turn gray at the edges. He was at least forty pounds overweight and taking on the distinguished college professor look. Oliver had studied to be a teacher and began his career teaching college physics. He was now director of the department at the local college.

"You're dressed to kill," he said.

Erin turned about for him to see the entire ensemble. Asha had given her the outfit for Christmas so she could wear it for First Night. The dress was a bright red African print that billowed out but tapered in to tight pants around her ankles. Her midriff was belted with a wide band of solid white cloth that extended from her breasts to her waist. The sleeves were swells of fabric that made her aware of her posture. They, too, tapered tightly at her wrists. Her hair was completely covered by a gèlèe, a wrapping of cloth, that, if extended, was just over five yards. It sat on her head like a crown, and the weight made her aware that she should keep her head level.

"And look at you," Erin replied. Oliver wore the traditional loose-fitting male outfit of white tunic cloth that folded into tucks at his shoulders and pants that became progressively tighter as they reached his shoes. "Are you presiding tonight?"

He nodded. "It's a duty I enjoy." He looked around. The room was nearly filled with people. "The celebration appears to get larger each year."

"More people become aware and take the time to attend. Once they've been to a ceremony, they return. This year we have a lot of people returning who used to live here."

Erin thought of Raimi. She was acutely aware of his possible presence tonight. She could see people beginning to take seats. "The crowd is assembling."

Oliver smiled at her. "I guess I'd better take my place."

He left her, and Erin found her family. She took the seat next to Asha and her parents. A hush fell over the room when Oliver stepped up to the podium. The people who would help in the ceremony took up posts at their assigned positions, and the first night of Kwanzaa officially began.

Oliver officiated, explaining the principle of Umoja: unity of family, community, the nation, and the race. Then he poured the libation and lifted the kikombe to the room in symbolic reverence. Most families had already performed this ritual before coming to the ceremony. Erin was startled when Alicia Marie Allen walked across the stage with her father, who lifted the little girl in his arms and guided her hand as she lit the first Kwanzaa candle.

It was traditional for a child to light the candles. This helped teach them the seven principles of Kwanzaa. Erin's surprise was that she was now sure Raimi was in the room. She hadn't seen him come in, nor had she seen Laurel, but they were certainly there.

She spotted Raimi seconds later. He lounged against the wall, his posture relaxed, his attention on the stage. Erin held her breath. How long would it be before someone recognized him and their eyes immediately sought her out? As if he could read her thoughts, Raimi turned to stare at her. Quickly she looked away, her face suddenly hot, her heart pounding in her chest and her mouth tingling from a remembered kiss.

The speeches couldn't last forever, even if Erin wished they had. Soon people were closing up chairs and assigned teenagers were stacking them against the wall. Erin moved out of the way, allowing the dance floor to be cleared. She wandered toward the back of the room, not daring herself to turn around and look at the place where Raimi stood. She didn't know if he was still in the same place. When he looked her way, she'd turned and not trusted herself to look again.

"When did he return?" Asha came up next to her. Erin

didn't look over her shoulder, but she knew exactly who her sister referred to.

"I saw him this morning at the store."

Asha looked directly at her. Erin kept the fact that they had been together not two hours ago at a diner to herself. Asha hated Raimi for what he'd done to Erin at the prom.

"You should have thrown—"

Erin caught her sister's arm and interrupted her. "Asha, leave it. It happened a lifetime ago. We were kids then, and none of us are the same today."

Asha studied her face. "Erin, I thought you'd gotten over him years ago."

"Of course, I'm over him," she lied. Before he kissed her she might have been able to convince herself she was over Raimi Price, but a few seconds in her life had proven her wrong. Asha looked at her for a long moment, then Erin let go of her arm.

Behind them the music resumed, and couples quickly covered the dance floor. Asha was captured by her current heartthrob, and the two of them moved to the area designated for dancing. Erin kept herself busy at the food tables. She refused to look around the room, keeping her attention on straightening the tables and sweeping away imaginary crumbs. With all the aromas that had told her she was hungry, the last thing she wanted now was food. She wanted to get out of here. As soon as it was within etiquette's approval, she would leave. Escape. Get away from the scrutiny of the crowd and the presence of Raimi Price.

Luck wasn't with her. In that space of time when the music stopped and the small band began another song, she glanced up and directly into the eyes of the man she least wanted to see. The hush in the room was audible, at least to her. Raimi didn't smile as he walked toward her, his steps purposeful.

"Dance with me?" he said, extending his hand.

Time must have stopped, she was sure. Nothing happened. She couldn't tear her gaze away. If she did, she was sure she'd find everyone in the room looking at her. And thus how could she refuse, knowing what they were all thinking. She took his hand. An audible gasp reached her ears.

Raimi didn't seem to notice anything out of place— even the backing away of the couples on the floor giving them room. Erin shot her sister an anxious glance for help. She didn't want to be hanging out here alone. She and Asha had never been psychic, but tonight she hoped the blood connection between them would communicate her need.

The music began. The sensual strands of a Barry White love song conspired against her. Raimi turned her into his arms. She slid as easily into his embrace as butter does sliding across a hot skillet. All the sizzle and fire of the initial contact racked through her system, and she melted. They were alone for several turns that felt like an eon before Asha and Tom joined them—and others, taking the signal, crowded onto the floor.

Erin felt delicious in his arms. She relaxed against him, closed her eyes, and let the music carry her away. This was how the prom should have been. With the two of them dancing in the dim light with a glittering ball overhead. Tonight there was no mirrored ball, and the women were colorfully dressed in African prints, not chiffon and satin ball gowns. The men wore no tuxedos, but in Erin's mind everything receded to a dream state. This was what she wanted it to be.

So it was.

"Have I told you how gorgeous you look?" Raimi whispered in her ear. "I'm sure every man here is jealous of me." He pulled her closer. "And I like it."

Erin couldn't speak. The emotion in her throat cut off speech. All she could do was stay in his arms and follow the flow of his body as they danced. She hoped the music would go on and on. This was one dance she never wanted to end.

"When I first saw you tonight, I didn't recognize you. You look so different from the way you did when you got out of the car earlier today."

"It's the dress," she offered.

"Are you going to surprise me every time we meet?"

"As long as they're good surprises," she countered.

The music ended and they separated. Erin looked around. Her mother and father were staring at them, and Asha's gaze was also trained on her. Erin was too scared to check the rest of the gym. Did everyone present remember who she was and what the man who'd held her so close in his arms had done to her in this very gym?

"Uncle Raimi!" Alicia ran toward them, and Raimi turned to gather her in his arms. Erin took the opportunity to return to her station by the food tables.

Asha came to her the moment she stopped. "Liar," was all she said. Then she walked away and back to the dance floor.

Erin didn't need to question her on the significance of the single word. She knew exactly what it meant. She might tell herself she was over Raimi Price, but she wasn't. She wasn't sure she would ever be.

Erin went through the rest of the night avoiding him. She'd go in the direction opposite from the one he chose. She spoke to and smiled at everyone who brought up his name and commented on them knowing each other in high school.

"Yes, he does look just as good as he did then," she'd said. "I don't know how long he'll be in town," she told someone. "It is a shame to have their house standing empty," she commented.

She had to get out of here. Finally enough time had passed that she could leave without drawing comment. She saw Asha near the door and went to her. Raimi was far away, and his back was to her. This was the perfect time to go.

"Asha," she called. "I'm leaving now. I'll see you at the store tomorrow."

"Erin, it's early. Why are you running away?"

"I'm not running away. You know how busy these days are. I need to rest before tomorrow, that's all."

Asha glanced around. Erin knew she was looking toward the broad-shouldered black man who'd nearly cleared the dance floor by stepping onto it. Erin, despite her resolve not to look, turned in the same direction as Asha looked. He was still standing on the other side of the gym. Several women surrounded him. Erin felt a twinge near her heart.

"He's always drawn a crowd," she said a little cattily.

"That he has, but it isn't really his fault."

Erin stopped in the middle of putting on her coat. "Asha, you've always disliked him."

"I know. Mostly because of what he did to you, but that was a long time ago."

"So . . ."

Asha didn't answer immediately. "So I saw the way you looked at him."

Erin could have denied that her sister had seen anything. She could have made up something to tell Asha, then she could have told her the truth. But she wasn't ready to admit to anyone that after sixteen years Raimi Price had walked into her life and . . . what?

"He doesn't remember me, Asha."

"What?" Her sister glanced at Raimi and back at her.

"This morning he looked at me without the slightest idea of who I was or that we had ever met before. In fact, when he left the store, he asked Anne Marie who I was."

Erin couldn't help the disappointment that went through her each time she thought of the truth of that. She'd pictured him feeling sorry for what he'd done to her, but in the ensuing years he hadn't given her a thought.

Erin started for the exit. She pulled her keys from her purse and held them.

"I'll see you tomorrow."

"You're not leaving?" Raimi's deep voice stopped her like a paralyzing drug.

"I have to be up early tomorrow," she said, turning to look at him.

"Let me drive you?"

"There's no need. I have my car." She held up her hand, the car keys dangling from it. Asha took them.

"Drive her home," she said to Raimi, then turned to look at her. "I'll bring your car around in the morning." With that she left them. Erin took a step and stopped. It was no use running after Asha. She'd just have to leave with Raimi if she didn't want to make a scene—and she'd played one scene in this gym already.

Moments later Erin sat in the warm confines of Raimi's car. It was sleek and dark and fast . . . like him. She had no idea what kind of car it was. She couldn't tell a BMW from a horse-drawn carriage, but it was the kind of car she would expect him to drive. They were quiet for the short ride. Erin didn't feel uncomfortable but this wasn't the most companionable silence she'd ever spent.

He pulled into her driveway and turned off the engine. What had happened earlier in this same car immediately jumped into her mind. Suddenly she no longer needed the heat from the car's system to keep her warm.

"Do you mind if I come in?" he asked. "I want to talk to you."

Erin turned to look at him. Concern was on his face.

"Sure," she said, feeling a little apprehensive. He hadn't asked where she lived. He'd driven directly to her house, as if he'd been there before. It is a small town, she reminded herself. If he'd asked her name in the store, he could very well have asked where she lived.

Inside, Raimi took off his coat and dropped it on a chair

by the door. Erin placed hers on top of it. She moved across the room and turned to face him. Raimi wondered if she needed space.

Her tree stood in front of the picture window. The fireplace was draped with a garland, which was entwined with tiny white lights that blinked on and off. Inside the hearth the ashes of a dead fire remained. On the coffee table was a Mkeka. On top of it was a kinara and some dried fruits representing the mazao.

"Can I get you something to drink?"

Raimi shook his head. "Sit down."

She took a seat on the end of a wing chair.

"Raimi, what's wrong?"

He took a step forward and sat on the end of the sofa near her. "Asha is your sister, isn't she?" He knew the answer before she nodded. "We went to school together. Graduated the same year."

"I know," Erin said.

"I know, too, Erin."

"Know what?"

"Tonight when I saw you in the gym, I nearly didn't recognize you."

"It's the outfit," she offered. He thought it was an excuse and that even she didn't believe a dress could hide her identity.

"It's not the dress." She was beautiful. She'd been beautiful this morning in the store under the fluorescent lights and later at the diner under the harsh lighting of the bulbs and the silver and neon reflections—but in the dim light of the gym, memory returned to him as it had in his nightmares for the last sixteen years.

"Then it must be the makeup."

"It was the gym."

He saw her visibly recoil. It was a slight movement, but he'd expected a reaction and had been looking for it.

"What do you mean?" she asked.

"I mean, sixteen years ago I took you to the senior prom—and I left with Margaret Foley."

Erin held his gaze, but he wanted to drop his. He wanted her to say something, scream at him, get angry, do anything except sit there staring. He felt small. He knew she'd looked familiar, but he couldn't place her—not until Laurel reminded him that he knew a lot of people at the celebration. She pointed out Asha Scott and said she was sitting next to her sister, Erin, the owner of Scott's Department Store. At that moment Erin stood up and started toward the back of the gym, the same direction she'd headed when Margaret Foley had appeared—and he'd left Erin standing alone on the dance floor.

Memory came back to him like a knife cutting into his brain. He wanted to relive that night, end it differently, not spoil the dreams of a young girl. He knew she had a crush on him. The entire school knew it, but he'd been blinded by Margaret. She was like a siren where he was concerned. He could see nothing but her. When they argued and broke up just before the prom, he'd asked Erin. Then at the prom Margaret had come, and he'd gone with her. He was seventeen and unconcerned about his actions, even though he knew it was wrong. All he could do now was apologize.

"The prom was a long time ago, Raimi. I've long since forgotten it."

Raimi's eyes caught a picture directly behind her head. He recognized himself, sixteen years younger. "You're trying to make this easy for me. I'm ashamed of what I did, and I have no excuse for it. It was wrong and I knew that, but . . ."

"But you were young and in love with the best-looking girl in school. Who could blame you for that?"

"You could." He paused. "Don't tell me you didn't hate me after that?"

"I won't." She stood up and walked to the fireplace,

her back to him. "I hated you for a long time. I'm not sure I haven't stopped hating you."

Raimi was sure. No one could have kissed him the way she did and still hate him. He thought it best not to bring that up.

"I never thought I'd live it down," she said, turning back to him. "The whole town knew. I couldn't go anywhere without people looking at me as if I had leprosy. School was awful. Whenever a dance was scheduled, I'd get teased about which boy would leave me this time."

"Erin, I'm so—"

"That wasn't your fault, but I blamed you nevertheless."

"A lot of those dances you wouldn't even go to," he told her. "Laurel told me. She said it was terrible—the things that people said behind your back."

Erin smiled at him. He stood and went to her. "I didn't know what they said behind my back. To my face was bad enough."

"Why didn't you leave?"

"I couldn't. My parents were both very sick. We discovered my mother had diabetes, and my father had suffered a heart attack. Asha was already three hours away in Washington, D.C. Someone had to be here to take care of them."

"I wish I could change things," he said inadequately.

Erin sat down and took hold of his arm. "Don't wish that. It's past. Let's let it stay there. Besides something good did come out of it. By staying here, I found out I'm a much stronger person than I thought I was—and I got the idea to open the store, and I'll never be sorry for doing that."

He stared at her. "You're a remarkable woman." He meant every word of that. He'd met plenty of women in his time, women trying to make it to the top, climbing over everyone in their effort to get to the corner office of the executive suite. Women who were dependent on someone else, women who wanted no responsibility, but Erin Scott made them all pale. She was strong, exuding that strength through a quiet beauty that made him want to stick around just to see what she'd do next. "I'd like to make it up to you."

Erin's eyes opened wide. "How are you going to do that? You can't restage the prom."

"I thought I'd ask you to spend Kwanzaa with me."

He held his breath. She didn't answer. Was she thinking about what it would be like when he left at the end of the week? Would she have to go through the small-town gossip after a few days in his company? Of course she would. He knew that. He'd lived here, but he'd left and moved to a large city where you spoke to your neighbors only in passing. You didn't socialize with them or stop them on the street or even come together for annual holidays. Here you did . . . and here was where Erin lived.

"I'd like that." He heard her whisper.

Chapter Three

Erin rarely ever overslept. This morning she'd heard her clock radio. Gladys Knight had been singing "Midnight Train to Georgia." She couldn't remember hearing the end of the song or turning off the music. She knew now it was an hour past the time she usually got up, and she rushed around trying to cram a shower, makeup, dressing, and breakfast into twenty minutes.

Rushing, she finished in thirty-five minutes, forgetting breakfast. She'd get a muffin in the coffee shop. Jabbing her arms in her coat, she went through the front door. She'd crossed the porch and headed down the stairs before remembering Asha had her car. Her sister had promised to bring it to her this morning, but Asha's clock didn't work the way the rest of the world's did. Erin frowned. She hated being late. She turned to go and call Asha, then stopped when she heard the dark tones of Raimi's voice.

"Good morning," Raimi said. He leaned against the front fender with his arms and ankles crossed. In the cold morning air, he looked as if he'd just gone out for a stroll.

"Is that coffee?" Erin spied the bag next to him on the car hood. If she hadn't been happy to see him, she was grateful he had the insight to buy coffee.

"I take it you're the kind who's no good until after the second cup."

"I'm an absolute bear," she agreed, accepting the Styrofoam cup he handed her. Removing the top, Erin took a sip of the hot liquid. When she lowered the cup, she saw it was diner coffee. He loved diner coffee, he'd told her.

"What are you doing here?" she asked.

"You don't have a car. You need a ride to work, and I need to get some materials to make my niece a Kwanzaa gift."

"I didn't expect you'd buy it this early. The store won't be open."

He pulled open the door to the passenger side of the car. "I know the owner. She's got a key."

Erin smiled and got inside.

The drive was short as it had been the previous night. Erin didn't speak. She sat and watched covertly as Raimi drove. He looked great in the morning, she told herself. He wore a flight jacket of worn brown leather and brown wool slacks. Blue jeans, which seemed to be the uniform of the twentieth-century man, weren't Raimi's style—and style he had, not to mention sex appeal. Each time Erin saw him, she thought of sex, of being in his arms and having him hold her. Song lyrics and cliches that seemed so true and applicable to him came to mind. She started to hum "What a Difference a Day Makes."

"Has the town changed much?" Erin asked a moment later.

"Downtown is the same. I suppose it will never change."

Erin nodded. She looked at Main Street. It was the same as it had been when they were in school. A few stores had changed hands or had become something different, but for the most part nothing had been torn down or replaced or renovated.

"The condominiums along Plainsboro Road were a surprise."

"Dotty Carson and Ellis Parks live over there. Remember them?"

Raimi glanced at her and nodded. "I played basketball with Ellis."

"They have twin boys. One of them is a champion swimmer. Dotty thinks he might make the Olympic team."

"I'll have to try to get over and see them before I leave."

Erin could have asked then and there when that would be, but she didn't. She didn't want to know. He'd asked her to spend Kwanzaa with him. He'd be here at least until New Year's Eve. She wouldn't let her mind think of anything past that.

"Have you been visiting a lot?"

"Not much. Laurel and Alicia kept me pretty busy when I first arrived. I got to see several people last night at the First Night celebration."

They pulled into the parking lot, and Raimi parked. As had become habit, he came around to help her out of the car.

"Where will you be today?" he asked.

"I have to work a shift in housewares."

"Why are you doing that?" He frowned. "Don't you have enough employees?"

"Sometimes more than enough. This is a family time of year. Some of the women are single moms with children home for the holidays. Others want to be with their loved ones. I try to let off as many of them as possible, but this is also the busiest time of the year. So I pitch in just as my entire office staff does."

"I said you were remarkable last night."

"I'm not remarkable. I just know what it's like for your family to need you."

They walked toward the employee entrance. Erin led him through the back hallways of the store. Boxes lined the walls with inventory they'd brought in to cover the holiday period. By the end of the week, everything would be back to normal, and she'd have closed another year.

At the employee elevator she stopped and pushed the button. "Have you got anything in mind for your niece?"

He shook his head. "She did love the doll I gave her this morning before they left for Delaware."

The elevator door opened, and they got in. Erin pushed four. "She's a sweet little girl."

"I wish I could see more of her."

"You don't live that far away." She wanted to ask him how long he would be here, but she didn't want to hear the answer. She wanted him to stay but knew better. He had a job in New York, a life there. She was part of a different existence, and she knew nothing would bring him back here.

The elevator doors opened quickly, and they got out. The fourth floor had crafts on it. Erin smelled the eucalyptus, scented silk flowers, and perfumed-candles. At times the combination could be overwhelming, but this morning it was like walking into a fragrant garden. She spied Willa Morris. Willa was from Jamaica. She'd been in the United States for twenty years and spoke near-perfect English, but the flavor of the islands was still present in the rhythm of her speech patterns. Erin loved hearing the lyrical way she spoke.

"Willa, you're in early."

"Good morning," she said, coming over to them. "The pandemonium at my house drove me away. Three college students, music and football—I needed someplace to hide."

"This is Raimi Price. He used to live here. Raimi, this is Willa Morris. She runs this department. She has one son in college who never comes home without bringing extra guests."

"I can't fault him," she said. "The boys couldn't go home for the festivities, and we've got plenty of room." She smiled a toothy grin at Raimi. "So I hear you're visiting for the Kwanzaa period."

Raimi frowned questioningly.

"Small town," Erin explained. "Everyone knows everything, even the number of breaths you take."

"Do they know I kissed you?" he whispered loud enough for her ears only.

Erin's face grew hot. She pushed away the thoughts coming forth and spoke to Willa. "Raimi wants to make a Kwanzaa gift, and he needs some direction. Is it all right if I leave him with you?"

"Of course," she said. "I'll take the best of care with him."

Erin looked at Raimi, intent on saying good-bye, but the warm look in his eyes had her wanting to melt.

"I'll see you later," he said.

Erin nodded. She went back the way they had come, but she couldn't help looking over her shoulder. God, she thought, what a difference yesterday made.

"Hey, got a minute?" Asha poked her head in the door of Erin's office and came fully inside. "I heard you were taking a break and thought I'd find you here."

"I don't think people are waiting for the January White Sale, judging by the number of comforters and sheets I've sold this morning." She slipped her feet out of her shoes and rested them on the end of her desk. "My body is not designed for this torture. How do people do this every day?"

Asha slipped into a chair in front of the desk. "You used to do it every day and then come to the office and do accounts, inventory, orders, employee schedules, accounts payable and everything else that needed doing around here."

"Those were some fun days." Erin never thought she'd be able to smile at those days, but today she could. "Asha, thank you for helping. I can't tell you how much I appreciate your giving up your holiday to fill in for me."

"Stop it." Asha raised her hand, palm out. "What is family for if you can't call on them when you need help. After all, how many times did I hear that Ujima means helping our brothers *and* sisters?"

Erin knew her sister wasn't helping out only to fulfill the Kwanzaa principle.

"And one of these days, I'll make you pay me back."

They both laughed. Her sister had worked one of the shifts in the jewelry department to allow the clerk who regularly worked there to visit her family in upstate New York. Erin didn't know whether she could call what Asha did work, since her sister was a gems expert by profession. She loved getting out from behind the designer's bench and actually seeing the people who bought and wore her jewels.

"Working here has been more fun than work anyway," Asha continued. She got up and walked around the desk, then perched on the end near Erin's raised feet. "How'd you enjoy last night?"

Erin looked at her sister, careful to keep the emotions that were jumping in her blood from spilling out and reflecting themselves in every part of her being. "As usual, I enjoyed the ceremony—"

"I'm not talking about the ceremony, and you know it."

"You mean Raimi?"

"Yes, I mean Raimi," she mimicked.

"I wondered about your behavior. I thought you disliked him."

"I did for a long time."

"When did you stop?"

"Last night when I saw the look in your eyes. If anyone wanted to eat a man alive, it was you."

Erin felt her ears grow hot. Had she been that transparent? She pulled down her legs and sat forward.

"Don't worry," Asha continued. "No one noticed it but me."

"I'm sure all of Cranbury noticed and remembers."

"Do you care that they remember?"

Erin didn't know. She'd been virtually in Raimi's company since she knew he was in town. He'd been the last thing she saw last night and the first thing this morning. Even while she worked, she couldn't keep her mind off him. Thoughts of seeing him again made her blood sing. She wanted to be with him, even if the town did know.

"I don't think I care," she said more to herself than her sister.

"If you want him, Erin, I say go for it."

"He's not going to be here past Kwanzaa," Erin told her. "He has a job in New York, a life in New York."

"You say that as if New York were the end of the world. People from here commute to New York every day. And of course, people have been known to commute from New York to Cranbury." She paused. "Or even from someplace in between."

Erin thought she should put the brakes on this conversation. "Asha, Raimi is visiting for only a short while. It's not like he's planning to stay."

Erin had to keep reminding herself of this too. Raimi was here for Kwanzaa. When it was over, he would return to his life in New York, and she would stay here.

"I don't know how true that might be." Asha pushed herself off the desk and walked around it. She faced her sister with a mischievous grin.

"What do you mean?" Erin couldn't stop her heart from lurching. Did Asha know something about Raimi?

Asha went to the door and pulled it open. Erin stood up. Blood beat through her veins. Did she really want Raimi to stay? Could they have a relationship? After all these years was he really the man she wanted, or had that image she had in high school been something she wished it could be? Sixteen years had passed. They weren't the same people any longer. Life had given them different experiences, and she'd never really talked to him about anything . . . she never *talked* to him at all. They hadn't even been friends. They'd spent several hours together yesterday and this morning. He didn't come to Cranbury to find her. He didn't even remember her!

"Oh, I went over to see that piece of land you're trying buy for another store."

Erin didn't want to talk about the land. She wanted to know what information Asha had that she was keeping to herself, but she wouldn't let her sister know how anxious she was. It was one of her characteristics. She'd become so used to hiding her feelings that even hiding them from her sister was second nature.

"What did you think of it?" she asked instead of the question she really wanted answered.

"It's in a great location, good access roads, large area for a parking lot, and the separate day-care facilities will work well for both shoppers and working mothers. I think it will work on all the levels you've designed."

Erin smiled. She valued her sister's opinion. She had encouraged her to open the department store when she'd proposed the idea to her family. Her mother thought she should accept the job offer at a nearby pharmaceuticals company, but Asha told her it was her life. If she failed, she could find a job then, but not going after her dream was failure in itself. And she hadn't failed. Scott's was her baby, and her mother had told her she was proud of her accomplishments. She'd told her that the first year when

Scott's made so little money and she was working night and day.

Of course, the store was a lot different today. She initially bought the entire warehouse, a five-story building, but had only enough money and inventory to renovate the first level. Year by year she used all her energy and all her profits to add additional departments and expand onto the upper floors. Now the entire building was occupied, and it was time to branch out.

"There is just one little thing I think might present a problem," Asha interrupted her thoughts.

Erin raised her eyebrows at her sister's comment.

"There is another bid for the property."

"Another bid. Whose?"

"Ostensibly it's from a tool-and-die company looking for property to build another plant."

Breath threatened to leave her body. "Ostensibly? What does that mean?"

"The head of the tool-and-die company is an old friend of both yours and mine." She paused, and Erin felt ice water pour into her veins. "Raimi Price."

"What could Raimi want with that land?" She hadn't meant to ask the question aloud, but she had and Asha answered her.

"Why don't you ask him?"

Chapter Four

By the time Erin left the store, she'd worked up enough steam to restart the Philadelphia–South Amboy train lines that used to service this part of the state and for which the nearby town of Cranbury Station took its name. Asha had returned her car earlier, and at the end of her shift Erin drove straight to Raimi's house—at least the house his parents had owned when they lived here. She wasn't sure whether Raimi or his sister owned it, or if they shared ownership, but the tom-tom system of communication told her this was where he was staying.

She turned into the lane. Brainerd Lake flowed through Cranbury. The lake was man-made, although few people knew that. Unlike other lakes, it wasn't land-locked but connected to the Millstone River that eventually flowed to the Atlantic Ocean. Erin could see it through the window, but she stared unseeing at it, unconscious of the beauty of the setting sun, the twinkling Christmas lights reflected in the early evening's depths, or the darkening of the sky as it turned into streaks of purple and pink before slipping quietly into the water to await morning.

While developments and condominiums had grown up around them, Raimi lived in the part of town untouched by the encroachment of progress. Erin liked it here, but tonight she didn't think about the twinkling lights in the windows, the huge candles on porches, or the life-size sleigh outlined with a floodlight on the lawn of the huge house at the end of the lane. All she thought of was the double-cross Raimi Price had played on her.

Slamming the door to her car, she barged up the stairs of the wide porch and pushed the doorbell with enough force to break it. She didn't think of the pain it was doing to her finger. Inside she could hear the chimes going off. She paced back and forth between the two white columns that divided the porch into equal measures. Breathing hard, she could see her breath congeal in the cold air.

"This is a surprise," Raimi said, opening the door. A wide smile split his face.

Erin whirled around to face him. "When were you going to tell me?" She glared at him.

"Tell you what?" The smile quickly left his face.

She brushed past him into the foyer. She went ahead into the living room. Erin had never been in this house before, but the room was easy to find off the center hall. She didn't take time to look around. "When were you going to tell me the reason you came back to town was to bid on a piece of land? Land you knew I was already trying to purchase."

"What are you talking about?"

"You know very well what I'm talking about. I'm talking about a hundred-and-twenty-five-acre tract of land in Hopewell Township, which I nearly had a contract on until you decided you wanted it."

"What a minute. Are you saying you have a bid in for that land—and that I knew about it?"

"That's exactly what I'm saying. You came here already

knowing all about my wanting that land. I've wanted it for years."

"I haven't been here for years."

She placed her hands on her hips. "I'm well aware of that."

"Just what does that mean?"

"It means nothing. It means that I live here and you don't. I work with the people of this community, and you just come in after sixteen years of absence with your corporation and your money and dangle it in front of the realtors. You can have anything you want, and you decide that tract of land is it."

"Erin, you're being unreasonable."

He took a step toward her. She recoiled and he stopped.

"This plant will provide jobs for hundreds of people. It will lower the tax base in this area. How can you argue against that?"

"My store will also employ people. It will give the people of this community a job. Single mothers will have jobs and an affordable day-care center, where they can leave their children and know they will be safe and fed and cared for by a staff that not only includes teachers but also doctors and nurses. Can you say that about your tool-and-die company?" She paused to draw in breath, then continued. "It will give them a sense of purpose and let them know they can support themselves and their families. A tool-and-die company needs specialized employees. They want experienced people who can work the first day. You're not willing to hire and train, to give people a chance."

"We can't do that. The products we make have to be done to precise specifications."

"Well, let them do it in New York and stay out of here." She crossed her arms over her breasts and turned away. Her face was hot, her ears burned, and her heart pounded in her head. She should leave. Why was she still here?

"This can't be the only place you can build a store."

She whipped around like she'd been spun out of rodeo rope. "Nothing is absolute, Raimi. There's land everywhere, and if I don't get this, I'll certainly find something else—which is exactly what you could do. Your company can find whatever they want. Why did you pick Cranbury? You didn't come here to renew old friendships. You came back for the land. Why don't you go somewhere else?"

Erin regretted the words as soon as she'd said them, but it was too late to take them back. Raimi stiffened. She could see every nerve in his body stand stark still as he stared at her. His hands balled into clenched fists, and he stood cold like a statue.

"You don't just mean the company, do you? You mean why don't *I* go away?"

Erin stood her ground. She wanted to back down but didn't. She allowed the electrified silence to speak for her.

"This isn't about land, is it, Erin? It's about you and me and that prom."

"This has nothing to do with the prom. It has to do with you trying to steal a plot of land that I had a valid bid on."

"Screw the land! This is about us."

"There is no *us*. Except for that one date sixteen years ago, I've known you barely twenty-four hours and—"

Raimi moved with lightning speed. Before Erin knew his intentions, he'd banded one arm around her waist and pulled her against him. The other hand he dug into her short hair and pulled her mouth to his. The kiss was hard and fast, but not fast enough to prevent her from going limp in his arms. Every inch of him defined itself in equal places against her outline. Her arms curved around him, and she pulled herself closer if that was possible. His mouth softened, then lifted. He looked at her, his eyes dark and filled with need. Then he kissed her again. This time she had no resistance. Her mouth opened under his. Her heart rate shot up. Heat generated around her, threatening to boil the blood in her system. And her mind went south. She could think of nothing save the sensations Raimi created in her. Nothing about the prom penetrated her consciousness, nothing of their years apart or of the barbs she'd taken over his treatment of her. The only thing she knew was that she wanted to be in his arms.

He released her slowly, keeping her against his body, but pushing her back enough to look into her eyes.

"Now," he said, "tell me there's no us."

Erin pushed herself out of his embrace. She wobbled a moment as she stepped back before regaining her strength. Erin understood when she was beat. Raimi had the upper hand, and there was nothing she could do about it except maybe exit with a little dignity. She was good at exits where he was involved. When he'd left her standing on the dance floor, she'd moved without disturbing anyone. Then Oliver Rendell had been there, and he'd taken her home. Tonight she'd leave under her own power.

"There might have been an us once, Raimi. But we've lost the opportunity. Enjoy yourself for the time you'll be here. I don't imagine we need see each other anymore. Good-bye, Raimi."

Raimi stared after her. He felt beaten, like he could do nothing right where Erin was concerned. Back in high school he'd made a bad decision, and he seemed to continue with bad decisions over and over.

He hadn't placed the bid to spite her. He didn't know she already had a bid when he'd suggested they build the plant in Hopewell. He'd put the incident of the prom out of his mind. He'd never believe the girl he'd taken would grow into Erin Scott. They'd been searching for an expansion site, and Raimi had grown tired of the rat race. He'd suggested the land because he wanted to come home, return here. He'd planned to run the place himself. He wanted to come home. But now he found his personal reasons for bidding on the land would destroy his chances of being with the woman of his choice . . . and Erin Scott was that woman.

Chapter Five

Skipping the Kwanzaa celebration tonight was at the top of Erin's list after her encounter with Raimi. She paced back and forth in her bedroom, reliving the awful scene she'd had with Raimi and how she'd let him kiss her. Let him, she thought. That was a laugh. He hadn't done it alone. She'd kissed him, too, wound her body around his as if he were a lock and she his personal key. Every logical thought she ever had flew to the four winds when he'd pressed his mouth to hers. She didn't want to see him again. The only place that was sure to happen was at the Kwanzaa program in less than an hour. She was going to have to be prepared for that.

Barring illness or breaking something vital, she had to be there. Asha, generally a calm, controlled individual except when she had to speak in public, needed her family for support. Tonight she would be explaining the principle of Kujichagulia, and Erin had to be on the front row. Forcing herself to calm down, she dressed. Tonight wasn't as formal as First Night, so she wore a navy-blue suit with a kente cloth scarf that draped over her left shoulder and dipped down her back to her calves.

Checking her reflection in the mirror, she left her bedroom. She had no reason to remain any longer. It was time to go. Erin wondered how many of the citizens of Cranbury already knew about Raimi's company's bid? How many of them knew Raimi Price had walked into her life and made a mess of it—again?

The drive was shorter than she expected. She could have kept going till morning, and that wouldn't have been enough time. Taking a deep breath, she squared her shoulders and entered the high school gym. Raimi was sure to be here already, if not then he'd appear before the ceremony ended. This morning she'd been willing to spend Kwanzaa with him. She wasn't sure she wouldn't have been willing to spend her life with him, but tonight her world had changed. Tonight her heart thumped at the prospect of seeing him over the expanse of the gym.

"I'm so glad you're here," Asha said when Erin had taken her coat off and left it at the check room. The lighting in the gym was about the same as last night. The huge middle candle in the kinara was already lighted. Asha would light the second candle after she explained that Kujichagulia meant self-determination, that the definition of ourselves should come from within and not without. Erin wondered about her own definition and if she were defining herself or if she'd let Raimi do that to her sixteen years ago.

Raimi entered at that moment. She and Asha stood near the door. He nodded to Asha and said good evening. To Erin he only nodded. She felt herself stiffen at his presence. She knew he'd be here, and he had a perfect right to attend the ceremony, just as she had. He passed them and went over to Oliver Rendell.

"What was that all about?" Asha asked, jerking her head toward Raimi.

"Nothing," Erin answered.

"I thought you two were—"

"No," Erin interrupted a little too fast. "No."

"It's that land, isn't it?"

The two of them began walking toward the center of the gym. "Asha, you know that's why he came here. His company is bidding on the land, the same tract of land I've been trying to get for years. They'll get it too. I talked to Carl Linert after you left my office this afternoon." Carl was the real estate agent Erin dealt with. "He told me their bid was significantly higher than mine, and that I should look for something else."

"Carl always was a weasel," Asha said under her breath. "So what are you going to do?"

"There isn't anything I can do. I suppose I'll have to find another site. It's just that I've done a lot of work on that area: demographics, zoning, contractors. Now I'll have to begin all over again."

"I'm sorry, Erin."

Erin tried to smile at her sister. "It's all right. I guess I'm so disappointed because I convinced the people owning that land to sell it and then to have it pulled out from under me by a friend . . ." She left the sentence hanging.

"A friend, Erin? Is that what you consider him?"

Erin looked at Raimi then. His back was to her as he talked to Oliver near the front of the room. He was the best-looking man she'd ever seen. For years she'd told herself she hated him. That after the prom and her school days she could never feel anything for him except hate. Yet she'd also made a fantasy of him. He was the man of her dreams—the one she compared every other man to and secretly the man she wanted. For sixteen years she'd done this. Then yesterday morning he suddenly appeared before her in the store, and the reality of him remained intact.

"Not after tonight," Erin finally answered her sister's

question. She brought her attention back to Asha. The confused expression on her face asked for more. "I went to his house tonight and told him we didn't need another tool-and-die company here. I told him I thought he should leave town and take his company with him. So you see, even if we could have been friends I made sure it would never happen."

"He doesn't have to leave because you said so."

"I know. I can't run anyone out of town." Least of all a man of Raimi's size, she thought but didn't say. "I also told him I didn't want anything more to do with him."

"Did you mean that?"

Erin didn't answer.

"Erin, I know I don't live here all the time, but I know that you were in love with Raimi when we were in school."

Erin opened her mouth to speak, but Asha stopped her.

"Don't deny it. I'm not blind. I saw your face when you told me he'd asked you to the prom. You were so excited. It was like another person had taken over your body. Nothing before had made you that happy and since that night no man has compared to the image of Raimi."

"You knew?"

"I'm your sister, and we grew closer with age. I always felt you'd get over him. That it was taking you a little longer than other women but all first loves take a long time to get over. Then he walked in last night and I knew."

Erin cautioned herself to look at him again. He'd moved to Clarice Markham. She looked at him as if she were hungry and he was dessert. Erin felt jealousy slice through her like a hot knife through warm wax.

Oliver came over as the ceremony was about to begin. Erin took a seat next to her parents, and Asha went on the stage. Raimi sat next to Clarice, and Erin tried not to notice.

The program went off without a hitch, and Asha's speech had no sign of nervousness. She made a ceremony of lifting the little boy and helping him light the Kujichagulia candle. The rest of the night was spent talking to friends. There was music but no dance floor, and after an hour or so of visiting everyone would begin to leave. Erin wouldn't wait that long. She'd talked to Janey Devore, whom she'd known since grade school. She met Katherine Ames, who was here for the holidays with her husband. They lived in Florida now, and she talked about missing the cold weather.

True to her request, Raimi didn't come near her the entire night. Erin felt the strain of being in the same room with him and not being able to talk to him, especially since everyone she talked to invariably looked from her to him. A few of them mentioned his name, and several even made reference to the prom. Erin kept her smile in place and laughed in all the right places, while inside she wanted to run away. It wasn't the comments people were making that bothered her. It was the fact that Raimi was in the room. It was the kiss they'd shared in his car yesterday and the one he'd taken tonight. Everything now seemed to revolve around him. She wanted to be with him. She wanted things to be different between them, but it seemed they were living on different planets. They didn't speak the same language, and they didn't travel on the same plane. No matter how much of an attraction existed between them, it wouldn't be enough to make them friends or lovers.

"Ah, Erin, just the person I'm looking for." Carl Linert came up to her. He was forty-something, balding, had pale blue eyes and the remnants of blond hair. He stuck out in this room of African-Americans like a white elephant, but Carl was political and this gathering represented future sales to his business. He always appeared at gatherings. She had to give him credit for coming here, although he wasn't the only Caucasian in the room, just the only one who stuck out.

"Hello, Carl," she said, keeping all the anger out of her voice. "What brings you here?"

"I always attend these ceremonies."

She nodded.

"I also wanted to ask if you'd like me to check on that other parcel of land we discussed this afternoon?" He went into his salesman mode. "You know, land around here is being snapped up all the time. I'd hate for you to lose out a second time."

Erin wanted to throttle him. The last thing she needed right now was a reminder about the land. "Go on, Carl. Check on it."

"You'll—"

"Carl." She stopped him. "I was about to leave. You can give me any details about it later."

She found Asha and her parents and told them she was leaving, using the excuse of the store and a full day tomorrow. Her mother kissed her cheek, and Asha threw her a look she'd rather not interpret. Erin headed for the coat room. As she slipped her arms in her coat, Raimi came up behind her.

"Let me help you." He grabbed the side of her coat and helped her on with it. For a moment his hands rested on her shoulders. Erin was confused. She felt heat rush through her. Even though his hands weren't against her skin, it felt as if they were. She turned and behind him she could see several people looking at them. She didn't know what to say, so she said nothing. She pulled her coat together and buttoned it. Then she looked at him, and her throat went dry. "Good night," she said and walked away.

Raimi wanted to catch Erin and force her to understand, but he couldn't. There were too many people staring at them, and from what she'd told him and what he knew from his sister, Erin hadn't had an easy time living here after he left her at the prom. His returning here and getting involved with her had only revived old memories, and people could be harsh even when they didn't intend to be. He'd been on the receiving end of a few comments this evening. He could only imagine what Erin had taken . . . and because of something he had done.

He was back to do it again.

Raimi couldn't believe her feelings made such a difference to him. He couldn't believe after two days he was so sure of wanting to spend time with her. A lot of time. She'd nearly knocked him off his feet when he first saw her, and each time he'd seen her since the feeling escalated. What bothered him was every time he got near her, he did something that complicated her life for the worse.

He looked at her retreating back and wanted to go to her, run over and make everything better. He couldn't. The decision on the land wasn't totally his, but he did have influence. If he wanted her good opinion, and he did, he was going to have to resolve the land deal. Taking it away from here, moving the factory to another location, would mean he went there too. Giving her what she wanted could take him away from what he wanted.

Her.

The road would need to be widened to accommodate the increased traffic. Water was no problem, but getting the heavy equipment down that hill might be tricky. Raimi assessed the value of the land that both he and Erin wanted. He could find nothing his company would have to do that she wouldn't. They might be able to put more pressure on the township to upgrade the road, but then Erin was a part of this community. She had friends who wouldn't need pressure. All she needed to do was smile at them, and how could they refuse. That smile raised his blood pressure. It could certainly get a variance if she needed one.

Behind him a car turned into the small parking area. Raimi turned around. From the road you had to know this space was here. The road between Hopewell and Rocky Hill was narrow and winding. Along both sides century-old trees flanked the roadway, extending high as they reached for the blue sky above them. This lot could hold no more than a few cars. It couldn't be seen from the road until you'd passed it. So Raimi wasn't surprised to see it was Erin. She stayed in her car when she saw him, the engine running. Her face told him, she hadn't expected him to be here or she wouldn't have come.

He went over to her and opened the door. "Looks like we both had the same idea." He offered his hand to assist her. She took it without hesitation, extinguishing the engine at the same time. Standing before him in boots and a green suede suit, Raimi wanted to hold on to her hand, but he dropped it as soon as she cleared the door. "This is one of the few times we can be together without the eyes of the town on us."

Erin smiled.

Raimi wanted to touch her. He wanted to go back sixteen years and change everything that had hurt her, but he knew he couldn't do that. He and Erin had begun a path that night, one that led them to this plot of red dirt on a hillside in Hopewell. Raimi looked again at the ground falling away from them as it arced down a hill covered in the wheat-gold-colored winter grass.

"Tell me about the store," he asked, turning to watch Erin.

"I'd planned to have it sit right over there." She pointed to her right and about halfway down the hill. "The main store would have six floors and look much like the buildings you see along the main road. We wanted to keep the rustic look. Over there,"—she pointed again toward the

right but further down—"that's where the day-care center
for employees would be. The day care for store clients
would be in the building next to the store, connected by
a tunnel. Parents could drop off their kids and shop, then
return to pick them up."

"Convenience, it's a good concept and one that will
make people want to shop here."

"It was my secretary's idea. She has a small child and
whenever she needs to shop, she says her child really ham-
pers her. Providing mothers a safe place to leave their
children would benefit both the store and the mothers."

Raimi liked the way she cared about people. It was one
of the things he missed about living in New York. People
didn't really have time to care about each other. Of course,
he knew his neighbors, and they looked out for each other,
but no one went out of their way to be friendly the way
they did here.

"You'll more than likely get the land," Erin stated. She
stood stiff and distant, pausing as if she had to force the
words to be natural. "Your bid is much higher than mine.
We both know that." She turned away from him then and
looked at the valley below them. Raimi could see the anger
in her. He recognized the coiled anger, the kind that rent
the inside of you, but on the outside you looked as calm
as possible. It was the same look he'd seen on a gym floor
as he turned to follow Margaret Foley out the door.

Raimi took a step toward her. She turned when she felt
him getting close.

"Tell me about the plant you're going to build here."

Her voice was tight, and he had the sudden feeling of
losing a dream.

"Erin, I didn't come here for this. I'm sure there is
something that can be done."

"I'll find something else," she said. "There's plenty of
property around here for sale. I've already talked to Carl
Linert. He's looking into another site for my store."

He knew now that she'd planned on this land a long time. Everyone in town knew, and they didn't mind giving him a few details when he mentioned it. Asha had gone as far as showing him the model Erin had had developed. She'd gone much further than his tool-and-die company. Her heart was invested here, while all he had was money and a multinational company. He felt like a thief, an interloper sneaking in under disguise and taking what wasn't his.

"There is another parcel for sale over on Route 1. It'll be just as good as this is."

But not as picturesque, he thought but didn't say.

"Erin, I'll talk to my company. We can find another place to build a plant."

She tried to smile, but he saw the difficulty in that. It's as if she heard his words but put no strength in them.

"You already have a contract. I'm sure the sellers won't settle for my offer now that they've had yours. It won't matter if you pull out. They'll raise the price when it's relisted. It will all be a waste of time."

Erin turned and headed for her car. Raimi reached out and took her arm. She stopped but didn't look at him. Her eyes remained on the hard earth beneath their feet.

"Look at me," he said.

She raised her eyes slowly, but they eventually connected with his.

"I'll do what I can."

She nodded and moved to pass him. He stepped directly in her path. Raimi took her face in his hands and lifted it until she met his eyes. God! He wanted her. He'd never wanted anyone as much as he wanted this woman—and he wanted her smiling, not looking at him as if he'd killed everything that was alive inside her.

At that moment he knew he had to change things. He'd done this to her, however inadvertently.

For a long moment neither of them spoke. He still held

her face in his hands. Leaning toward her wasn't something he had to think of doing. He just did it. Fear had him trembling, but he moved closer, cutting the distance between them by small fractions, certain that if he moved too fast he'd lose the fragile thread that connected them. He could feel the heat of her, discern the same trembling that pulsated through him. Like himself, she was fighting something inside, wavering over a decision. He wanted to help that decision, wanted it in his favor. His mouth was only an inch from hers. He could taste her breath, feel the warm heat of her mouth as she anticipated the kiss. One hand moved into the short crop of hair at her nape.

Then as he homed in on her mouth, she turned her head and his kiss landed on her cheek. He held it there, slipping his arms around her and holding her close.

He could feel everything happening to her, the intensity with which she held herself, the moment her arms raised and she relaxed, the tears that slid from her eyelids. Then her arms lost weight like they had suddenly turned to water. They slid away from him, and when she stepped back he didn't stop her. She didn't look at him, didn't speak. She walked toward her car, got in and backed out of the small parking area.

Raimi watched her go with trepidation. He turned back to the land. Wars had been fought over real estate, and now he and Erin were locked in a kind of war.

Well, he didn't want to fight it.

Chapter Six

An early night was just what she needed. Erin pulled the wrapping from her hair and combed it back into the style she'd worn for several years. She'd gone to her parents for the ritual exchange of gifts. Her smile had been in place and no one, not even Asha, seemed to realize she wasn't really having a good time.

Since Raimi had kissed her this morning, she'd been disoriented, unable to concentrate. Ujima was a big night at her parents' house, and she went loaded down with gifts she'd made. They had a big meal and celebrated. Her father presided over the home program. When the family decided to attend tonight's ceremony, Erin drove herself back to the small house she occupied.

Folding the yards of multicolored cloth, she placed it in the drawer. Slipping off her shoes, she re-racked them in the closet that got smaller and smaller each year. As she prepared to remove her dress, the doorbell rang. Erin groaned. She knew it was Asha coming to interrogate her. Padding barefoot to the door, she pulled it open and stopped as she prepared to refuse Asha's request to join her. Raimi stood bathed in the porch light. He wore a dress suit, and his grooming appeared more formal tonight than it had on other occasions. As always his handsome features took her by surprise.

For a moment Raimi looked as uncomfortable as she felt, shifting from one bare foot to the other. She hadn't expected to see him. He was the main reason she'd avoided going to the celebration.

"Do you think I could come in?" he asked.

Regaining some of her composure, Erin stood back, holding the door completely open. "Of course," she said. "Come in."

She closed the door and faced him. He carried his coat over his arm and a box wrapped in brightly colored paper with fabric ribbons of silver and taffeta in his hand. She reached for his coat, and he handed it to her.

"Go in," she said. He went toward her living room and she took a deep breath, taking her time hanging up his coat. It held some of his body heat, and she forced herself not to bury her face in it. She loved the way he smelled. This morning when he'd held her, she drank in the essence of him. That same essence lingered on his coat. What was he doing here, she asked herself, trying to force her mind to forget this morning, yesterday morning, and all the times the two of them had been together. Closing the closet door, she joined him. He stood in front of the fireplace between the facing sofas. His back was to her, and he looked at the photos on the mantel. The one he held in his hand was the one her parents had taken of them just before they left for the prom. Erin knew it well. The outdated dress and hairstyle were preserved in time. The smile on her face was enough to light the room. She felt foolish about it being there, but then she never expected Raimi Price to ever stand in this room. "Can I get you something to drink?" she asked to divert his attention.

"Coffee?"

She nodded and went to the kitchen. Hoping to have some minutes to herself, she was surprised when he followed her into the spaciously lit room and even more surprised when he set the photo on the kitchen table.

Preparing the machine with coffee and water, she was conscious of Raimi's silent presence behind her. It made her uncomfortable. She didn't like the feeling. Turning to face him, she took the offensive. "Why are you here?" Always wanting to know exactly where she stood, Erin never beat around the bush.

"You didn't come to Ujima tonight."

She shook her head. Her mouth was suddenly dry. Did he think she'd avoided the gym to avoid him? That was exactly the reason she hadn't gone. She didn't want to face him, not after this morning and after the kiss and the way he'd held her. She could fight him with the land. She could even lose the land. That wouldn't bother her in the least. It was his tenderness, the hurt in his eyes that undid her, melted her insides and made her want to rush into his arms.

"I went to my parents'. We celebrated there."

Behind her she could hear the gurgling of the water as it dripped into the pot.

"Were you avoiding me?"

"Why would I want to avoid you?"

He took a step closer. Erin instinctively moved back.

"Because of this morning and the other morning. Because of the way you felt in my arms. Because I find it impossible to stay away from you."

Erin hadn't expected such a revelation. She was speechless. Did he mean it? Could she trust him? Her heart screamed at her, telling her this was her dream. This was what she had wanted all her life. Yet her brain gave her a totally different interpretation. He was the same man who'd left her at the prom. The same man who'd returned unexpectedly into her life and turned it upside down. The same man who'd double-crossed her. This was the man who wanted her trust. Dare she give it?

She turned back to the coffee. Mechanically she opened the cabinet and took down two mugs. Raimi came up behind her and took her shoulders, pulling her back against him. He buried his face in her hair and kissed her on the side near her ear. Sensations spiraled through Erin. She fought to maintain her hold on the cups in her hands.

"Tell me you feel the same way I do," Raimi whispered.

Erin groaned. She did feel the same. She'd wanted nothing more than to have her life and his follow identical paths, but something held her tongue, wouldn't let her say it. She loved him. Closing her eyes, she let her head fall back against his shoulder. She had always loved him. From that first moment in school when she'd seen him, she knew he was the man of her dreams, but she had never been in his thoughts.

Could they be together now? Had their lives moved along the same parallel or converging planes? Were they now closer to being one or were they simply traveling through this particular time together? After the season ended, would he ever think of her when he was back in New York? Would this be only a Kwanzaa memory, hidden and forgotten among the many memories of a lifetime, or would she be the crowning memory, the one that wouldn't go away, wouldn't be denied? She was confused. She had no way of knowing what to do.

Raimi took the decision out of her hands. He turned her around and this time gave her no chance to decide. His mouth took hers hard and fast. His tongue pushed past her teeth and sought the sweetness inside. Any decisions she could have made were postponed as sensation attacked her system, replacing her blood with a rapturous flow of thrill like a carnival ride. She felt as if they were flying on a high ride that took them to the brink of danger but kept them in place.

Erin returned his kiss. Her arms circled his neck, pulling her body into contact with his, a procedure she was sure would cause them to spontaneously combust, but she no longer cared. She no longer had any control over what happened to her, and she didn't care. She was in love with Raimi. She'd always been in love with him. She loved the way his mouth felt on hers, the way his body fit with hers, the way his hands traveled over her back evoking sensation, calling emotions she had no previous knowledge existed. Her nerve endings craved his touch, reached for him, converted his touch to pleasure and dove into the pool without thought.

She heard him groan as his mouth lifted from hers. "If you want me to leave," he said, his voice heavy with emotion. "You're going to have to say it now. I'm on a short fuse, and in a moment I won't be able to go."

Erin looked at him. She knew her eyes were full of the love she felt. She knew she wanted him, had always wanted him, and knew this might be the only time they would ever be together. In the future he could be only a memory, one that glowed hot and bright whenever she chose to display it, but tonight she would make that memory.

Her hands slid off his shoulders and down his arms. She watched the movement as if it were in a dream. At the end of his arms, she took his hands in hers and turned toward the stairs.

The coffee was forgotten.

Raimi kicked the door to her bedroom closed and turned her around. Erin put her hands on his waist and looked up at him. He wasn't watching her but looking at the semidark surroundings. Her house predated the Civil War, like most of the homes in town, including his own. Behind her stood a queen-size bed dressed in a Kwanzaa comforter of bright colors: red, black, and green. The

fireplace burned low from hours of absent attention, yet
it provided a golden glow to the room. A tabletop Christmas tree sat on the circular table in front of the window
next to the fireplace. The mantel drape of gold held a
miniature kinara on a kente cloth bed. Colorful bulbs hung
from the drape, and tiny white lights and garland flanked
both sides of the ornate fireplace. The room held mementos from previous points in Erin's life: photos, a silk flower
basket that looked like a wedding remembrance, a mug
from Disney World, a small replica of a cruise ship. Raimi
felt a sudden loss. Where had she collected these things?
Who had been with her? A sudden rush of jealousy caught
him when the knowledge entered his brain that he wished
he had been with her to make those memories.

When his eyes came back to her, his heart was in them.
He didn't just want to make love to her, he wanted to be
part of her life, part of this room and the love that lived
here. He wanted to be part of the memories that the Disney
cup could bring, part of the smile that formed her lips
when no one knew what she thought. He took her face in
his hands as he'd done this morning on the top of the
windy hill. Raimi had never been afraid of anything, yet
Erin scared him. His heart thudded in his chest as he slowly
lowered his mouth to hers. His arms closed around her,
holding her carefully, as if she were a priceless jewel, something to be cradled and desired, something that needed
special handling.

Erin was shorter than anyone he'd ever been involved
with, but she fit perfectly against him. Raimi lifted her off
the floor as he deepened the kiss, his mouth devouring
hers, giving and taking, lifting only to reposition itself and
begin the torture he was willing to endure throughout
time. Holding her against him, he felt the length of her
frame. She was soft and warm and smelled of something
sweet and flowery. Her breasts pushed against his chest as
her arms circled his neck. The erotic movement drove

him past the edge of sanity. He lowered her to the floor, allowing her body to slide over the sensitive areas of his, sending sensation off the Richter scale. It was all he could do not to shout out loud, releasing the pent-up frustration that overwhelmed him.

Walking her back to the bed, he slid his hand up her back, along her spine with a slowness that surprised him. At her nape he found the zipper and lowered it. He could hear the ripping effect as the teeth separated. He touched the bare skin of her back as he slid the instrument from top to bottom. She shuddered when his fingers raked along her back. Her skin felt like fire to his hands, burning his fingers, sending fiery sparks from her nerve endings to his. Electricity arced up his arms until he was ablaze.

Stepping back, he peeled the dress from her, never breaking contact as he pushed the sleeves down her long arms and over her hands, first one arm and then the other. It fell to her waist. He gasped at the sight of her, dark as brandy in the gold light of the dying fire. The yellow hues of the dress reflected on her smooth skin. His throat was too dry for words. Only a guttural sound escaped him. He pushed the dress over her hips, letting his hands linger on her curves until he knew he'd drive himself mad with need if he continued. Finally, the fabric pooled at their feet.

Raimi wanted to see all of her, and she seemed content to let him undress her . . . one agonizing piece of clothing at a time. She still wore the tight ankle pants that completed the outfit. She reached down and unhooked the ankle buttons, freeing the bonding cloth to escape over her feet. Then she placed her hands over his on her waist and pushed the pants to the floor. He pulled them off one leg at a time.

His breath left him when he straightened to find her clad only in bra and panties, Christmas red. Her stomach was flat, her small breasts peeked over the tops of her bra cups. Her waist beveled inward, perfect for his hands, for dancing or pulling her forward, perfect for kissing. Her hips rounded gently into long legs that went on forever. He remembered their one prom dance. He had held her thin, angular body and swayed to the music. This body was different—there were no hard angles here, and he certainly wanted to dance with it.

Quickly he dispensed with the remainder of her clothes, then his own joined hers on the floor. Erin pulled the comforter back and got into the bed. Sheets with the same jungle print that beat in his veins settled over them as he joined her there. He pulled her close, kissed her eyes, her cheeks, worked his way to the soft spot of her throat that beat a pulse equal to the rapidly flaring one in his own throat. He listened to her sounds, learned her movements as his hands moved with precision over her hot skin. When he reached her breasts, she arched forward. Her nipples were hard and dark as red wine. Her eyes closed when he touched them. Sensation seemed to run through her that made her body reach toward him for more pleasure. He gave her what she wanted, wanting to give, wanting to make this night the best in her life, wanting to make sure no other man had ever loved her the way he intended to love her.

Her arms came around him, and her legs angled over his. He felt her body convulse as he touched her in the most sensitive place. He rubbed himself against her, holding in the need to plunge inside her, listening to the animal sounds that came from her at his touch. Again her hips arched, reaching for him, seeking to join with him, communicating her need in primal messages that men and women had used since they first walked this undiscovered country. Her hands ran the length of him, every inch quivering as her nails brought to life the erotic awareness of his union to her. Every centimeter became a river of fire that burned to his very core. Finally, she took him in her hand. He couldn't stop the shout that came from his throat. No voluntary pressure produced it, only the sudden impact that she caused with fingers that couldn't know their worth. It was instinctive. Sensation shot through him like a burning bullet discharging. He'd never known such a feeling. No on had ever done this to him and never this fast.

He took her hand and moved it. Pinning it on the side of her head, he took her mouth fiercely as if he couldn't go on breathing without help from her. He rolled onto her, spreading her legs and replacing the open area with his own body. He entered her smoothly, hearing a near whimper she couldn't hold in, as heavenly pleasure promised to take them to a plane neither had visited before. Paradise loomed before them, a magical place, reserved for them only. Ecstasy rocketed through him, pushing him forward as the timeless rhythm began.

He wanted to go slowly, take the pacing down a peg, but when Erin's legs wrapped around him and pulled him into her all hope was lost. He felt the snap, like a bullwhip, inside him as he lost control and nothing could stop him from racing, reaching, hungering for the goal he sought. Nothing could keep him from trying, not even the thought of dying here, could stop him from taking her to that place that loomed only a step away, that utopia that was theirs for the asking and he was asking.

Erin didn't recognize herself, not the way she was acting with Raimi. She'd never been aggressive in sex, but she found herself meeting his hard thrusts, kneading his muscular buttocks, and guiding him into the place that made her crazy. Her legs had never been this strong, this forceful, this controlled as she sought the push and pull of a thousand centuries of love. Her ancestors before her, all the Scotts, her entire heritage had produced bloodline after bloodline until it brought her to this night, this place, and this man. She joined with him, knowing they were on the brink of forever. They were locked together as inexorably as a medieval dungeon. Raimi's hand felt hot on her skin. She drowned in the aura that surrounded them, fanned the flames they created, and fed on them like a perpetual motion machine. The faster they worked, the greater the flame, the faster the burn. She didn't want it to end even when she felt the coming, the knowing, the knowledge that the end was a brilliant light just over the rise she'd been scaling—knowing that Raimi would go there with her, knowing the two of them would explode if they didn't get there and flying as fast and fiercely as possible.

With a crash she felt it, the blast, the discharge and answering report, the eruption, detonation, the convulsion of all that embodied her. She knew the sweeping pleasure that rocketed through her, taking her and Raimi, joining them into a single unit and showing them the pleasure that two people could experience.

Suddenly he collapsed onto her, spent and disoriented. She'd never known anything like this, and knew as long as she lived never again could anyone, except Raimi, take her to the heights the two of them had just scaled.

Erin ran her hands over his back and into his short-cropped hair. She reveled in the feel of him, him inside her after sex, after love, after the wonders of the universe had been revealed to them and they slowly descended back to earth. She lowered her legs, feeling the roughness of his hairy ones against her smoothly shaved skin. Would her life ever be the same again? Could the sun rising tomorrow be the same as it had been today? Would life go on as it had for centuries? She couldn't believe it could. Tonight her world had changed, metamorphosed. Surely it would be evident to every living soul that the two of them had altered the world.

Erin woke feeling lazy. She stretched, remembering last night. Her body felt tight, different, wonderful. She reached for Raimi. He was beside her. Her hand smoothed over his stomach. His muscles grew taut at her touch. Without opening her eyes, she smiled and pushed her legs over his. She heard him moan and opened her eyes. Instead of his face, the gift he'd brought with him last night sat on the pillow between them.

"What is this?" She pushed herself up, pulling the sheet to cover her nakedness.

"It's your Kwanzaa gift."

He was beautiful, she thought, pushing a hand through her short tousled curls. She wondered what she looked like. Was her hair standing up? All her makeup had surely been washed away by Raimi's kisses. Her eyes probably looked small and unappealing, but she didn't care. Raimi looked at her as if she were the most beautiful woman in the world. She felt beautiful.

"Since you didn't come to the celebration last night, I couldn't give it to you." He reached up and pulled at her hair. "Open it." He pushed the box toward her.

Adjusting the pillows and the sheet, she placed the box in front of her and pulled the ribbons. "Did you wrap this?"

"Guilty." He smiled.

"No help?"

"Well, I had to take classes but I managed to learn to tie a knot."

Erin grinned then pulled away the wrapping and lifted the lid. Inside yellow tissue paper covered the gift. Moving it aside, she caught her breath. Lying in the folds of the colorful paper was an angel. She pulled it out. It was a candle. Several candles. Somehow they'd been molded together then dressed in Kwanzaa colors and cloth. Erin felt tears gather behind her eyes, and she blinked them away. She could say nothing. Raimi's Kwanzaa angel had completely taken her by surprise. He'd made it for her. She looked at the delicate fabric and ribbons and then at

Raimi's hands. Had those hands produced something as beautiful as this? She loved it. Emotion took her voice, and she could say nothing. It was the most beautiful gift she'd ever received. And he'd given it to her.

"Say something," he said.

"Did—did you make it?" she managed over the knot in her throat.

"I didn't melt the wax and form it, but I did everything else."

A tear fell then. She raised her hand to her mouth. "It's beautiful." The angel's face had been made with inlays of gold thread. Crafter's pins formed her smile. The dress, made of the same cloth Erin had worn on the first night of Kwanzaa, covered the body. Guilt gripped her. She remembered her words to him that first day in the store when she accused him of buying his gifts. And he'd made this wonderful present. It was more than she could hope for. Pushing the box aside, Erin went into his arms.

"Thank you," she said through sobs. "It's the most wonderful angel I've ever seen."

Raimi turned his face into her shoulder and kissed her bare skin. When he spoke, his voice was low and hoarse. "You're the most wonderful angel I've ever seen."

Chapter Seven

"**Y**ou know, over the past few days that I've been here, I'd say that's rapidly becoming your favorite song," Asha commented with a lifted eyebrow. Erin looked at her, and Asha hummed a few bars of "What a Difference a Day Makes."

"Oh," she said. Erin couldn't keep from smiling. She'd hummed that song about a million times since Raimi had come into her life. Erin could have told her she'd never been in love before and being with Raimi had changed everything about her. Yet she held it in. For the time being she wanted to hold on to her love, wrap herself in it, feel the warmth of true love, and not share it with anyone but Raimi. She left Asha's unasked question hanging in the aromatic air of her kitchen.

Tonight it was just herself and her sister for dinner. Asha tossed a salad while Erin completed the final preparations on the roast she'd made.

"I'm glad it's just the two of us tonight. We never have enough time together," Asha remarked.

Erin carried the main course to the dining-room table.

Asha followed her. "Well, you have a busy life traveling the world, and I have Scott's to take care of."

She slid into her chair, and Asha took the seat next to her as she placed the salad with the other food. The table was laid with bone china place settings and crystal wineglasses. Asha poured the wine she'd brought into the glasses. She lifted hers in a toast. "To Nia," she said.

"Nia," Erin answered and clinked her glass with her sister's before taking a sip. "I really have enjoyed your help at the store." Erin filled her plate with the succulent meat and added a helping of roasted potatoes, mint jelly, and broccoli with cheese sauce. She didn't often eat like this, but roasted potatoes and mint jelly were Asha's favorites.

"You know I don't mind helping out once in a while."

"I know. I just want to go on record as saying I appreciate it. At least with you in the store I can spend more time with you than if I'd worked all day and saw you only in the evening."

"Especially since we know where your evenings have been spent lately." Asha placed a potato in her mouth and closed her eyes as if she'd never tasted anything so wonderful in her life. When she opened them, her expression was definitely teasing.

"I haven't spent that many nights with him." Erin's ears heated up at the thought of the last one she'd spent with Raimi. Upstairs was the Kwanzaa angel he'd given her. She could spend many more nights in the same manner. Then she looked at Asha and halted her thoughts.

"Let's see." Asha looked at the ceiling. "He's been in town four days and you've spent—"

"We don't have to count them." She stopped her. Had it only been four days? She'd known him all her life. It seemed the last few days had been months, even years long, or maybe they were years in the making.

"I'm leaving in a couple of days," Asha declared, nipping her thoughts that seemed to run toward Raimi every chance they got.

"I know. We'll have to make plans to get together regularly."

"So is Raimi," she reminded Erin.

Erin stopped, her fork partway to her mouth.

"New York isn't the end of the world," she said. "Many people commute there every day," Erin replayed her sister's words.

"You've never been a commuter, and so far neither has he. Have you talked to him about it?"

Erin shook her head.

"You're in love with him." It was a statement.

Erin swallowed. "I think I've been in love with him since we were both in the cradle." She took another sip of her wine. "I told myself I hated him. For years I tried to forget him, but when I'm really honest with myself, I know he's the reason I've found fault with every man who's ever wanted to get serious. Somehow I never got over him."

"Are you sure it's real now? Could Raimi just fall in the category of . . . unfinished business?"

Erin didn't immediately deny it, although she could have. If he'd been unfinished business she'd have known that last night. He was definitely business of the current variety.

"Can I take that as a no?"

"It's a definite no." Suddenly Erin was angry. She held it in, knowing her sister had her best interests at heart. "You know it was you who threw me at him on First Night. Now you change your mind and think I should go back to being the spinster aunt."

"You're not even close to being a spinster or an aunt." She lowered her voice. "I just don't want you to be hurt."

In the flash of a second, Erin saw her life without Raimi. She knew what it would be like when he left, and she didn't kid herself that he wouldn't leave. They had only a few more days together and then he'd be gone. Back to his world of precision instruments while she worked at selling everything from perfume and fur coats to toys and tools.

"Erin." Asha's voice was soft. Erin recognized it as the serious voice, the one she used when she meant what she said and nothing would change her mind. "I remember what you went through back in high school. I don't mean the teasing. That was horrible, but the feelings you tried to hide from us all. Mom and Dad didn't know half of what you were going through, and you wouldn't tell anyone, but I knew. I know he avoided you, too, after the prom. Then he was gone, and you were still reeling from the promise of what you wanted. I just don't want you to mix up what you really feel and what you want to feel."

"Don't worry. I'll be fine. If he doesn't stay here, I'll be fine."

"No, you won't. You'll be devastated."

Erin looked shocked.

"Even if I weren't your sister, I'd be able to tell how much you love him." She paused a moment. "Erin, you positively glow when you're around him. The mention of his name changes you."

Erin dropped her head. She didn't want her sister to see any of the things she'd mentioned. She knew they were true. Love had done that to her, and there was nothing she could do about it.

"Asha, I'm a grown woman. I'm not that sixteen-year-old who couldn't deal with life after the prom."

"Aren't you?"

Erin pulled her fur coat closer around her. She was dressed for the weather, which had turned colder overnight. She had on her warmest coat, a matching hat, and boots. The ensemble had graced the window of Scott's last season, but fur never went out of style. So she was as fashionably dressed today as anyone. She stood by the lake, watching the water flow. It moved slowly, going toward its eventual end in the Atlantic Ocean. Some long-ago civics class told her the lake had been named after a Presbyterian missionary to the Seneca and Delaware and Lenape Indians who used to inhabit this area.

Like the lake and its waters' flow, her mind moved to Raimi. Erin wanted to put off thinking about him leaving. She didn't want to discuss the subject with him or even mention it. Unfortunately her subconscious had crept in once or twice to remind her of the inevitable, then Asha had brought the subject to a head. Trust Asha, she laughed to herself. Good ole, straightforward, never-beat-about-the-bush, Asha. She'd tell you the truth whether you wanted to hear it or not. This was something Erin didn't want to hear, but the words had been said and she couldn't forget them, couldn't put them behind her or out of her mind. So she'd ended up here by the ever-present lake. It was a mainstay in her life. Sometimes she even thought it gave her strength. Some of the—no, all of the important decisions she'd made in her life had been made near this body of water.

Raimi *was* leaving in a few days. She could no longer deny it, even to herself. The most she could count on was having him here until Imani.

The world became normal the day after Imani, New Year's Day. People began putting the holidays behind them, decorations came down, new goals were set into motion. She wondered what Raimi's goals were. Did any of them involve her? Should she hope that he—She stopped that thought. It was useless to speculate. She couldn't get into his mind. As close as she felt to him, she couldn't read his thoughts. If she looked things straight in the eye, she'd realize she'd known him for only a few days. Back in high school he never even looked at her. An underclassmen and too shy to approach him, she'd been floored when he asked her to the prom. He was the big man on campus, while she was only a sophomore, with a huge crush on him. Maybe Asha was right, and she'd really only fallen in love with love, with a youthful dream, not with a man.

What was she going to do when he left her? Yes, she was a grown woman, but her heart was the same as that sixteen-year-old's heart. She'd be devastated as Asha had predicted.

"I thought I'd find you here."

Erin turned, surprised to see the subject of her thoughts. "How did you know where to find me?"

He ran his hand over the fur covering her arms. "It's where you used to escape to when you saw me coming. For the month that school was still in session after the prom, whenever you'd see me coming you'd avoid passing me by escaping here." He looked at the water. "By this lake. Once I'd passed and you thought it safe to come out, you'd go on. Do you know I used to look for you here when I went by?"

"Why?"

"I wanted to talk to you, tell you I was sorry. I just didn't know how."

"And I didn't give you the chance." She remembered avoiding him, in school and out. He was right about her hiding by the water. At least she thought she'd hidden.

He pulled her close to him. She let him embrace her, but she didn't raise her arms to return the affection.

"What are you doing here today?" he asked.

"Thinking."

"About me, I hope." His voice had a lightness to it, and his mouth smiled at her.

Erin nodded but returned none of his good feelings. "You were at the forefront of my thoughts."

He scrutinized her face. "It doesn't look as if the thoughts were pleasing." She said nothing, only stared in his eyes. "Let's walk." He turned her away from the main road and headed her down the narrow path along the water's edge.

For moments no one said anything. Erin thought how idyllic the setting was: winter, the water, lovers. What more did they need?

"Why don't you talk about it?" Raimi prompted.

For a moment Erin didn't say anything. She didn't know if her voice would let her speak without the emotion that his presence evoked. "I suppose you could say I was thinking of the future." She glanced at him. "Not the distant future. Only a few days from now."

"What happens then?"

She stopped a moment and stared at him for any sign that he was teasing her. She found none. "The season ends," she said. "You return to your life in New York and—"

"New York is only a few miles away. It's not like we'll be unable to see each other."

"Raimi, you know long-distance romances don't work, even when the distance is only fifty miles."

He stopped walking and turned her around to face him. His hand sank deep into the fur at her arms, and he held her in place. "Are you trying to tell me what we have is only a holiday romance? That this will end as soon as the New Year marches in?"

"Wasn't that the plan? We agreed to spend Kwanzaa together. Nothing was said beyond that. I assumed our lives would return to their previous course."

"Can you do that?" His hands tightened on her arms. Erin refused to let him know he was hurting her. "After the other night?"

Erin dropped her eyes. "I don't want to talk about that night."

"Well, I do." He pulled her closer. "It changed my life. You can't tell me it didn't change yours." He shook her slightly, then said in a lower voice, "I've never known anything like what happened when we made love. You can't throw that off."

Erin stiffened, staring at him without moving. She didn't know how long she could hold out against the feelings that careened inside her. Luckily Raimi dropped his hands before her resolve collapsed, letting her go as if something about her had become rank. He made a sound she couldn't describe, then turned and walked away. His back was ramrod straight, stiff as an overstarched shirt. Erin wanted to run after him, tell him she was wrong, sorry for what she'd said and what she'd implied. She loved him. She wanted him to know that, know that nothing could stop the feelings he induced in her, that he didn't even have to be present to cause her body to tremble. She could convulse with only the thought of him, but she did none of those things. She knew better.

She wanted to run after him, beg him to remain here forever, but she couldn't. She was afraid. The night they made love hadn't just changed his life, it had rocked her world. And it scared her to death. She'd thought she'd loved Raimi before, but what he'd done to her that night told her she'd never known the depth of feeling that one person could have for another.

She had it for him.

She didn't even think she could remain in his presence without giving herself away. She'd heard about, read about, the power that love gives to another person, but she'd never experienced it, hadn't really believed it existed. Raimi had shown her how wrong she could be. He had her heart. He didn't know he had it, but she'd willingly placed it in his care—and now it frightened her how badly he would hurt her when he left.

This was why she watched his back as he retraced their steps along the paved walkway that led back to Main Street. Something old, inborn, instinctive, held her back, kept her from following her heart and running to him, telling him that she loved him, that for her entire life she had loved him and that she didn't expect any man she ever met to affect her heart in the same way Raimi Price affected it.

Love wasn't easy. Erin knew that now. It was probably the hardest thing on earth—harder than criticism and pity from well-meaning townspeople; harder than starting a business with no money, no help, and with the possibility of failure greater than success; harder than following the crowd; and much harder than being alone.

Chapter Eight

Raimi lay on his back, lifting the heavy weight. Over his head he pushed a hundred-and-sixty-pound barbell up and down, breathing out each time he brought it down, then strained to repeat the action. He could bench-press nearly his own weight and not break a sweat, but he couldn't handle one skinny little woman. And he couldn't keep his mind off of her. Every time his mind opened up, he'd find her there. Something would trigger her image: a single word someone said, a place they had been, a memory they'd made together.

Raimi wanted to hit something. What was wrong with her? How could she not be affected by what had happened between them? How could she not feel what he felt? She'd picked a fight on purpose. Why? Everything had been going fine. They'd spent a wonderful night together. He refused to think of it in any way other than what it was: a life-altering day, the most wonderful day he'd ever had in his entire life. And she had the nerve—Breath whooshed out of him as he lowered the barbell, almost forgetting how much it weighed and letting it fall too fast. At the last moment he caught himself and set it in the frame. Sweat poured off him as he sat up.

Physical exercise usually made him feel better, but not today. Today Erin Scott had a stranglehold on his mind, and no amount of weight lifting could relieve the lock she'd put on his heart. So why was she acting like this? Why was she fighting him off, pushing him away?

"Damn," he cursed aloud. He stood up and headed for the shower. He knew why. It was that prom again. He'd deserted her once. She probably thought he'd do it again. Why wouldn't she? It was his history, at least the only one she was familiar with. After he'd moved away from here, he'd changed. Maybe she had something to do with that, but while he was here he'd been a high school student. He'd had many girlfriends and thought nothing of them. Being on the basketball team made girls flock to him as if he were a magnetic pole. Margaret Foley was only the last of them. The *flavor of the month,* he grinned as he turned the shower on. That was how his friends used to refer to his girls. He and Margaret had been seeing each other only since the beginning of basketball season, but he was enamored of her, so much so that he left Erin on the dance floor to follow Margaret out. He regretted that action, but no amount of guilt or wishing could ever change what he'd done to her or what he'd been. In college he'd changed. His studies required a lot of time, and he had less of it for women.

Erin didn't know him. Neither of them knew each other well. He knew only that he couldn't imagine being without her. Not after they'd made love. His body reacted at the mental picture that formed in his mind when he thought of them on her bed. He stepped under the hot water, knowing he could cool it with the degrees of temperature his skin could produce when he thought of her.

He was different now. The high school jock was gone. Raimi didn't even recognize that he could ever have been that man. Today he was a one-woman man. Although he hadn't been serious about anyone in more years than he cared to think about, he did have many female friends and never wanted for dates or sex. But with Erin it hadn't been the same. He had wanted her, almost from the moment his niece pointed to her in the crowded store, he'd felt a connection between the two of them.

He couldn't accept that she would throw away what was developing between them. Raimi reached for the soap and began lathering his body. In the midst of soaping up, he stopped. Fear! He'd been afraid. Maybe she was too. Could that be why? Could she be fighting the same unfamiliar feelings he'd experienced when he saw her, touched her, made love to her?

It would never work, Erin told herself. She'd told herself this since this morning when she'd gone to the lake. After Raimi left her there, she'd run the litany over in her mind. He wasn't the man for her. She knew that. Then why was it three o'clock in the morning and all she could do was pace this room and remember the two of them in that bed.

She couldn't sleep in it now. Not after she'd been in it with him, not after what had happened when they were together. Each time she closed her eyes, she'd see him. Her arms would reach for him, and when they closed on nothing but air, she could hardly contain the painful cry that rose in her throat.

Now she paced the room, staring out the windows at the front lawn. Her mind came up with nothing concrete, nothing that would get her past the situation she found herself in. Raimi would be gone in a few days. She could survive those days. Somehow she could avoid him. When he left, her life would return to normal. She'd told herself this more than once today. She'd survived it when she was sixteen. She could do it again.

The words ran through her mind, but they didn't register. She was unsure of their truth. How long would it take for her to forget? Before he hadn't kissed her. They'd shared a car ride, a dance, and a glass of punch. But now, now she'd kissed him, been in his arms, knew what it was like to have him hold her, caress her, make her feel as special as an African queen. And foremost he'd made love to her, wild, abandoned love. The kind she was sure would happen only once in a lifetime. When he left, she'd die inside.

"I'm not going to be able to take it," she told the empty room. Then quickly she pulled off the nightgown and robe she was wearing and pulled on jeans and a sweater. Not allowing herself to think or change her mind, she knew what she was going to do. She had a lifetime to be one of the living-dead. While he was here she wanted to live, to be alive, in his arms, with him loving her and her loving him. She knew the consequences. They would be the same regardless of whether she spent her time with him or not, so she'd take the chance.

A light snow had begun when Erin pulled onto Main Street. It wasn't sticking. The ground was only wet. Her car flew through the deserted streets. She'd have no defense against a cop who might stop her for traveling fifty in a twenty-five-mile-an-hour zone, but she had continued toward the house she'd been in only once.

It was set back from the street, and when she pulled up the winding driveway minutes later, everything was dark. Not even the Christmas lights were on. All signs that someone lived there had been extinguished. Her headlights hit Raimi's car inside the open garage. Erin braked, letting her car slowly roll to a stop in front of the open garage door. Everything went dark when she turned off her car lights. The darkness closed in on her. She shivered slightly but got out of the car anyway. The silence was just as close as the dark had been. She went through it, heading toward

Raimi's car. It seemed unusual to find the door open. It was cold and snowing, and a reasonable person would close the garage door.

She looked inside the interior. It was empty. She sighed with relief. For some reason she expected to find him sitting there in the cold and darkness. Looking up, she spied the door to the house. It was slightly ajar. Her heart began to pound. Something was wrong. She could feel it, yet she pushed the thought of leaving to get help away from her mind. Whatever was wrong she knew she had to find out. If Raimi was hurt, he could need her right away.

Inside it was dark, but her eyes had adjusted, and she could see as she moved through the back of the house. Her movements were stealthy as if she expected a burglar to jump out and accost her at any moment. She continued her quiet tour until she was in the front hall.

Suddenly the light went on, and she jumped. A tiny scream erupted. She whirled around, looking for the source of the light. Panic grabbed her heart and squeezed. Raimi stood on the last rung of the stairs. He'd pulled on a pair of jeans and nothing else. Erin's mouth went dry. She hadn't expected to be found as if she were a thief. Her mind still had him in the overcoat he'd worn in the park or one of the sweaters she'd seen him wear, even the suit he'd had on during First Night. The last thing she expected was to find him bare-chested wearing jeans, zipped but unbuttoned, riding so low on his hips that she knew there was nothing between him and the denim but her riotous imagination. God! she thought, he could make a statue blush.

And she was no statue. She was flesh and blood, and at the moment that blood was boiling. She'd forgotten all about the open garage and her belief that something sinister might have happened. All she could think of was the denim and what it would feel like raking across her naked skin, especially at that point where the teeth of the zipper separated. Heat washed over her body. She wet her lips and swallowed the dryness that was as scratchy as sandpaper.

"What are you doing here?"

"I thought . . . that is . . . the door . . ." She glanced over her shoulder. "It . . . was . . . open," she stammered. "I thought something might have happened to you."

"You came to rescue me." A sardonic twist pulled at his lips.

Erin scanned the area around him. She couldn't keep her eyes anywhere safe. His bare chest spoke of hours of workouts. Muscles defined as cleanly as if they'd been chiseled ran up his arms, across his chest, and into his neck.

"At this hour?" He checked the time on his watch. "What do you really want?" he asked. His voice was gruff, and she stepped away from it. Pulling herself together, she tried to speak. Words didn't come. Even the tightness of his voice didn't stop her wayward mind from running the course of them being together. She could almost feel him, know the heat of his touch and how together they created a world unto themselves. She wanted that world again.

"I want—" She stopped. "I want you to make love to me."

Raimi's eyes narrowed. She realized she'd said it out loud. She could see his jaws tighten. Corded muscles pulled across his chest. Erin had the feeling he was trying to see into her mind, determine what direction she was using this time. After what she'd said by the lake this morning did he believe she was sincere—or had she killed anything he might feel for her? For an eon he said nothing. The gap of time growing between them had her curling her hands into tight balls. Hadn't he heard her? She couldn't say it again.

Raimi could have turned to stone as still as he stood at the foot of the steps. He raised his eyes to hers. Erin looked at him expecting ridicule. What she found was passion.

She felt rooted to the spot. She wasn't sure the world revolved about the sun any longer or that the hours still moved from one to two and beyond. She knew only that between them hung a need so brutal and so earnest that neither of them was able to break it.

She thought she moved first, but Raimi was beside her so fast it could have been him. He grabbed her arms and pulled her close to him. His arms closed around her and his mouth descended on hers greedily. She wore the fur coat she'd had on this morning. Raimi brushed the hat off her head and sheathed his fingers through her hair. His mouth was hot and wet. Kisses rained over her face and neck, coming back to her mouth. His hands raced up and down her back through the coat. Erin dropped her arms and let the coat fall to the floor. Steel bands embraced her in a prison she had no wish to escape. He pulled her closer to him, the contact so perfect it was hard to separate the places that made them individuals. With only a little more effort, she thought, they could become one person.

With the coat gone, Raimi slipped his hands under the barrier of her sweater. She gasped as hot hands made contact with her skin. Fire burned her skin, turning it into a railroad yard of seared tracks. She reveled in the feel of him. Her body curved around his. She rubbed against him, throwing her head back as she felt his body grow against hers.

Her hands sought his bare skin, then raked down his sides and hesitated for a moment on the waistband of his jeans. She felt the intake of air that went through him when her hands started to move closer together.

"Erin." His voice was a strangle of sound. She heard it, but it was the only coherent word that came from him.

At the zipper she stopped, taking in a long breath of air. Raimi buried his hands in her short hair and held her mouth to his. She dug her hands into his pants, not stopping to release the zipper. His shout went into her mouth. For a moment she let her fingers rub against the length of him, feeling the hardness, feeling that tremble that passed through his body and into her hands. Then slowly she removed one hand and pulled the zipper to the bottom. With the other hand she pulled him out and placed the tip of his penis in the palm of her hand.

His breath was ragged, and he squeezed her tighter and tighter. She was keeping him standing, bearing his weight for as long as he could stand the torture. He groaned and grabbed her hands, pulling them free of contact. Then lightning struck. He pulled her sweater over her head, unsnapped her jeans and pulled them and her panties down her legs in one exaggerated movement. Her clothes and shoes came off at the same time. Then he dropped his own jeans and pushed her to the floor.

She lay on the fur coat. His mouth took one breast. Erin gasped at the elation that bolted through her. Her nipple thickened to a hard nub as thousands of minute nerve endings craved the rapture that he was teaching it. She heard her own sounds, not recognizing her voice or the deep-throated grunts that came from her. Raimi had control of her, control of everything. He knew everything about her, every place that could drive her crazy—and he was taking them one at a time. His mouth moved to her stomach. She made a cave of the area but he followed it, tasting her as he went. Erin cried his name. She could feel the wetness between her legs. Her body arched toward him. Her hands dug into his legs, his back, his buttock. She wanted him.

"Now," she pleaded in a whisper.

Raimi wasn't ready to release her from his torture. He brought his mouth back to hers, pushing her further into the fur pallet. He settled himself in the space between her legs. She lay back, breathing hard, then took Raimi in her hands for the second time and guided him to the one spot on her body that was made completely for him. Raimi drove himself deep into her. Her body instinctively closed over him, her muscles contracting, pulling him in and holding him for a moment before he pulled back. As he repeated the stroke, she felt the pleasure his movement created. She helped him, joined him, spurred him on, setting the rhythm as the two of them began the sex dance.

She threw her arms around his neck and wrapped her legs around his waist. The action opened her body, and Raimi took advantage of it. He filled her over and over again, his body grunting with each stroke. Then she felt the world tilt. It was inside her and he was inside her. She felt Raimi's change, too, knew they were on the brink and that they would cross it together. The sounds between them were animalistic, base and primal. The heat was so intense, Erin could see the flames, knew the golden glow of its color, felt the fire and tasted the smoke. She became one with Raimi and one with the fire. They didn't reach a crossing. They exploded in a conflagration of intense heat and powerful love.

Erin wasn't aware when her breathing returned to normal. Everything around her was new. She was like a baby learning her surroundings, experiencing new feelings and new textures for the first time. The fur at her back was a soft bed. She knew every individual pelt as it caressed her back. Her head, pillowed on one of the sleeves, gave her dreamy eyes a close-up view of Raimi. He was new too. Love was a bright new planet on which they lived. She couldn't imagine her world without him, without the magic they made when they came together.

She was still wrapped in Raimi's arms, and his body was still joined with hers. Around her the air chilled skin he didn't have a prior claim to. She didn't shift, didn't want to break the spell that captured her.

Raimi moved then, rolling away from her and crouching on his knees. She purred as he wrapped the coat around her, then lifted her off the floor. For a moment he held her gaze, his eyes showing as much love and passion as her own. When he moved, she rested her head on his shoulder, her hands smoothing over his arms and back. He carried her up the stairs and into his room. The lights were off, the bed rumpled. Gently he laid her on the sheets and pulled away the coat. Then he got in with her and pulled the covers over them.

Erin shifted closer. Raimi's arms wrapped around her, and one hand settled over her breast. A feeling of total contentment descended over her, and she closed her eyes.

Raimi's chin topped Erin's head. He brushed her hair away from his face then pulled her body into contact with his. He didn't ever think he'd let her go again. No matter what she said or thought, she was his—and he'd make her understand even if he had to prove it to her every day.

Raimi heard her even breathing and knew she slept. For a long time he remained awake, holding her, listening to her, breathing in her scent, replaying the way he felt when he turned the light on and discovered her in his house. Lying awake earlier, he'd heard something and gone to investigate it. He'd forgotten to close the garage door and lock the outer entrance, but Cranbury was a place without bars on store windows. It was a nice place to live and raise children.

Had that been what he'd subconsciously thought of when he suggested his company buy the land in Hopewell? Had he wanted to come here, find Erin, make up for what he'd done to her? He smiled and rubbed his thumb over her nipple. Even in sleep her body reacted to his touch. She stirred but didn't awaken. Falling in love with her, however, had never been part of his thoughts, whether conscious or unconscious.

Now he had fallen in love. Tonight they'd made love, wild, passionate, spontaneous love.

And without a condom . . .

Chapter Nine

"**D**o you think Scott's can spare you today?" Raimi asked when the sun was rising high in the sky.

Erin turned to look at him, a seductive smile on her mouth. "What did you have in mind?" She kissed his chest. A tremor went through him. "I'm already late. I haven't even called my secretary."

"Where will she think you are when she tries your house and you don't answer the phone?"

Erin ran her tongue over his flat nipple. It beaded in her mouth. Raimi tried to concentrate, but just as his body had reacted to hers last night and every night since he'd returned, he closed his arms around her and let the excitement of her touch flow through him.

"I don't care," she whispered.

Neither did he, and he proceeded to show her exactly how much he didn't care.

"This is what you wanted to do?" Erin held on to Raimi's arm as they walked down Main Street. "This is what I took the day off for?"

"So we could stroll through town as if it were a warm Sunday in June? Yep, that's the reason," he replied.

Raimi had taken her into the hardware store, the drugstore, and the bookstore. They'd peered through the windows of Cranbury Publications closed storefront, a tiny hometown newspaper, and stopped to review the names of soldiers, who'd lost their lives in World War I, on the memorial across from the lake.

She knew what Raimi was doing. It was called staking a claim. She liked it, liked the feeling of being his, being with him and not caring that everyone in town knew about it. By noon they all would know anyway. She was as sure of the rumor mill as she was of the space shuttle going off on time and with the same amount of precision.

Erin wore the only clothes she had. Over them the fur coat, hat, and boots kept her warm. The lightly falling snow from last night had covered the grounds and the road. They walked through slush, Raimi's arm always around her or her hand tucked through his arm.

"Can we go back now?" Erin shivered.

"I think it's safe enough now."

"Safe! You know everyone in town will be talking about us after this walk."

"I'm counting on it."

Erin didn't ask why. She smiled to herself, feeling wonderful. She didn't mind the world knowing they were a couple, a unit, a thing, lovers—that she was the happiest woman on earth and it was all due to this man. They turned back toward Raimi's house. There she could pick up her car and go home to shower and change, or she and Raimi could go back to bed.

The thought made her stumble. He caught her and pulled her close. Snowflakes coated his hair, a couple caught in his eyelashes. Erin reached up and brushed them away. He caught her hand and pulled it to his chest. Lowering his mouth he kissed her, on Main Street, in full view of the town if they cared to look. Erin didn't know if anyone was looking, and she didn't care. The only important thing was she was where she wanted to be, where she'd always wanted to be.

His lips were cold, but they warmed her blood. All the way to her toes, heat scorched her body. She wrapped her arms about his neck and returned his kiss with everything she had. Inside her, her heart swelled to bursting capacity. A happiness she'd never known surged within her, and she knew nothing could equal this elation, this need, this overflowing vessel of love that pulled them together like opposite poles of a magnet.

Chapter Ten

Raimi squired her around all day. In fact, he hadn't let her out of his sight for more than a few hours since she'd awakened in his arms this morning. Their stroll through town had taken them back to her house where she changed and they'd gone to a late breakfast at the diner. Afterward they'd spent the day visiting the area, walking through Princeton, visiting a miniature train exhibit in Flemington, then having dinner at an out of the way inn in Hopewell, not far from the land they both wanted.

Erin hadn't thought about the land in a while. It had paled in importance next to the man whose hand she held as they mounted the stairs to the high school for the Sixth Night program. She'd never been happier. She knew what she'd find when she went inside, and tonight she was glad, glad to flaunt her heart, to put it on her face and sleeve and let the citizens of her city share in the happiness she felt.

They took seats together. Erin held on to his hand. She wanted to pull it to her breast and hold it there. She wanted to be alone with him, make love again, do all the things she'd fantasized about in the intervening years. Raimi turned and smiled at her then. Her face warmed and the heat spread through her. Erin had never understood this kind of love. She'd thought she loved Raimi in high school, but her mind had known nothing like this. The books she'd read, the movies she'd seen, nothing had touched her emotions or her feelings the way she had been touched in the last week. She couldn't believe he'd been here less than seven days, and she felt this strongly.

She smiled up at him as the program began. Pulling her thoughts away from returning to bed with Raimi, she listened to the program speaker. Tonight the lesson seemed to be just for her. Kuumba, meaning creativity, doing what we can to leave the community better than it was when we inherited it. Erin had no doubt that her life would be like that—that she and Raimi were on a course that could only get better.

Raimi tightened his grip on her hand. Erin brought her attention back to him as people around her began to move. The program was over, and Erin hadn't heard much of it. She'd been daydreaming, thinking of the two of them. When their chairs were taken, she moved out of the way but not away from Raimi. It wasn't a night for dancing, but like all Kwanzaa events there was music and food. Erin couldn't eat another bite, but she swayed to the recorded music that came through the sound system.

Raimi was taken away by one of their friends, and she found herself facing her sister.

"You don't answer your phone, your car is parked in someone else's driveway, you go walking down Main Street with a stranger—"

"Stop it." Erin laughed at her sister standing in front of her with one raised eyebrow and her hand on one hip. "I suppose everyone in town knows?"

"Only about the walk down Main Street. In a place

where very little happens, you've become the talk of the town."

Erin frowned. She'd never liked being the center of attention.

"I tell you, they're like little bees buzzing the news." Asha looked about the room. Erin's gaze followed hers. Several people smiled or waved at her. She returned the greeting. "I suppose they've always wished you and Raimi well," Asha continued. "You'd be surprised at the people remembering what he did to you at the prom." Asha raised her hand when Erin would have protested. "However, they forgive everything in the face of true love." Asha paused then. "I'm happy for you, Erin," she said. "You deserve to be happy. I'm glad you found him."

Carl Linert joined the two of them.

"Hi, Carl," Asha said.

"Good evening." He included both of them in his greeting.

"Are you enjoying yourself?" Erin asked.

"It's quite a gathering," he said, not committing himself to an answer. Erin didn't think he understood any of the principles of Kwanzaa, especially the one on economics and helping each other. Yet year after year he attended. Maybe at some point something would rub off on him. She could only hope.

Asha made an excuse of helping out at the refreshment tables and left them.

"I have something to tell you," Carl said the moment they were alone. "I'm still trying to find something you might like, but that tract of land we discussed on Route 1 already has a contract. The sellers say it's firm."

Erin took the news without a flicker. Yesterday she would have felt another betrayal but not today. What a difference a day makes, she thought.

"Don't worry about it, Carl," she said. "I have complete

faith in you. You'll find me something." She smiled and moved away.

Erin sought Raimi then. She was always conscious of his presence, but in a room this size with so many people blocking her view she'd lost track of him. Scanning the crowd, her good cheer was suddenly doused with water as cold as Brainerd Lake. She found Raimi.

In the arms of Margaret Foley.

Erin's heart stopped. She could feel the walls closing in. She'd never been claustrophobic, but she felt as if she were in a small room, one where all the air was being sucked out. She could no longer breathe. She reached for something solid to hold on to but found only air. Then she pulled her hand back to her breast. Forcing herself, she breathed normally.

Asha had just mentioned the prom, and like a nightmare from her past Margaret had shown up. Erin moved. Her feet still worked. She crossed the room and joined the small group of people who had Raimi and Margaret as their center. She had her arm around him the same way she'd draped it there sixteen years ago. They were again the king and queen of the prom. And she was the outsider.

"Erin!" she said when she saw her. "Erin Scott. My, how you've changed." Unlike Raimi, Margaret recognized her immediately. The tone in her voice said Erin's change hadn't been for the better. She couldn't have hurt her more if she'd cut her with a knife.

"How have you been, Margaret?" Erin's voice was stiff and formal.

"Just fine." she smiled. "I was just telling Raimi here that I've moved to New York. We'll be able to see each other often since we'll both be living in the city." She turned to smile at Raimi. "I've heard you run a little store here."

"Yes," Erin replied.

"It's not a little store," Oliver Rendell explained. "It's the largest store in this area, and it draws people all the way from New York."

She looked at Erin. "You must be proud."

Erin didn't answer. She wanted to get out of here. She wanted Raimi to take her home, to tell this woman that he was with her.

The music changed at that moment, and on came a song that had been popular when they were teens.

"Oh, Raimi," Margaret exclaimed. "Remember that?" She looked as if she could capture the music. "I know there isn't any dancing tonight, but this was our song." She turned and opened her arms, then moved into his. They danced away from the small crowd, leaving Erin subject to the stares of the group.

She felt like she did at the prom when Raimi left it. History was repeating itself. Erin could almost hear the room talking about her, pitying her, and after today . . . Everything had been perfect today. Well, perfect was over. This was reality, and again she'd let herself forget that. She wouldn't forget it again, and she wouldn't wait around for them to leave her stranded. This time she'd be the one to leave.

"Oliver?" She faced him. He'd been her rescuer before. It was only fitting to ask him to do it again. "Would you give me a lift home?"

Erin couldn't face going home. The house was too lonely, and she didn't want to be there by herself, not after she'd been there with Raimi. Oliver dropped her off and she went inside, promising him she was fine—when her world had come crashing down on her. She got her car out as soon as he was gone and started to drive. She had no particular destination in mind, just the need to move, feel, and think. She rolled down the windows and let the cold air blow in.

She found herself in Hopewell, on the same hill where she'd found Raimi only a few days ago—the same hill where he'd kissed her cheek. She pulled in and turned off the motor, turned off the lights. Everything went dark except small points of illumination in the distance. Taking a deep breath, Erin knew she didn't feel any better. She would never feel better where Raimi was concerned. She questioned everything about him, about *them*. Had they really been that good together? Did he feel the same way about her that she felt about him? She thought he had. This morning when he'd walked her down Main Street, staking his claim, when he'd kissed her in front of the war memorial and let the whole town see, she was sure of him, sure of his feelings. But now that she thought of it, he'd never said he loved her, never declared anything verbally. Yet his actions, what were they? Wouldn't a reasonable person construe that they were in love, or at least falling in love?

She had no claim on him. He was here only for Kwanzaa. When it ended tomorrow, he would leave and return to New York. She'd known that in the back of her mind. The fact that she was here and that she wanted him to stay had nothing to do with reality, and she was out of the fantasy now. Margaret Foley had been the dose of cold water that washed away the blinders she'd been wearing.

Reaching for the ignition, Erin turned on the engine and backed out of the space. She drove slower this time, driving aimlessly. She didn't know how far she'd gone until she saw the sign that read WELCOME TO PENNSYLVANIA. She passed it and headed into central Philadelphia. It was late, but the city was alive. Building lights were still on. The street lamps made pools of light on the ground, and floodlights illuminated the historic buildings. Finally she grew tired. It was time to head back. She had no need to rush. There would be nothing waiting for her. Tomorrow she had only the town's pity to look forward to, but she could face it.

The car lights hit him in the face the moment she turned into her driveway. Raimi sat on the porch steps leading to her house.

"Where have you been!" He wrenched the car door open as soon as it came to a stop. She gathered her purse and turned her legs out of the car. She hadn't expected to see him. "Do you know what time it is?"

Erin stood up. He stepped back to give her room. "What difference does time make?"

"You've been missing for hours."

"But I did come back," she said, driving the insult of his past defection home.

She went up the stairs to her porch, searching the ring in her hand for the key to the front door. She wanted to get away as fast as possible. The blood in her system was pumping fast, too fast, and her heart was pounding. What was he doing here? She expected him to be with Margaret.

"Don't walk away from me." Raimi grabbed her arm and turned her around. She snatched her arm away.

"I didn't walk away from you. From where I was standing, you were the one doing the walking."

He took a deep breath. A pang of guilt rushed through Erin. She pushed it aside. She wouldn't feel guilty. She'd done nothing wrong. She was the victim here, and she wouldn't let him reverse the role.

"Are you all right?" he asked

"Of course, I'm all right. What are you doing here?"

She opened the door and went inside. He followed.

"Worrying myself sick," he muttered, and she had the feeling he hadn't expected to say that aloud. She looked at him, made eye contact. He looked awful, as if he'd spent a sleepless night. She knew about his night. It was exactly the same as hers. Her heart went out to him, then she steeled it against the feelings that threatened to soften her. She couldn't afford to be soft. He was leaving in two days anyway. Why should she make it hard for herself. Let him think he'd been nothing more than a diversion, someone to spend time with over Kwanzaa.

"Why?" she asked at his previous comment. "Margaret Foley is back in town. Shouldn't that make a difference?"

"What's that supposed to mean?"

"It means you can drop me again. You have the better woman at your beck and call. Margaret is free. Oliver told me she's divorced, and she already lives in New York. The two of you can take up where you—"

"Where we left off sixteen years ago." He finished the sentence for her.

"Exactly," she said.

For a moment they stared at each other. Anger hung between them as tangible as gauze.

"Go on," he urged. "While I've been sitting out there waiting for you, you've had enough time to get good and angry. So get it all out."

"All right, I will." She took off her coat and threw it across the back of a chair. "For a while I thought there might be a you and me, but I know better now. Margaret was the catalyst that brought the message home." Crossing her arms, she went on, "Tomorrow is Imani. The last day of Kwanzaa. You go home the next day, and the world returns to normal. It will continue to spin on its axis, and in a few days no one will even remember you were here."

She turned from him then.

She didn't hear him move. Moments stretched between them.

"Won't *you* remember, Erin?" His voice was soft, caressing, sexy, unraveling. She'd been prepared for shouting, anger, angst, even an unreasonable declaration . . . but tenderness, that she hadn't expected. Why didn't he call her out for leaving him? Why didn't he go home, call her on the phone where she could hang up on him, where she wouldn't have to look at him and feel the things that went through her mind when she saw the anguish on his face? Why didn't he do anything except steal her anger with a velvet soft voice that challenged her?

She felt him move, knew he stood behind her. "Erin," he whispered. "I love you."

Erin gasped, the hairs on her neck stood up. She felt his breath, warm on her skin. She turned around, backing away from him.

"Margaret means nothing to me. She hasn't since that prom night sixteen years ago. The mistake I made that night hasn't stopped haunting me. I want it to." He took one step forward and stopped. "I never thought I'd feel like this. I'm breathless every time I see you. All you have to do is smile, and my insides turn to water. You mean everything that was ever good and decent in my life. I've never told another woman I loved her." He paused. His eyes were filled with desire, and his voice was thick with emotion. "Erin, I love you."

She softened. She wanted to rush to him, but she waited. She'd been immobilized by three little words. She'd dreamed of hearing him say them, had formulated how she would react, had rehearsed what they would say to each other. But now that the play had an audience, she was tongue-tied, lost.

"When I got here and found you, I felt as if I were returning home, coming back to the place where I belonged. As the week has gone by, I've fallen more in love with you than I could ever be with any other woman. I know you can't forgive me for what I did to you, but I want you to know how I feel."

Erin felt tears in her eyes.

"I can't expect you to feel the same way," he said. "I

know there may never be an us. You've told me that, but for the record I want you to know that I want there to be a you and me. It took so long for us to find each other. Let's not let something as insignificant as Margaret Foley kill our chance at happiness."

It was her decision. Raimi was giving her the choice of accepting or rejecting him. Tears spilled from her eyes, washed down her cheeks. How could she refuse such an offer? Even if she hadn't been in love with him, he would have won her over with that speech. She made her decision in a nanosecond. "I love you, too," she said, emotion gathering in her throat. "I've been in love with you since grade school."

She took one step then flew into his arms. His mouth was on hers, devouring her, drinking her in. Their lips smashed against each other's, teeth gnashed together as frenzy engulfed them. Raimi's arms crushed her to him. She loved him, he loved her. The litany played over and over in her head.

He lifted his mouth for breath.

"I love you," Erin said again. She felt free to tell him . . . finally. After sixteen years of carrying a secret, she could finally voice it. "I wonder how long it will be before the entire town knows."

"They already know," Raimi informed her, stealing another kiss. "I told them when I left Kuumba tonight that when I found you, I'd never let you go."

Erin hugged him closer and let her head rest on his shoulder. "You actually said that?"

"Yes." She felt his chin move as he rested it on her head. "It appears"—he pushed her back and looked into her eyes—"that I had the backing of the entire town when I told them I wanted to marry you . . . if you'd have me. Will you have me, Erin?"

She nodded. "Oh yes, I'll have you."

Chapter Eleven

Feast day! The gym was packed. First Night and Last Day brought out the crowds. There was barely enough room to move around. Of course the band took up room, the dance floor had been relaid, and the event was catered so there were tables and chairs that hadn't been there before. Erin and Raimi moved slowly through the crowd, stopping to talk and smile as they made their way to their table. Raimi had hold of her hand, or he had his arm around her waist. Erin didn't care what people thought about them. She knew only she'd never been happier. It showed too. She overheard people whispering about them when they turned to resume their trek to their table.

"She's always been in love with him."

"Look at them. Love was never more visible."

"Remember when we looked like that?"

Erin could only smile. If love had an aura, she and Raimi were radiant with it. Everything looked wonderful. Everything had a solution. Even the land they both wanted was unimportant as long as they had each other.

"Hello, Erin." Mrs. Danner stopped them. "I haven't

seen you in a very long time." She took Erin's hand in her bony one. Mrs. Danner had lived next door to Erin's family when she was a child. They'd been neighbors until Mrs. Danner became too old to live alone. She now lived with her son in western Pennsylvania.

"It's so good to see you again." Erin kissed her on the cheek.

"And you"—she looked at Raimi—"you're Jake Price's boy."

"That's right, Mrs. Danner." He took her hands in his and kissed her too.

"You two married yet?" she asked. Mrs. Danner always came to the point quickly.

Erin, embarrassed, tried to hide her face, but Raimi answered her, "No, ma'am, not yet."

"Well, I hope it's soon. You know she's been in love with you since the third grade."

Erin dropped her eyes. Raimi trained his gaze on her. He spoke to Mrs. Danner, but he looked directly at her. "No, I didn't know that." He turned back to the old woman then. "But I'm glad you told me."

"Now you do something about it," she commanded in a manner that only the very old are allowed.

"I will."

They moved on when Mrs. Danner took her seat. Raimi slipped Erin's hand under his arm and held it to his side. Erin felt the warmth of his skin through the coat. She felt special, loved. He made her feel as if she were a queen.

Asha waved them to the table where she sat. Erin pointed toward her, and she and Raimi headed in that direction. It wasn't easy getting through the group. It seemed everyone had heard the news about them and wanted to offer congratulations.

"I never thought we'd get here," she told Asha as she took her seat. No one else was at the table. Erin's parents would arrive later, and Asha described herself as between gentlemen callers at the moment. Erin knew she could have come with any of the men in town who still held a torch for one of the popular women who'd once lived here. Still she decided to come alone.

"It is crowded, and you two have given the town something to talk about." Asha smiled that I've-got-a-secret grin. "And what better time than on Imani?"

Faith, Erin thought. Imani meant faith, to believe in ourselves and our fellow man. She believed in Raimi. She'd always believed in him, even when she thought she hated him.

"I wanted to be the first," she said. Asha held a small box in each hand. She offered one to Raimi and one to Erin. Erin's eyes widened at the small white box with gold ribbons. She loved presents. Like a child, she'd never gotten over the joy of a surprise. She took hers, quickly pulling at the decorations. They came off easily. Opening the package, she found a velvet ring box inside. She looked up at Asha. Raimi was holding the same kind of box in his hand.

Asha was a jewelry designer. Erin loved her creations and knew whatever was inside would be gorgeous. She and Raimi lifted the lid at the same time. A small piece of paper fell on the table. Erin picked it up and opened it. She read it and looked up at Raimi, who'd read his. They exchanged the slips of paper. His read the same as hers: *IOU one wedding band designed by Asha.*

"Asha, thank you." Erin was on her feet, hugging her sister.

"Thank you, Asha. I'm looking forward to having you as a sister-in-law." Raimi kissed her forehead, and she patted his arm.

"This is my only sister," she told Raimi. "Make her happy."

"I'll do my best."

She nodded and stood up. Her eyes were nearly as wet as Erin's. "I'm going to find someone with a less emotional subject to talk about," she commented. "It's getting awfully wet and misty over here."

Erin fingered the small sheet of paper as her sister walked away. She and Raimi would get to design their own rings. She liked thinking of them doing things together, beginning together. Coming in tonight was different than any other time Erin had ever entered this gym. She felt the magic, the fantasy, the way she'd wanted with all her heart for that night to be sixteen years ago. She felt as if she were being given a second chance.

The program didn't begin with a speech or the lighting of the final candle in the kinara. It began with music. The band played, and Raimi asked her to dance. She went into his arms as light as a cloud. They circled the floor, swaying to the music, nothing beneath them but air. She could look only at him, not caring if people saw how she felt. She was in love. If they'd never been this happy, she wanted them to know that this kind of happiness existed outside novels.

Raimi kept her close all night. They danced together, visited with old friends, shared the meal that provided more food than any one person could eat, laughed, talked, and danced again. She should have become tired, but she didn't. She'd waited a lifetime to be with Raimi.

Erin hummed to herself as Raimi drove the short distance to her house. She couldn't believe the way her life had changed in the last week. He parked in her driveway and turned off the engine. She didn't move. She continued to hum her song, the standard that was quickly becoming her signature song.

"It does," Raimi said.

"Does what?"

"Make a difference," he said. "One day made so much

difference in my life—and all I can say is, I'm so glad I found you.''

Erin smiled, emotion welling up in her chest. Raimi leaned forward and kissed her on the mouth. She could feel herself growing warm. She wondered if she would still feel like this in ten years or twenty . . . fifty. A smile curved her mouth as he pulled back.

"I have a present for you," Erin said.

Raimi's eyes opened wider. She could see them in the dimness of the car.

"Not that," she said with a small laugh. "Come on inside."

The fire had burnt down, but the room was welcoming as Erin had never known it to be. She'd always felt at home here but with Raimi in the room, it was more than a room. They were more than a couple. She'd loved him a long time, yet didn't know the depth of feeling that one person could have for another.

Erin dropped her coat and picked up the box she'd left on the small table. Raimi sat down in the chair and took it. She sat on the coffee table, facing him. Carefully he opened the box, taking his time as if they had all night. Erin bit her lip, wanting him to rip away the paper and find what was inside.

Finally he reached it. Inside was a book. He pulled it free of the tissue paper.

"You made this?" he said.

She lifted her hands and twirled them in front of him. The book had a cloth cover she'd made by covering thick cardboard with batting and fabric. The inside had pages that depicted the history of Cranbury, the lake, the old gristmill and the miller's house, the Presbyterian church, a map of Cranbury, and finally an embroidered replica of Raimi's house.

"You didn't do all this in a week?" He turned each page as if it were a painting by van Gogh.

Erin shook her head. "I've worked on it a long time," she said.

"Not for me."

It hadn't been for him when she'd begun it years ago, but she wanted him to remember Cranbury when he left. "I want you to have it."

"I'll treasure it always." He kissed her quickly. "I have a gift for you too." He pulled a rolled-up piece of paper from his pocket and handed it to her. It had a red and green ribbon tied around it. Erin pulled the ribbon and unrolled the scroll. Across the paper in large red letters the word CANCELED had been stamped. Erin looked at Raimi, a question openly on her face. Then she looked back at the paper.

"This is the contract for the land."

He nodded. "It's available to you. At your price."

She smiled wide when he told her that. "You're . . . not taking it?" she stammered.

"Maybe not," he teased.

"I don't understand."

"Well," he said. "There's a string attached to it."

He pointed to the ribbon. Erin followed the line and saw the ribbon stretch between them, then disappear inside his suit coat. She stared at it for a moment. Curiosity got the better of her, and she pulled the ribbon. He grabbed her arm and stopped her.

"What's the string?"

He let go of her hand. She pulled the ribbon again. Out came another scroll. When she unrolled this one, it was the contract for the other tract of land . . . on Route 1.

"You bought the land?"

"No." He shook his head. "My company bought the land. I'm taking over the vice presidency of the new division. I'm going to live here."

"Here!" Erin could hardly contain her surprise. "In Cranbury?"

He nodded. "In the house by the lake." He reached for her, pulled her from the coffee table onto his lap. "Will you live there with me? Will you marry me, be my wife, have my children?"

"We've never talked about children."

He cupped his hand around her jaw, his fingers extending into her curls. Pulling her mouth close to his, he whispered, "We'll talk about them later." His mouth took hers then. Fire spread through her as their breaths mingled. The tingle in her belly spread throughout her body. Raimi bent her back, holding her helpless in his arms. His mouth made love to hers, the kiss obliterated all but one thought. Erin could think of nothing other than little boys running through the house by the lake.

All of them looking like Raimi.

'Round Midnight

BY
DONNA HILL

Dear Reader,

I had a ball writing *'Round Midnight* and I hope you enjoy the lighthearted story of Summer and Tre and the eclectic world in which they lived. They were truly meant for each other.

Because of the devoted readership of Arabesque, *Winter Nights* was made possible. I cannot thank you all enough for your ongoing support of all of my work over the past ten years. I will make every effort to continue to create the stories that entertain, uplift and speak to the heart.

Many blessings to you all during this wonderful holiday season and throughout the coming year. Where will you be just *'Round Midnight?*

Until next time,

Donna
Donna

Chapter One

The control room was tight, like a pair of fifty-percent-off shoes you bought only because of the deal, even though you knew they'd be too small. The same cloud of air hung in the same place every day, building in size and strength with every exhale of onion, sour garlic, curry, and Tic-Tac breath. WKQR FM had to be the tiniest radio station in America, Summer thought, not that she had any to compare it with, but anything smaller was impossible to imagine.

Employees hustled in and out, turning sideways to get past each other to avoid becoming wedged between flesh and furniture. Most of the crew, the engineers, DJs and production staff stayed in faded jeans, T-shirts, and sneakers. Summer preferred casual but professional attire when she went on the air. Even though her audience couldn't see her, it made her feel better to know that she looked good.

She opened the door to the studio and stepped inside. She took a quick sniff. Danny D must've had curried chicken for dinner again. Danny was the celebrated host of Caribbean Beat—four hours of nonstop reggae. She popped a Tic-Tac in her mouth.

" 'Ow ya be feelin' der, doc?" Danny asked in his Jamerican patented dialect, leaving off all the "hs" in his words.

"Not bad." When she first arrived at the station nearly a year earlier, it had taken her months to decipher what it was he was trying to say to her. To this day, sometimes she still had to just play along, having long ago grown tired of asking, "What?"

A reggae remake of Babyfaces's mega-hit "Whip Appeal" pulsed through the speakers. *Hmmm. Non-stop reggae. You just gotta love it,* she thought. Or hate it. She hung up her Donna Karan leather jacket on the hook behind the door, and did a quick finger-wave to Leslie, her engineer, who was seated on the other side of the glass partition. Leslie had a job in the industry usually reserved for men. But then again, there had been many a time that looking at Leslie made you just say, "Hmmm."

Danny spoke into the mike, when he received his cue from Leslie to give Summer's intro. "Comin' at ya in about five with words for de 'eart and music for de soul is just 'Round Midnight wit Dr. Summer Lane. So stick around. Dis is Danny D signing off."

He removed his headset as an old Bob Marley classic wailed in the background. He eased out of the swivel seat and scooted behind Summer so she could slide into his place.

" 'Ave a good show, Doc," he said, moving toward the exit, his high-topped red, black, and green knit hat wobbling back and forth over a mound of dreadlocked hair.

"Thanks." Summer settled back and looked over the playlist of music that would provide her background for the evening and wondered who'd call her during the midnight hours.

It had been nearly a year since she'd come to WKQR and she'd heard just about everything you could think of—from "How do I keep my man from whorin' around?" to "What can I do about this rash?"

She doled out plenty of commonsense advice, laced with humor and topped with R&B. She had a song to go with "whatever ails ya." As a result her ratings were soaring through the roof. Her top-rated talk show had gone from two nights per week to five and the owner was begging her to sign a three-year contract. She wasn't too sure about that, though. Working at the station was fine for the time being, but with her thirty-fifth birthday coming around the home stretch, and with a relationship of her own non-existent, she wanted something more—and the pickings at WKQR were slim to none. Unfortunately the strange hours she worked kept her out of the social circle, and she slept during the day when the rest of the world was turning. Her biological clock was ticking.

When she'd given up her private practice, on the heels of a potential scandal and in the hopes of writing her "relationship" book, she quickly realized she needed an income until she made her first million-dollar deal. That was two years ago, and the few pages she had managed to crank out were beginning to look a bit yellowed around the edges.

How she landed her job at WKQR FM was purely by accident. She'd run into Carl Sloane, one of her old psychology professors from George Washington University, while she was window-shopping one day in Georgetown. He'd started telling her about this radio job he'd just turned down but thought she'd be perfect for it.

The last place she ever thought she'd be sitting was behind a microphone, giving advice to the lovelorn of Washington, D.C. She had a doctorate in psychology from George Washington University, for heaven's sake. But at the time her bank account had definitely dropped a few digits, and going back to private practice, getting calls from her offbeat patients all times of the day or night, was not at the top of her list of things to do. So she'd gone for the interview and never knew if she was hired because they were desperate to fill the time slot or because of her credentials—but here she was, a female Frasier Crane. *Does it get any better than this?* she thought, sarcasm dripping through her brain.

Leslie gave her the five-second countdown and her theme song, " 'Round Midnight," the Dexter Gordon version, began to play. She slipped the headphones over her sculpted haircut and leaned toward the mike.

"Welcome to my world," she said in her standard sultry greeting. "You've just tuned in to 'Round Midnight, the only place for late-night talk with a dash of soul. This is Summer Lane, hoping to give you the answers you're looking for. Tonight our topic is respect. How to get it and how to keep it. Think about it for a minute while we listen to Dru Hill's 'Sleepin' in My Bed.' Then I'll be taking your calls."

Tre Holland, the program director, saw the ON AIR light go out over the control room door. He was tempted to pop inside for a moment and say hello. It would be the decent thing to do, since Summer was the one who was carrying the ratings for the station these days—a phenomenon he could not understand. Why in the world would people tune in to some of the nonsense that came across the airwaves? He still couldn't figure out why someone who looked as good as Summer and who, according to the station owner, had degrees up the "yin-yang," would be sitting up in some radio station dishing out advice to all the nuts who called her show. Maybe she was just a little crazy, he thought—probably the reason why she only half spoke to people or practically looked right through you if you said anything to her, like she was trying to peer into your soul or something. He couldn't count the number of times he'd lied and said, "Good show"—since he actually never listened to it—and all he ever got was a vague

"Thank you." Then she'd walk right past him like he wasn't there.

And what kind of name was Summer anyway?

The ON AIR light lit up over the control room door.

Too late now. Oh well, can't say a brother didn't try. He turned sideways to get past one of the audio technicians and walked down the corridor to his office.

Summer knew he was standing there watching her. He did that sometimes, but she wouldn't give him the satisfaction of turning around. She'd already concluded that he was the distant sort, the type of man who was difficult to get through to. He'd probably been hurt by his parents as a child, shunned or ignored, which made him somewhat reclusive but still able to function well on the outside. She sighed, realizing that she was "doing it again," as her best friend, Kia, would say. "If you wouldn't spend so much time psychoanalyzing every man you meet, maybe they'd hang around long enough for you to find out what they're really like."

That's what she was afraid of—realizing too far down the line, after she'd gotten her feelings all tangled up with some man, only to discover that they were just like the kind of man the women kept calling her about. She didn't need that. But all the books, scientific studies, and clinical labels didn't keep her warm at night.

Tick-tock.

"We're back, and we have Jean on the phone," Summer said into the mike. "Jean, what's your idea of respect in a relationship?"

Jean began rambling on about the two men in her life and how she tried to be the best woman she could be to the both of them, but couldn't understand why they kept treating her so bad.

Summer wondered how this woman was able to juggle two men, and she didn't even have one to call her own. "Maybe if you were honest with them, you could get some honesty back. But, Jean, how can you expect to gain their respect if you're lying and cheating?" Summer asked.

"But I like them both," she protested.

"Do they both know that you're seeing someone else?"

"No."

"That's part of the problem. You need to set the record straight. You only get as good as you give, and that's pretty hard to do when you have to split yourself down the middle. Let's listen to Anita Baker's 'Giving You the Best That I Got.' Sister knows just what I mean."

She slipped off the headphones for a moment, stood and stretched. It was going to be one of those nights; she could feel it in her bones. She looked down at the phone lines. All eight of them were flashing, waiting for their turn to lay their problems on her, waiting for her to give them some miracle cure in their allotted three minutes.

Did she really ever help anyone? At least with her regular patients she could track their progress over a number of prescribed sessions. With this . . . you just never knew unless they called back, which was rare. Sometimes it all seemed so futile and pointless. She felt like such a fraud, like one of those roadside doctors who had a cure for everything in one of those little brown bottles.

Yet, as much as she sometimes doubted her effectiveness, they kept calling. So she must be doing something right. Or maybe they just liked the music she attached to their problem, which of course was the hook to the whole show. Sometimes she really had to dig deep to find the correlation between the caller's problem and the playlist. But she hadn't spent a fortune on her education to be a dummy. If there was one thing she was good at, it was thinking up something quickly to fit the situation. She'd mastered that unique skill in about the second grade, when she had to start coming up with explanations for why her parents never showed up for open school and class trips. She couldn't very well tell the teachers that her parents fought so much she could never get a word in edgewise to let them know what was happening in school. So invariably her sanitation worker father became the out of town corporate executive and her waitress mother was—to anyone who asked—the social butterfly involved in one of her major charity events and "couldn't possibly get away." Just thinking about Pat and Thomas Lane gave her a headache. It was a good thing they finally had sense enough, after seventeen years, to go their separate merry ways. She'd have a field day if she ever got one of them on her little couch.

Anita belted out her last alto note, and Summer was back on the air. "For those of you just joining us, tonight's topic is respect. I think the first step toward respect is respecting yourself and knowing what you will and will not tolerate from your significant other. How much will you take before you walk out that door? Let's ask Gladys. Then I'll take the next caller."

"If I Were Your Woman" by Gladys Knight pulsed, and Summer hummed along. She took three more calls, two from very irate men who strongly believed that the demise of male-female relationships was the result of women who wanted to be on par with men and not giving men their due respect as the head of the household. The one woman caller retaliated by saying that if she was making the money and a contribution to the household, what made a man's head any better than hers. Although on the air Summer always made a point of not taking sides, she secretly agreed with the woman. Times were changing, and women wanted their place in the world. They were just as competent as men and should be respected for their abilities. What she really thought was the problem was the man's inability to accept that and not feel threatened by a powerful woman.

That had always been her problem, she mused, removing the headset as her theme song played in the background. All the men she'd ever been involved with felt some macho compulsion to prove that she wasn't as smart as she thought she was. Which of course was a result of society's definition of male-female relationships. She just wished she could run across a man who was secure enough in who he was and what he was about and not feel threatened by all the letters of the alphabet that followed her name.

Was it her fault that she was driven, that she wanted more out of her life than to be a subservient housewife, a yes-girl? Humph, not hardly. She had no intention of turning into her mother. She needed a man who was her equal, if not educationally, at least emotionally. And most men were such babies.

She grabbed her coat from the hook, did the finger-wave thing to Leslie, and squeezed out of the control room.

Still wrapped in her train of thought, she figured male dominance would be a great topic for one of her shows. She was so involved in working out the details in her head, she almost breezed by the program director without responding to his usual "Good show" comment.

"Oh, thanks," she mumbled as an afterthought, subconsciously taking in his tall, athletic build—that overshadowed her five-foot eight-inch height by at least a good head—and his soap and water clean scent. She angled her body slightly to the side to get by, their bodies barely brushing. For a hot flash their gazes connected, and she noticed for the first time that his eyes were the color of cinnamon. She smiled vaguely, mumbled her standard "Excuse me," and continued down the narrow corridor.

Man, if she was overweight she'd have a real problem in this place, she thought for the zillionth time, making headway toward the exit.

Tre watched her unhurried but determined departure and had to admit he dug the way her just right hips swayed left . . . right as if they had their own secret beat, and wondered why he'd never noticed that before. Maybe it was because they rarely ran into each other, since he worked the overnight shift only a couple of times a month. But like all the other times, she'd barely responded and had looked at him as if he had two heads. Made him want to check a mirror or something—make sure nothing was stuck in the corner of his mouth. He was totally unaccustomed to women who virtually ignored him. He could understand the problems working relationships could cause with all the sexual harassment suits flying in and out of attorneys' offices, but how much did it take to be civil? She never associated with anyone on the staff. He never saw her at any of the local hangouts that the radio crowd frequented. She didn't talk much at the monthly staff meetings, but seemed to be sizing people up all the time, taking mental notes. *Wonder what she jotted down on him in her trusty doctor notebook?*

Maybe she was gay. That would explain why she showed no interest. That would be a waste. Regardless as to what he might think of her, the sister was fine. Almost the spitting image of that fly model, Beverly Johnson, only with short hair. Maybe she had a man and didn't want to be bothered because the brother was the possessive type. Yeah, he liked that idea better.

He stepped into his office and crossed the room to his narrow window, which gave him a bird's-eye view of their sorry excuse for a parking lot. She should be coming out any minute, and he wondered if someone was meeting her. *There she was.*

Summer stepped outside into the balmy September morning, took a quick look around the dimly lit, nearly deserted area then walked quickly to the miniature parking lot that could hold maybe six compact cars on a good day. Forget it if somebody decided to drive the family station wagon.

As she approached her gray Mercedes convertible, she pulled the car keys from her purse, took one more look around, and stuck the key in the driver's side door. Didn't make sense not to be careful. She'd read too many stories of women who were assaulted in deserted parking lots while they were busy fumbling for car keys in the bottomless pits of their pocketbooks.

Starting the powerful engine, she eased out of the lot, mindful of the space limitations, and pulled out into the street, her mind already on her next show.

Mercedes. Figures, he mused and turned away from the window.

Chapter Two

Just as he'd been doing for the past five years since his very ugly divorce from his high school sweetheart, Desiree, who mysteriously turned into the Wicked Witch of the East about two years into their marriage, Tre headed to his sister, Diane's, house for Sunday dinner.

Diane had warned him about Desiree from day one, but Tre hadn't listened. Once he got a taste of Desiree, the little dessert that all the boys at Lincoln High School were dying for, he was hooked. He had it so bad, he couldn't see straight. Desiree knew and played him like a flute. He'd walked down that aisle and out the church door with a big stupid grin on his face.

Every time he thought about it, he wanted to smack himself upside the head for being such a fool. "Can't nothing be that good," Diane had said a million times. But you couldn't tell him nothing. Nothing. At least until he came home early one day and found her in all her natural glory, toussling around in their bed with the guy from Federal Express.

When he'd pulled up to their town house and saw the

truck parked outside the door, he figured Desiree had another delivery from one of her many catalog purchases. Yeah, she got a delivery all right.

At least Diane had been decent enough not to say, "I told you so," even though it was in her eyes as bright as neon lights in Times Square, and subtly disguised in her cryptic remarks about the worthlessness of his life.

But after the divorce he was a changed man. He ran through women like old socks, never hanging around long enough to form any attachments. He liked it like that, and the women he dealt with didn't seem to mind, except for the ones who wanted something more, something deeper. Hey, that was his cue.

But there were those few times that he felt the urge for something more, something that had meaning. Especially when he saw how happy his sister was in her marriage of fifteen years, and the two beautiful girls she and her husband, Jeff, had. He had wanted that same kind of life . . . once.

But getting beyond the fear he had of being hurt again was enough to keep him out of the loop, even though Diane insisted that there were plenty of good sisters out there who were looking for a good man. Like she was insisting now.

"You just need to give yourself a chance, Tre. You been running the street hard for a long time. You need to settle down."

"Tried that, Di. Remember?" He took a sip of iced tea and peeked out of the kitchen window to see Jeff playing tag with his daughters. Something in his stomach tugged.

"We both know that Desiree was a tramp from the jump," she said, the distaste for her former sister-in-law as potent as sucking on a lemon. "Well, at least everyone did besides you. Anyway," she added quickly before he could get a word in, "those airheaded women you run around with are no brighter than a burnt out bulb. You need someone with some sense. A woman who can stand on her own two feet, has something of her own, and won't need to drain the life out of you."

"Maybe I like my life, ever think of that?" he asked without too much conviction.

Diane cut him a look from over her shoulder as she rinsed the dinner dishes and rolled her eyes. "Pleeze. Who you think you talkin' to? You work damn near six days a week, sleep with anything that will lie down. And if some of them hussies you brought over here bring you happiness, then you need to have your head examined. 'Cause you are crazy."

He had to laugh. If there was one thing about his big sis, she didn't bite her tongue, said just what was on her mind, whenever, wherever, and to whomever.

"Yeah, okay." He chuckled, settling back in the cushioned kitchen chair and stretching out his long legs. "What's your advice this week, 'Dear Abby?'"

"Why don't you ask that sister at the radio station? Dr. Lane."

He frowned, realizing that Diane had finally gone off the deep end. "What!"

She spun around and wiped her hands on a dish towel, her eyes taking on that neon glow that he knew meant trouble. She pulled out a chair from beneath the table and sat down opposite him. She leaned forward. "Why not? She's right there. And she gives great advice."

"Are you kidding? You listen to that nonsense?"

"Nonsense." She straightened, totally offended. "That's one of the few talk shows on radio or television that make sense and have class. The lady has style and a sense of humor. You should know that. Don't you listen to the show?"

"No."

"Figures." She sucked her teeth. "What does she look like, anyway? I was always curious about that. Every time

I've seen someone from the radio, I was truly disappointed. Their looks never met the standard of their voices."

He shrugged. "Let's put it this way, she wouldn't ruin your illusion."

"Hmmm," she hummed under her breath, watching her brother closely. "What's she like?"

"Wouldn't know—she doesn't say much. She's aloof and full of herself," he said, thinking about her lack of response to him.

"In other words, she's not all over you."

He cut her a look. "No. That's not what I mean."

"Oh yes it is, and you can't stand it. It's all over that handsome face of yours."

"There's nothing all over my face, Di," he insisted, but wondered what his sister did see.

She sat back in her seat and folded her arms beneath her breasts. "I still say you should talk to her. Call into the show, ask her how a man like you could find a good woman. Better yet, ask her out yourself."

"Now you're the one who's crazy." He chuckled. But he wondered . . . *what if?*

"When are you gonna get a day off, girl, so we can hang out?" Kia asked, running the blow dryer through her hair. "Folks have forgotten what you look like. And you need to stop hiding behind that microphone and get a life— stop worrying about everyone else for a change and concentrate on yourself. You ain't getting any younger," she shouted over the hum of the dryer.

Summer curled up in the corner of Kia's bedroom lounge chair, only half listening to Kia's ritualistic lecture. Every chance Kia got, she felt compelled to tell her how much she was missing because she didn't have a man in her life—as if she were some example to follow. Kia Taylor was, for lack of a clinical term, "a hot mama" who lived for the sole purpose of accumulating men: old, young, rich, poor. Didn't matter. But she had a heart of gold, which unfortunately was her downfall. The men she found herself involved with played on her kind, giving nature until they grew tired and moved on. But that obvious fact never seemed to bother Kia. She just pressed on.

The roar of the dryer stopped, and Kia sauntered in from the bathroom, her shoulder-length ink-black hair fanning out around her shoulders, creating a halo around her petite almond-toned face. She plopped down on the edge of her bed and stared at her friend. "I have this great guy that I'm dying for you to meet. He's the new account rep at the ad agency."

"Kia, please—the last guy you hooked me up with had a mama complex and thought that a woman's role in his life was to take care of him. I'm not trying to take care of a grown man. And that other guy actually had the nerve to tell me that too much education was a dangerous thing and couldn't understand why a 'beautiful woman like me' would want to waste my time with all those degrees." She sucked her teeth. "So if you're my friend like you claim to be, don't do me any more favors."

"You know what your problem is?" Kia went on, totally unperturbed. "You're too picky."

"Picky! Is it too much to ask that a man have a grain of common sense, some decency, and want more from me than just what's between my legs? That getting over isn't his middle name, and he doesn't feel threatened by the fact that I spent eight years in college, and people call me Doctor Lane, not *Ms.*? I worked hard to get where I am, to have what I've acquired. And I'm not going to pretend for the sake of the fragile male ego that I'm some shrinking violet who's just dying to have his babies."

"Yeah, that's all good, sister-friend. But look at you. You have a fly condo in Georgetown, a Mercedes worth more than my yearly salary, a wardrobe that would embarrass Ivana Trump, and three degrees. And not to borrow a cliche, but all that isn't worth anything when you have no one to share it with," she ended dramatically with a hand across her brow.

Summer bit back a smile. She wouldn't give Kia the satisfaction of letting her know just how right she was. *Tick-tock.* Maybe she was too hard on the men she met. Maybe she was too analytical, always skulking around in the corners of their minds, looking for the glitches in their personalities, their hidden phobias. Like her grandmother used to say, "Look hard enough for something, you're bound to find it." Invariably she always did.

But Lord knows, she just didn't want to wind up like her parents, trapped in a continual tug of hate and unhappiness, sticking it out only because it was the right thing to do, even though they'd discovered years earlier that they weren't meant for each other. And for that she blamed herself. She knew they stayed together because of her, waiting for her to be old enough to deal with their breakup. But the reality was, their staying together did more damage to her than if they'd separated years earlier.

So she'd gone into a profession where she believed she could fix things, make them right—help people to see what they were too blind to see on their own.

But how blind was she about the reality of her own life?

She snuck a peek at Kia, who was busy giving her hair the standard one hundred strokes. And Kia was happy, actually happy. She did what she wanted, enjoyed her life to the fullest. So maybe Kia didn't have a Mercedes, or a condo and three degrees, but she got more pleasure out of her life than anything Summer could prescribe.

She sighed as she watched Kia prepare for her date, humming to Chaka Khan's "I'm Every Woman." Maybe she should start thinking about making some changes in her life.

Kia's phone rang, and she heard her friend's voice drop to that seductive low, and she just knew it was a man on the other end. She heard her girlish giggles and tried to recall the last time she'd actually giggled with a man.

Couldn't remember.

"Sure you don't wanna come?" Kia asked, suddenly standing over her.

Summer blinked and looked up. She forced a faint smile. "No. Thanks. Maybe next time."

"Yeah, yeah." She fastened the belt on her silk robe. "You said that the last fifteen, twenty times I asked."

"And I meant it all those times."

Kia shook her head and padded to her overstuffed closet.

Summer hauled herself up to a sitting position, then stood. "I'm gonna head on home. Talk to you during the week."

"Yeah, you say that all the time too. If I didn't call and practically drag your behind out of that beautiful house sometimes, we'd never get together."

Summer felt a mild stab of guilt, but it didn't last long. Kia was a master at it, some quirk in her personality Summer had concluded, and she'd learned long ago that the best tactic was to ignore her. She picked up her purse from the foot of the lounge chair and got her jacket from the hall closet.

Kia followed her to the door. Summer turned, giving her friend a long hug.

"Have a great time tonight."

"Oh, I will. No doubt about that. Otherwise what's the point?" She grinned. "Still wish you were coming, girl." She braced her hand against the door frame.

"No, that's okay."

"Yeah, I know, another time." Kia pursed her lips and put her free hand on her hip. "Sure hope there's an eligible somebody at that station, 'cause, girl, I swear you don't go anywhere else to find him."

"Maybe I'm not looking, Kia. Maybe I like my life the way it is—my independence."

"Yeah, okay, but you're gonna be a I'm-not-looking-at-my-life independent old maid." She wagged her finger. "Don't say I didn't tell you so."

Summer's lightly glossed mouth curved up on one side. "Trust me, I won't." She turned, then tossed an "Enjoy" over her shoulder, before heading downstairs from the third-floor walk-up.

Driving home, Summer envisioned what awaited her when she arrived. Great furniture, some expensive artwork, a great view of Washington. Maybe some music if she decided to turn on her thousand-dollar-plus stereo system, a microwave dinner, and herself.

That was it.

Suddenly she didn't want to go there. Didn't want to walk into emptiness. But there was no place else for her to go.

For five years her private practice had been her refuge. She'd hidden behind her expert analysis and advice, never really having to offer anything of herself. At the station she could hide behind the faceless entity that she'd become to her thousands of listeners, never having to connect with the countless callers.

"Yeah, girl, go ahead with your b-a-a-d analyzing self," she said out loud. "Got it all figured out, huh? Now what are you gonna do about it? Take a pill and call me in the morning," she mumbled, pulling into her driveway. She stepped out of the car and looked up at the darkened windows.

"There's no place like home"

Tre's head was pounding. He blinked against the blinding light that attacked him from the bedroom window, rolled over, and was momentarily mystified by the bare behind he'd bumped into. He shook his head, trying to clear it, but the marching band started up in a direct path right between his eyes.

Slowly his night came back to him. After he'd left his sister's house, he'd decided to hang out for a while at one of the jazz clubs in Georgetown. They had a live band that was slamming. By the time he thought about checking the hour, it was almost 2:00 A.M. He'd consumed four gin and tonics and had convinced Carol—an old flame who'd come into the club unescorted—that they shouldn't let the evening end there.

Without putting up much of a fuss, she agreed, and now here they were—a heartbeat away from hiding their morning breath. Why did he keep doing this to himself?

He groaned, and the body next to his wiggled a bit closer. Gingerly he peered at his guest, but all he could see was a mass of curly auburn hair that peeked out from the top of the quilt like spiral macaroni.

He turned his head and checked the digital clock: 7:15 A.M. If his memory hadn't abandoned him totally, he had a 9 A.M. meeting with the owner and a staff meeting at 11:00 A.M.

He tapped Carol lightly on the shoulder. She moaned. He tapped again—this time she jumped up as if she'd been shocked.

Red hair was everywhere. Literally. He saw several wayward wiry curls lying on the pillow she'd just vacated. He almost wanted to pick them up and hand them to her—maybe they fastened back on her head, some kind of way. But he thought better of it. No sense in starting the day off on the wrong foot.

She stared at him wide-eyed for a moment, as if she, too, were trying to figure out what was going on.

"Uh, I have to get ready for work. Can I drop you somewhere?"

Carol ran a hand across her makeup-smudged face. "I must look a sight," she mumbled.

He'd withhold a response. That was one of those trick comments that women used to see if they could catch you off guard. Yeah. He was hip to that one.

"Listen, I'm gonna take a quick shower. Or you can go first." He checked his watch as if to emphasize the need for expediency. "I really gotta get moving."

"I'll straighten up in here while you shower," she offered. She turned and spotted the AWOL curls perched on the pillow like candy at some fancy hotel. She snatched them up and dared a glance at him.

Tre sort of shrugged, half smiled, and raised one eyebrow all at the same time. "Be back in a few," he said and hurried off into the bathroom.

Closing the door securely behind him, he pressed his back against it and shut his eyes. A vision of Carol and all the other countless women danced before him, congealing into one big blur.

Was this what his life had come to?

Summer had spent a restless night. Images of her as a shriveled-up old woman set out to pasture had dominated her dreams. Sometimes she was in a faded green muumuu, sometimes it was pink, but every time she was alone. And if she looked toward the horizon, just above the smooth sloping hilltops, she'd see Kia skipping along with a trail of men behind her, like the pied pipetress of D.C., or something.

She splashed cold water on her face, then stared at her reflection in the mirror. What would she tell a patient if they'd described that dream?

"In my professional opinion, Ms. So-'n-So, you need to get a life." She stuck out her tongue at her image and proceeded to vigorously brush her teeth and hopefully get herself in the frame of mind for the monthly staff meeting.

* * *

All the usual suspects were in what passed for a conference room when Tre arrived for the staff meeting, following his brief one with the station's owner, Stan Howard.

Stan was hunched over a mound of papers in his usual seat at the head of the wobbly six-foot table, furiously puffing on a cigarette, although he'd banned smoking in the building a year earlier. Danny D was slouched in a corner chair, bobbing his head to whatever was blasting through his headphones. The distant beat could be heard at least three feet away. Paul Douglass, the station manager, who should have been fired ages ago as far as Tre was concerned, was looking bleary-eyed in a seat next to Danny. Jordan Michaels, who listeners said sounded like the legendary radio DJ Frankie Crocker, and who vaguely resembled him, was at the refreshment table pouring a cup of coffee. Leslie, who looked surprisingly feminine today—must be the earrings, Tre thought absently—sat on the right-hand side of Stan.

And then there was the lovely Dr. Lane, who stood out in the crowd like a candle in a blackout. Impeccable as always, and reserved as usual, she wore—some designer something, he was sure—a pearl-gray suit that looked like it was made just for her. She barely looked up from the notes she was taking when he entered the room, and for some reason the sting of her dismissal bothered him more than usual.

Probably using us as case studies, he silently grumbled, and pulled up a chair closest to Stan.

"Good," Stan said, the instant Tre sat down. "Now that we're all here, except for the morning shift that is, we can get started."

Stan went into a monolog about the budget, how well the station was doing, and upcoming contracts. He praised the hosts of his evening programs for keeping the ratings up and expressed his strong belief that in another year, WKQR would be able to take a nice healthy chunk of the market share.

Tre had heard all of this during his early morning sit-down with Stan, so he was only pretending to pay attention. What he was really doing was taking—on the down-low—glances in Summer's direction.

On the surface she seemed to be into what Stan was saying, nodding her head at all the appropriate points, taking those damned notes. But looking at her, really look-ing, he could tell she wasn't the least bit interested in what was being said.

It was in her eyes, the way she didn't actually look at you. He wondered if that was a technique she'd mastered in dealing with her patients in order to maintain some sort of objectivity, or was it simply her personality: distant and unreachable? What would it take to light a fire in Summer Lane?

"Tre, you want to pick it up from here?" Stan asked, turning the meeting over to Tre.

Momentarily jostled from his musings, he made a short show of straightening his tie, which he wore only for these shindigs, and reshuffled the papers in front of him in a attempt to buy himself a couple of minutes to collect his thoughts.

He cleared his throat, and all eyes turned in his direc-tion.

"Stan and I met earlier this morning to discuss doing something a little different for the holidays, a way to boost the ratings."

Everyone seated around the table leaned forward a bit, knowing that when ratings went up, it was often reflected in their paychecks.

"It may sound like New Year's is a long way off, but it's only a little over three months away. What we decided to do was air live on New Year's Eve from the jazz club Blues Alley on Wisconsin Avenue."

Everybody started talking at once. The room bubbled with excitement. Even Summer seemed a bit more animated. Tre held up his hand. The group quieted by degrees.

"This is the deal. We plan to run live from ten to eleven forty-five. Then at your regular time, Summer, eleven fifty-five, you're going to come on with the countdown and some soulful advice for couples in the new year." The group chuckled, and if he didn't know better, he'd swear she blushed. "Everyone's gonna have their fifteen minutes of fame," he continued. "What we want to do is get all of our hosts to put together a ten-minute playlist of the top hits for the year for your segment."

Again the group began talking all at once, the excitement pumping through the air like a string of greatest hits.

Tre smiled, seeing the enthusiasm of the team. It's what had propelled WKQR from near obscurity to number four in the ratings since he'd taken over as program director. The station had needed a new surge of energy, some reorganization, and some sense of what the listening audience wanted to hear. He met the needs of the station and the audience.

Since he'd come on board a little more than three years earlier, the sound of the station had evolved from all gospel and talk to an eclectic blend of R&B, reggae, talk radio, and jazz. There was something for everyone. His only holdout had been bringing Summer onto the program lineup. Stan insisted that the station needed a "help" segment and had originally hoped to get Dr. Sloane from George Washington University to fill the ninety minutes. But when he declined, Tre couldn't have been happier. He'd wanted to add a classic R&B segment similar to 98.7 KISS FM in New York, which was spiraling off the ratings chart.

Then along came Summer, highly recommended by Dr. Sloane. He wouldn't have given the show a snowball's chance in hell, but she'd gotten in there and pulled it off. 'Round Midnight was their most listened-to show, according to Arbitron, the national ratings bureau.

He still couldn't figure it out. Why would anyone want to call in and discuss their business over the radio? Guess it was the same bizarre mentality behind those nuts who showed up for the television talk shows.

"How soon will you need our playlist?" Jordan Michaels asked, derailing his thoughts.

"As soon as you can start getting it together. I'll need to time everything out. Leslie, you and I will work on that part."

She nodded.

"Also as part of the promo, we'll be selling tapes of the show. So put your best out there." He looked around. "Any more questions, suggestions?"

Everyone at the table looked at each other, then at Tre, shaking their heads.

"Good. I'm done. Stan?"

"That's it for me, people. Keep up the good work." He stood and the staff began to file out.

Tre gathered his notes and stood towering over Stan's white-haired, perfectly cropped natural. Stan was a small man in height and girth, but he carried his compact frame with authority. Often Tre was reminded of a black Napoleon whenever Stan Howard entered the room.

"I think that went well," Stan said, slipping into the suit jacket he'd draped on the back of the one good chair in the room.

"Yeah. Too bad we didn't videotape our fabulous duet. We could just run the tape for the morning crew this evening."

Stan chuckled. "See ya later."

Tre followed shortly after and, since he didn't have to

be back at the station until six, he decided to take a walk around the corner and have an early lunch at Houlihans, a favorite local bar and restaurant. He was likely to find someone he knew hanging out.

Stepping into the semidark, almost classy interior, Tre adjusted his vision as he slipped out of his brown leather jacket and was quickly shown to a table, just far enough away from the door to avoid the flow of traffic, but close enough to see every face that came in.

He ordered a burger, medium well, and a side of fries. Loud murmurings of his sister, Diane's, warnings about his eating habits bounced around in his head. "And a Diet Coke," he said to the waitress, handing back the menu, his way of appeasing his sister.

Tre settled against the red leather cushion back of his seat and took a long, languid look around, sizing folks up along the way.

Just as he was about to turn his attention back to the place mat that boasted twenty-five trivia questions, his gaze landed on Summer, who was almost tucked away in a corner of a booth.

What captured his attention was the slick cap of slightly wavy black hair set against a near flawless almond complexion. The soft light, the sparkle of the chrome decor, and the red leather background seemed to magnify her natural beauty. And she was a beauty, he had to admit—maybe a bit on the odd side of the street, but a beauty.

Yet observing her outside of the only environment he'd ever seen her in, she seemed different somehow, more vulnerable, soft, less reserved.

It was almost as if she'd telepathed his thoughts when she slowly looked up from the book she was reading and turned in his direction.

A brief flicker of recognition momentarily widened her dark eyes, and then it was gone. She pushed a short smile across her lips and went back to her reading.

How can someone be that indifferent all the time? Tre fumed. Doesn't she ever exhibit any emotion, engage in idle chitchat? The unanswered questions tumbled through his head, ticking him off by the second.

He was two seconds from just marching over there and setting her stuck-up—

"Here's your order, sir," the waitress said, placing the platter of steaming food in front of him.

For a second he glared at the waitress then mumbled his thanks.

"Lucky for her," he grumbled under his breath, stabbing a french fry with his fork, but he'd suddenly lost his appetite. He looked up again, and Summer was taking back her credit card and her tab from the waitress.

With an easy grace she slid out of her booth, retrieved her leather jacket from the brass hook above her head, and proceeded toward the door.

Tre felt like jumping up and shouting, "Can't you even stop to say hello!" when she looked toward him, flashed a perfect smile, and strolled out toward the exit. His hot-air balloon slowly deflated.

He watched her weave her way out of the restaurant and couldn't for the life of him figure out what it was about that woman that got his temperature rising. He took a long, cold swallow of his Diet Coke, having every intention of pushing her to the back of his mind, and found he couldn't. Plain and simple, the mysterious Dr. Summer Lane piqued his interest and had for quite some time. What to do about it was the question.

Chapter Three

Summer stepped out of Houlihans into the early afternoon sunshine. The building parade of pedestrians, out for a quick getaway from offices and apartments, tumbled onto the historic streets. She slung her Coach bag over her shoulder and strolled down P Street in search of nothing in particular, peeking in store windows, stopping for a moment to take a look in an antiques store. She knew she should go home, get some sleep, so she could sound like she had some sense when she went on the air. But she didn't feel like it. She wanted to do something. Didn't know what, just did. But she also wanted someone to do it with.

She stopped at the corner for a red light, undecided about what to do next—get her car from the lot and go home or continue on her destination-less stroll—when a car horn caught her attention. She usually didn't pay much mind to honking horns. She thought it was a rude way of getting someone to notice you, especially if safety wasn't the offender's concern. But something made her look, and she couldn't have been more surprised.

Tre Holland.

He rolled down his window. "Can I give you a lift somewhere?" he shouted over the noise of flowing traffic.

For a moment, she was caught between mystification that he should turn up like that—first the restaurant and now here—and curiosity about the man in general. She couldn't remember ever having a conversation with him, other than brief encounters at the job, and her catching him watching her performance when he thought she wasn't looking. But she'd always liked his take-charge attitude and, since the other night, when they'd brushed past each other in the corridor, he'd somehow found a little haven in the recesses of her mind. Maybe this was her opportunity to put all the nagging little assumptions she had about him to rest. Besides, what else did she have to do today?

She hesitated a beat then walked toward the car. She bent down and met his gaze. A short shock rippled through her body, when the most engaging smile greeted her.

"Hi. Looks like we just keep running into each other," she said.

The light turned green, and impatient drivers immediately began honking. She opened the door and slid onto the soft, brown leather seat. The interior smelled of cologne and old leather.

Tre pulled out into traffic, giving the driver behind him the finger. He glanced at her out of the corner of his eye. "Oh, sorry about that."

She smiled. "Don't mind me. I'm the worst."

"Could it be that the sedate, always together Dr. Lane loses it?" He chuckled. "I can't believe it."

"I have my moments." She focused on her hands and tried to ignore the deep pulse of his voice and the funny way her insides felt when the subterranean rumble of his laughter echoed through her body.

"Where can I drop you?"

"My car is in the company lot. I was indirectly heading that way."

"To the lot it is." He made a left-hand turn and headed down Pennsylvania Avenue. "So what did you think about the plan for New Year's Eve?" he asked when he realized she wasn't going to say anything.

"It sounds like a great idea. What made you think of it?"

He shrugged. "Believe it or not, that's my job—to keep coming up with innovations and keep up with the competition. I figured this was a way to gain a wider audience."

She nodded.

Silence.

He turned on the radio, feeling unreasonably nervous. He took a quick breath. "We don't get to talk much."

"No, we don't."

She wasn't going to make this easy. "So how do you like WKQR? You've been there, what, about a year?"

"It'll be a year in January. I like it. It's fun, actually. But sometimes I wonder if I'm really doing anyone any good."

He glanced at her. Summer Lane never struck him as someone unsure of herself. "Your ratings should be a good gauge. You're all Stan talks about."

She smiled. "I know ratings are important. It's what will make or break a program. But for me it's more than that."

"What is it for you?"

"I've always been an achiever. Looking for a goal and finding a way to accomplish it. Even though I try my best to point the listeners in the right direction, there's no way I can determine if what I'm saying makes a difference."

"Then why do you do it?"

Now he was getting personal, and she didn't know how much of her personal reasons she wanted to share with him. She knew he was the one who'd tried to keep her from coming on the air in the first place. Maybe this was a way to find an excuse to get her out: lack of commitment to the job. "It still gives me a chance to reach people I wouldn't have been able to reach through my practice." She turned to him, wanting to put him in the same hot seat she'd just vacated. "Why do you do what you do?"

" 'Cause I love it. I love the challenge. I love beating the competition. I love reading the ratings and seeing us climb the charts because of some new twist I've come up with for programming. I love pushing the hosts to give it their best and then they do."

"In other words, you love it."

He chuckled, and she felt that deep rumble in her stomach again.

"Yeah, I guess you could say that."

The parking lot loomed ahead, and he knew their brief interlude was about to end. He didn't want that. "What do you do for fun besides give out advice?"

Uh-oh, where was this going? "Listen to music mostly."

"Yeah? So do I. Do you ever go to any of the jazz clubs?"

She swallowed. "I haven't in a while."

He pulled into the lot.

"My car's over there."

She pointed in the direction of her Mercedes, and he had the sudden sensation that he was out of her league. He pulled up behind her car.

She turned to him. "Thanks for the lift."

"Sure. No problem." She put her hand on the door. *Well, bud, you gonna go for it or what?* She opened the door. "Uh, maybe we could hang out one night. Before your show . . . or after." *Now you're babbling.*

Her heart knocked. She swallowed then turned to look at him. *Why not?* "Let me know. Maybe we could work something out."

Be cool. "I'll do that."

She nodded, gave a tight smile, and slipped out. "Thanks again," she said a second before she shut the door.

He backed up his Honda Accord and let her out. She waved as she pulled away.

"You just asked the great Dr. Lane out on a date. And she sort of said yes." He smiled. "Maybe you're not out of her league after all."

Summer pointed the car in the direction of home, but her mind was still on her encounter with Tre Holland. She replayed all the times she'd ever seen him, spoken to him, seen him interact with others. When she added it all up, the total was "nice guy." People seemed to like him. He earned the respect and loyalty of the staff. He had a passion for what he did and, like her, could be single-minded about it. He was handsome, in a rugged sort of way. Not polished like most of, well, the few men she'd dated. And then there was that *"somethin' somethin'"* like Maxwell sang about that just stuck with her.

Kia's words rang in her head: "Sure hope there's an eligible somebody at that station . . ."

Tre?

She wasn't one for speculation—but, hey, you never know.

Summer took the long route home, driving in and out of the narrow Georgetown streets, along Pennsylvania Avenue. She took a peek at the White House and wondered what new scandal was brewing behind the ivory walls, breezed by the Federal Triangle, back up Sixteenth Street, and home.

Stepping into her apartment, she was momentarily surprised by the flash of melancholy that greeted her at the door. She tossed her bag on the glossy, circular table in the foyer, hoping to add the unwanted sensation to it. Slipping out of her jacket, she absently added it to the array of clothes—long, short, furs, leathers, wools, and suedes—that filled the walk-in closet from end-to-end.

Summer meandered into the spic'n-span kitchen, done in muted tones of mauve and peridot-green. Every cooking gadget imaginable graced the sleek, rectangular room, hung from ceiling racks and lined the pale green marble countertops. Besides her passion for music were gourmet and ethnic cooking. A glass and wood cabinet that stood six feet tall in a corner of the kitchen contained rows and rows of cookbooks and volumes of recipes that she'd gathered over the years and had written down. She'd decided long ago that her penchant for fine food had to have come from the years she suffered at the hands of her mother's tasteless, unimaginative meals.

She opened the fridge and sighed as she pulled out a can of cranberry juice and pushed the door closed with her foot. When she got right down to it, she was tired of fixing for one; not accepting invitations to events because she didn't have a date; rolling over in the morning to the cold, empty spot beside her; and buying slinky Victoria's Secret lingerie and not being able to show it off except in front of her bedroom mirror.

She plopped down on the mauve and green patterned cushion of the kitchen chair and felt the powerful current of "woe is me" try to suck her in like an undertow. She took a long swallow of her juice, straight from the can. She couldn't let that happen, especially since she would always tell her patients not to let their problems get the best of them. They had to be in control of the situation, not the other way around.

"So what about me?" she asked the empty, picture-perfect room. Briefly she shut her eyes—and there was Tre Holland, peeking at her through the glass door in the control room, watching her in the restaurant, giving her a lift.

He did sort of ask her out. Maybe she'd take him up on it if he brought it up again. 'Cause it sure had been longer than she wanted to discuss when she'd last been on a date.

She told him to let her know, so the ball was in his court. If he was really interested, and not just being nice, he'd ask again.

She tossed the empty can of juice in the recycle bin and went into her bedroom. Stripping out of her clothes, she tied a silk scarf around her head, and slipped under the covers.

Office relationships always spelled trouble. Hold on, girl. An *almost* asked out on a date did not add up to a relationship. She shut her eyes. But maybe it could, she thought. She wished. He was kind of fine. She snuggled down under the covers.

And then what?

Tre found himself whistling as he headed home. He figured he'd catch a few hours sleep then go back to the station for his late afternoon meeting with the morning crew.

He thought about his brief but enlightening interlude with Summer. When he went back to the station later on, he'd check her monthly schedule and see which Friday or Saturday night they were both free. Or maybe they could do the jazz brunch thing on a Sunday. Now his next step in the master plan was finding the time to ask her out. Their schedules rarely matched, and he already knew he wasn't on night duty for the next two weeks.

Calling her at home was an option, since he knew he could just check her personnel file and get the number. But he had a very strong feeling the good doctor wouldn't appreciate that. No. He'd wait for the right time. When the time came to take her out, he wanted it to be special.

Yeah, he was feeling real good.

Hmmm, wonder what dear Diane would have to say about this?

* * *

"Get outta here. You and Summer Lane? I don't believe it," Diane said, wiping her hands on a dish towel. She pulled up a chair opposite him at the kitchen table.

"Well, it's not a date . . . exactly."

"What exactly is it?"

"I sort of asked her out, and she said to let her know."

Diane nodded slowly as if the steps to the solution to a mathematical equation finally made sense. "Oh, I see. You sort of asked her out and she kind of said yes. So the two of you may get together. Is that about right?"

"Now maybe you know why I keep you out of my business. Your mouth." He tried angry on for size and found it didn't fit, not with Diane's sheepish grin and eyes jut like their mother's twinkling back at him.

Diane tilted her head to the side. "You really like her, huh?"

He shrugged and pushed away from the chair and stood. "I don't know, Di. I mean there is something about her. We've really talked only once, but in that short conversation she erased everything I'd been thinking about her. She's not all stuck-up and stuck on herself like I thought."

Diane stared at her brother's sharp profile. Ever since their parents died, when she was in her second year of college and Tre was in his second year of high school, she'd felt committed to seeing about his happiness. Right up until now. It was obvious Tre had *a thing* for Summer. She'd never seen him half step or unsure about anything, especially a woman, unless he somehow felt intimidated in some way, found a woman who could challenge him. She knew that's why he dealt with women who didn't have much of a brain or any real ambition. As much as she hated to admit it, her ex-sister-in-law Desiree was the only woman she'd ever known who'd given Tre a run for his money. Unfortunately, as a result of her trifling self, Tre tried to stay as far away from any woman who even vaguely presented him with the notion of being all he could be. And she was pretty darn sure that's what was scaring him about Summer Lane.

"So what's the next step?"

"Just have to wait for the right time. It's not like we see each other every day." He knew that explanation sounded weak, but what could he say—that he was scared that when he finally got around to asking her out, she'd say no, and he'd look and feel like a complete fool? No. He couldn't tell Diane that. There was no way he was going to ruin his invincible image in her eyes. It had taken time to scrape off all the tarnish after Desiree, and he still caught Diane's not so subtle comments about that fiasco even now. No sense in giving her any more mementos for the archives.

Tre took a long swallow of his grape Kool-Aid, the kid's favorite. He'd already checked and double-checked his and Summer's schedules, and it didn't look good for the rest of the month. The two nights per week that she was off, he was on duty. But maybe he could . . .

"Aren't you the program director of that place?" Diane asked.

"Yeah. And?"

"So use your head, baby bro, program yourself right into her life."

His thoughts exactly. But he wouldn't let Diane know.

"For those of you who've just tuned in, you're right in the middle of 'Round Midnight, with me, Summer Lane. You just heard from the classically soulful sounds of Marvin Gaye's 'Distant Lover,' " Summer crooned into the microphone as she watched the board flash with callers on hold. Tonight's topic was knowing the difference between great sex and real love. It took all she had to keep from cracking up when one woman, who called herself Ann, said real love *was* great sex, and all the women in the room with the caller whooped and hollered in agreement.

"Our next caller is Basil. Hey there, Basil, what's your take on tonight's topic?"

"I think the whole love thing is overrated. Some of the women I've been closest to I was never in love with, and the couple of women I thought I loved dogged me out. Love sets you up to be hurt."

"There are risks involved with everything we do, Basil," Summer responded. "I assume the women you said you were close with—you mean sexually. Correct?"

"Yeah."

"You were taking a risk there as well. For most people with a conscience, sex changes the fabric of any relationship. It creates an unspoken commitment between two people. As far as love is concerned, true love is a two-way street. Unfortunately it sounds as if the women you'd given your heart to didn't feel the same way. That doesn't mean you won't find a woman who will. And when you do, you'll know it. It sounds as if it was the wrong woman and the wrong time. Thanks for calling, Basil. And on that note, let's take a listen to 'Love on a Two-Way Street,' by the Moments."

Summer slipped off the headphones, stood, and stretched her arms over her head.

Tre peeked in when the ON AIR light went off over the door, and a sudden wave of heat moved through his body. He caught the outline of Summer's full body profile, precise enough to use as a cut-out. Her body blossomed, dipped, jutted, and curved in all the right places, defined by her all-black outfit that looked as if it were painted on.

"Hmmm," he hummed under his breath. She had about fifteen minutes before the end of her show. He was going to make it a point to talk with her before she left.

Slowly she turned her head in his direction, and he had that same feeling again that she was reading his mind. He felt exposed, as if all his erotic thoughts were blazing in neon on his forehead.

But then she smiled and that shift, like a wave rushing to the shore, swept through his stomach. Man, what was wrong with him? He smiled back as casually as he could, gave her a couple of hand signals, trying to indicate that he wanted to talk to her later. She frowned in confusion, then nodded her head. He pointed down the corridor, then walked off, turning slightly to the side as one of the production assistants squeezed by him.

By the time he reached his office, he realized his palms were sweaty. Annoyed with himself for getting all worked up over some woman, he roughly wiped them on his jeans.

"Get a grip, man. If you're acting like a sick puppy now, whaddaya gonna do when you take the woman out?"

"Say something, Tre?" Danny D asked, standing in the open doorway.

Tre looked up and felt even more like an idiot for having gotten busted talking to himself. He etched a stern look on his face.

"Just thinking out loud, Danny. Business." He started shuffling papers on his desk. "A lot on my mind."

"I hear ya. Good night."

" 'Night."

Danny sauntered off, and Tre plopped down in his seat. Would he be glad when this evening was over.

"Thanks for joining me tonight, sharing your thoughts and your vibes. Check us out tomorrow 'Round Midnight, when the topic will be infidelity and getting past it. Dexter take us out."

Her theme song played and she slid out of her seat,

depositing the headphones on the desk, just as Jordan Michaels stepped into the room.

"Hey, Summer. I caught a piece of the show." He grinned. "Good stuff."

"Thanks. Some real characters called in tonight."

"You handled it. I gotta tell you, I really admire what you do. It's got to be tough thinking on your feet like that, trying to patch people together in a couple of minutes."

His small, dark eyes zeroed in on her, and she'd swear his smile was more than casual. His long nose and thin lips reminded her of a predator, and she suddenly felt like the prey.

He made no effort to move when she tried to reach her jacket on the hook behind him. Yeah, they may have been in tight quarters, but it wasn't *that* tight.

"I was thinking maybe we could get together some time." He shrugged. "Go for a drink. Maybe dinner."

When it rains it pours, as her grandmother used to say. One minute she couldn't catch a date with a bait and hook. Now she had two offers in two weeks. However, smooth Jordan Michaels was definitely not her type, nor did she want to be added to his roster of conquests. She'd seen the string of women who flocked around him.

"That's really nice of you to ask Jordan, but I don't think so."

His small eyes grew smaller. "I didn't figure a big uppity doctor like you would be interested in me, but I thought I'd take a shot," he said, keeping his voice even, but Summer distinctly heard the underlying nastiness.

She arched a brow. "Sorry you feel that way."

"No need to apologize. I know where you're coming from." He flashed her a snide smile. "I guess all those stories about you are true."

Not again, her mind screamed. Her eyes widened for a

moment, but she refused to go for the lure. "If you'll excuse me, I'd like to get my jacket." She stared him down until he moved. "Thank you," she snapped and walked toward the door. Just as she opened it, she could have sworn he called her the dreaded "B" word.

That little encounter put her in a foul mood. What did she do to deserve that? she fumed, marching down the corridor. And what stories? She would have breezed right by Tre if there'd been room.

"Hi. Great show."

"Thanks," she mumbled and angled her body to get past him.

"Hold on a minute. I'll walk you out."

She didn't want to be rude, but at the moment she didn't want to be bothered either. "I'm really in a hurry, Tre and I have a splitting headache."

"No problem. I won't keep you. I just wanted to take you up on your offer. Thought we could get together Sunday afternoon. If you're not busy."

His smile seemed to soften her reserve. She looked up into his eyes and saw a gentleness there that she hadn't noticed before.

"I wish I could. But I can't. I really don't think this is such a—"

He held up his hand, halting any further explanation that he didn't want to hear. "No problem."

His smile had wilted a bit around the edges, and she felt responsible. But what else could she do? According to airhead Michaels, there were already stories circulating about her—which could mean an array of things. But still, there was no need to fan the flames by going out with the boss, as much as she wanted to.

"Have a good evening," he said and turned into his office.

"You, too," she mumbled and headed for the exit.

She should have explained, she thought, pushing through the exit door and out into the overcast predawn morning. She pulled her leather jacket tighter around her as a cool breeze blew by. He was nice enough to ask her out. The least she could have done was tell him that the reason she couldn't go out with him was because starting an office relationship was never a wise thing to do. She pressed the deactivation button on her hand-held car alarm and heard the telltale beep. Besides, if what Jordan said was true, that there were stories circulating about her, that was a headache she didn't need. The pain of false accusations had nearly ruined her career and had been the catalyst that propelled her to close up shop, combined with patient-overload.

No. She wouldn't risk that kind of humiliation again.

She turned the key in the ignition and slowly pulled out of the lot. Briefly she looked up at the building and saw someone's silhouette in the window. She wondered if it was Tre.

Tre moved away from the window and tried to push aside his boiling emotions. Did she suddenly wake up and think she was too good for him, or was she a tease that got a kick out of leading men on?

He sorted through some papers on his desk and put them in the appropriate folders, running through their previous conversation as he worked. Now he distinctly remembered her saying to let her know. He might be a lot of things, but hard of hearing wasn't one of them. Obviously, between then and now, she'd done a complete three-sixty.

Fine.

Probably a mistake anyway. He flipped off the light switch and headed out.

* * *

"I think you need to have your head examined," Kia said to Summer, totally exasperated. She piled their lunch dishes in the dishwasher and turned it on. Taking a seat opposite Summer at the table, she took a sip from her glass of Sprite. Kia stared at her friend. "Do you mind explaining why you told the man to take a walk in traffic?" She cupped her chin up on her palms and waited.

"That's not what I said."

"You might as well have. It all amounts to the same thing."

Summer blew out a breath. "I just can't risk it, Kia. Not after the last time."

"Summer, come on. All the rumors were unfounded. Your patient was a real head-case. And you know it."

"He may have been, but the damage it caused to my reputation and my practice took almost two years to recover from. And even then business wasn't the same. I still get those looks from some of my former colleagues when I run into them."

"So the plan is to hide behind your microphone and pretend to write that best-seller instead of picking up the pieces and pressing on?"

Summer rolled her eyes. "Who's the psychologist here, me or you?" Kia ignored her, but Summer knew Kia was right. It was the same advice she'd give to one of her patients, or one of her callers. But everyone knew doctors never took their own advice and made the worst patients.

"I am pressing on," she said in her defense.

"Right."

Kia's sarcastic tone was not lost on Summer. "What do you expect me to do now? It's a done deal."

"I'm fresh out of suggestions. And even if I had any, you wouldn't take them." She took a sip of her Sprite.

"I can't very well go back and say I made a mistake, can I?"

Kia knew that tone. Summer wasn't really asking a question, she was asking for approval. She'd known Summer so long, she could read her like a book. And for someone with so many degrees, you'd think she'd have sense enough to manage her own life. But she never could. It had always been easier to do it for someone else.

"Only you know what you want to do, Summer. It's apparent the man made enough of an impression on you to even have you talking about this. Go with what you feel. Take a chance."

"Just calling to see how you're doing, baby bro," Diane said, switching the receiver from her right to her left ear, as she pushed dirty laundry into the washing machine.

"I'm fine, Di," Tre mumbled, rolling onto his side and peering one-eyed at the bedside clock: 8:00 A.M. His sister had the uncanny knack for finding the exact moment his sleep was the most satisfying and waking him up. She'd been doing it since they were kids. You'd think she would have grown out of that nasty habit by now.

"Still asleep? Rise and shine. It's a beautiful Saturday morning."

He shut his eyes and groaned. He hadn't gotten in from roaming the nightlife until the sun crested the horizon, which he'd swear was just a few minutes ago. He pulled the pillow over his head.

"Yessss, I'm still asleep and intend to stay this way for as long as possible," he grumbled.

"I'm just checking to see what time you're coming for dinner tomorrow, and if I should set an extra place at the table," she hedged.

"I'll be coming. Alone. Thank you."

"I was hoping you'd invite Dr. Lane. I'm dying to meet her."

"Forget it, okay."

"What happened? Lousy date?"

"Forget it, I said."

"I can't. You know I can't. So you might as well tell me."

He blew out a breath, knowing from long, grueling interrogations of the past that Diane was as relentless as a pit bull once she set her mind to something. And she had obviously set her mind to meddling in his business this morning. "There was no date, and there won't be any. Satisfied?"

"No. What happened? Did you ask her out?"

"Yessss. And she turned me down."

Diane frowned. She'd never known a woman to turn her brother down. This Dr. Lane must have a lot with her. "Why?"

"How would I know?" Although it did seem that she'd wanted to explain, he didn't want to hear it. "Listen, you got your scoop for today. End of story. I don't want to talk about this anymore. I want to get some sleep."

"Fine. I'll see you tomorrow."

"Yeah. Yeah. Tomorrow." He fumbled for a few minutes until he was finally able to set the phone back on the cradle without taking his head from beneath the pillow, determined to get back to sleep. But he couldn't. Thoughts of Summer plagued him just as they had from the moment he'd met her. Sure, he'd been able to push her to the back of his thoughts, but there had always been something about her that, without warning, would become resurrected at the oddest times, even if it was something negative. And when he'd finally gotten around to pushing past the barriers he'd erected against her, she turned him down. Flat.

He felt like an idiot, even more so because he'd listened

to his sister. He punched the pillow. Unfortunately that didn't rid him of his frustration. He punched the pillow a few more times, rolled onto his belly, then pushed the pillow aside. He wasn't used to taking no for an answer.

He sat up. He wasn't going to start now.

Chapter Four

"Welcome to my world. This is Summer Lane coming to you just 'Round Midnight. Tonight's topic: saying you're sorry. Why is it so hard? I'll take the first call after 'I Apologize,' by the Whispers."

Summer looped the headphones around her neck and wondered if Tre was out there listening. After talking with Kia and having a good long conversation with herself, she realized how silly she was. For all she knew, Jordan could have been making up the whole thing just to get on her last nerve because she'd turned him down. And that ugly incident with her patient was a long time ago. She blew out a breath and took a look at the playlist.

She hadn't seen Tre since she'd said, "No thanks" a week earlier. And she'd been thinking about him ever since, hoping she'd run into him again, or at least see him at the station. She hadn't.

Maybe tonight.

"Welcome back to 'Round Midnight. You just heard from the Whispers with 'I Apologize,' which is our topic for tonight. Why do some people find it so hard to admit they're wrong and say they're sorry? We have Shelly on the line. Hi, Shelly. What's your opinion?"

"I think it's hard because sometimes we just don't want to be seen as weak, or having made a mistake."

'That's very true. Unfortunately many people take any act of softness or kindness as a weakness, and we don't want to be seen that way. But being able to admit that you're wrong takes a certain kind of strength. Thanks, Shelly, for getting us rolling tonight. Let's talk to James. James, what are your impressions?"

"Women make it hard," the caller grumbled, and Summer instantly knew from his tone that this was going to be "one of those calls." "They constantly want to throw whatever you did in your face. They never forgive or forget anything," he spat into the phone.

"I can't agree with that, James. You're painting all women as unforgiving. And that's not true. Perhaps you've just been unfortunate enough to run into the wrong ones."

"Yeah. Right. Blame it on the man. Isn't that always the case? The man gotta be the bad guy. You're just like all the rest, and you call yourself a doctor. You got a man, Doc?" He chuckled in a nasty tone.

Summer was getting a real bad feeling about this call and knew she had to get him off the line as soon as possible.

"Blame is not the issue here, James. It's facing up to mistakes and apologizing for them."

"Do you apologize when you're wrong, Doc?"

"I make it a point to do just that," she said, thinking about how much she wanted to tell Tre she was sorry.

"I think it's a mistake having you on the air. You want to apologize for that?"

"Tell you what, James, I'm sorry you feel that way. And thanks for calling. Next up is a song from way back that talks about the way it should be when it's all said and done: 'Stay in My Corner,' by the Dells."

The powerful voices of the Dells pulsed through the

small confines of the studio, and Summer wasn't sure if it was the vibration of the music or if her hands were really shaking.

That caller, James, if that was really his name, had actually rattled her. He was so angry, hurt by someone deeply. And because of the limitations of her job, there was no way that she could dig deep enough to find out what the real problem was. That's what was so frustrating at times. Her feelings of inadequacy. But he was so angry and . . . she felt as if his anger were directed at her.

The balance of the program was pretty uneventful. Most of the callers had the same complaint—their significant others didn't take their apologies seriously, or made it so difficult for them to say they were sorry. She did the best she could in the time allowed to offer advice, but that call from James had thrown her off balance.

Leslie gave her the exit cue.

"Thanks for being with me tonight. Join us tomorrow just 'Round Midnight." She turned off her microphone, slipped off her headphones, and stood. She gave Leslie the thumb's-up sign and took her jacket from the hook. She opened the studio door and walked right into Jordan.

"Had a rough night, I heard." He grinned.

"Nothing I couldn't handle," she tossed back, easing by him and getting a quick whiff of his cologne, realizing that she really didn't like it.

"Thought your job was to make the callers happy," he said to her back.

"Can't please everyone." She closed the door behind her and headed down the corridor. Oooh, she didn't like that man. He might have one of the smoothest voices on the air, but he could sure use some lessons in class—a trait he was sorely lacking.

* * *

Tre turned off the radio, his office lights, and went out the door—just as Summer walked by.

He stood in his doorway and watched her walk down the corridor, that slow seductive sway of her hips like a hypnotic metronome. He wanted to say something, hear what she had to say about the show. Tell her he'd tuned in and wondered how she felt about the angry caller. But he didn't.

Maybe some other time.

For the next two weeks James called every night. His verbal assaults on her, the show, the callers, and the topics were getting out of control. Leslie tried to screen the calls, but James would disguise his voice, change his name and slip through, identifying himself once he got on the air. It seemed as though he'd developed a personal vendetta against her, and it was totally dismantling her confidence and her concentration.

The worst part came about a week after the calls started, when she was called into Stan's office.

"See these letters on my desk?" It wasn't a question.

Summer sat down. She briefly glanced at the stack of assorted letters and unopened envelopes in Stan's IN box.

"Yes."

"They're all about you and your caller. Our audience isn't happy. And when my audience isn't happy, I'm not happy."

"I'm doing everything I can," Summer replied in her doctor-patient-soothing tone, even though her insides were a jumble of frayed nerves.

"Whatever you're doing is not enough. You were hired on the recommendation of someone I think very highly of. Your background indicated to me that you had experience in handling . . . these types of problems." He cleared his throat. "Don't get me wrong, up until now I've had no complaints. You know how I've felt about the way you took the show and ran with it. 'Round Midnight has been our number-one draw almost from the beginning." He began pacing the short expanse of the crowded room. "There's no other way to put this, Summer." He stopped his pacing, turned to face her. She had the sudden sensation of being hustled off to radio purgatory, that elusive black hole in the time slot when no one was listening.

"Your ratings are down. And if they keep falling . . . we may have to look at replacing the show."

Her heart knocked once, hard, then seemed to rush up to her throat where it stuck, pounding. She took in a slow lungful of air, giving the declaration an opportunity to wind its way through the labyrinth of her mind. This was worse than purgatory, where at least you had the chance to repent for your sins and be reassigned back to the Pearly Gates of primetime. This was most certainly the slow elevator to that other place, down below. Banishment.

Stan took a breath, then reached down on his desk for his pack of Newports. He lit up and blew a cloud of smoke into the air. He held the cigarette almost daintily between his fingers, Summer thought for an abstract moment, thinking the affectation so odd for someone who strutted around like Napoleon incarnate.

Stan pointed the cigarette in her direction as he spoke. "Do you have any enemies?"

Summer frowned. "Enemies? What do you mean?"

"Someone who might be out to get you, ruin your reputation. Someone who might be jealous, feel slighted—an old boyfriend. Whatever."

A parade of possibilities marched through her head, but the band kept right on going. There was no one she could think of who'd want to see her squirm.

"No," she finally answered, looking him directly in the eye.

Slowly he nodded. "We'll do what we can in engineering in terms of monitoring the calls, but if he gets through, you'll have to handle it. Maybe some people like the verbal sparring and nastiness from some of the other talk radio programs and the ones on television, but it's not what our listeners want. And the Arbitron ratings prove it."

Summer could tell by his stance that this meeting was over. She stood. "I'll do what I can."

"I'm sure you will. I'm depending on you to pull out of this. There's got to be something in one of those psychology books of yours that tells you how to deal with nutcases."

"They're not nutcases. They're troubled individuals," she gently corrected.

"Call 'em what you want. I just don't want them on my show."

"Thanks for talking with me, Stan. It'll work out."

"Hmmm," he mumbled, already absorbed in his next crisis.

Summer slipped out quietly, slinging her oversized purse on her shoulder. Her stomach had that fluttery feeling like the instant before a plane lifts off the runway, then dips and pitches until it settles at a comfortable altitude.

She couldn't let this happen to her again—have what she'd built, worked at, ruined by someone for no other reason than just because. She felt her eyes burn and begin to cloud over.

She wouldn't cry, not here. Especially here where she didn't have a real friend she could count on. As she passed the twisting, turning array of employees, she looked at each one with a critical eye. Maybe Stan was right about it being jealousy. Her show was number one, and she was sure there'd be no love lost if she got bumped down a notch or two. Or three.

Is it him? Her?

She turned the corner. She'd so insulated herself since she began working at the station, that there was no one she could turn to and get the inside stuff, find out if there were any plots being hatched against her.

The only person she could rely on was herself, and her skills at analyzing others, which unfortunately seemed to always fail her when it came to her own life and problems.

Summer pushed through the exit doors and out into the chilly October afternoon. A breeze whipped across her face and sneaked under her jacket. She quickly zipped it up. What she needed was a plan, she decided as the thoughts formulated in her head.

She looked up, seeing Misty's, one of the other local hangouts for the radio crowd. What she needed was some allies. The brief flicker of a smile teased her mouth. What better place to start than at Misty's?

When she stepped into the semidarkened bar/grill/ restaurant, sometime nightclub, the place was already packed with early lunchgoers, late breakfast eaters, and those who had nothing else to do but find out what everyone else was doing.

She fell into the last category.

Stepping farther into the less than plush space, she was stopped in her tracks by a buxom—the kind you see on Jerry Springer—waitress, slash, hostess who asked her how many.

It took all Summer had to keep her eyes focused on the woman's lackluster brown eyes and not the overabundance of cleavage that clearly did not want to be confined in whatever cup size they were in.

Summer blinked at the sound of popping gum. "Oh, just one, please."

The woman snatched up a menu from the stand and commanded, "Follow me." Which she did and with every step wondered how the poor woman didn't topple over face first.

She showed Summer to a table tucked in the back.

"Your waitress will be with you in a minute," she said, placing the menu on the table and nearly slapping Summer across the face with those launch missiles. Reflexes snatched her head back just in time.

Summer looked up. "Thanks."

Once alone, she casually scanned the crowd. She'd seen several of the radio staff on her way in, none of whom paid her much attention. Everywhere she looked, people were in twos and threes, enjoying conversation, sharing jokes and trade secrets.

She took a sip of her lukewarm water, realizing just how out of touch she'd become. Although networking and gripe-and-grin sessions were never her strong suit, the little skill she had at it had atrophied from disuse. There was not a friendly face in the place, and she knew she'd never made it easy for folks to just come on up and chat with her. So this was the price she was paying.

She was thirty-four years old, and the stampede of thirty-five could be heard in the distance. She had a luxury condo, top of the line automobile, clothes, art, and was a great cook. But she, as Kia diligently reminded her, had no one to share it with. And now she was also faced once again with the possibility of having to walk away from a job she loved with her tail tucked between her legs.

Where was the waitress? she almost asked out loud, the unfairness of her situation erupting like an uncorked bottle of bubbly. She looked up, her eyes scanning the shadows and shapes of the room and landed right on Tre, who was being led inside by the hostess with the mostest.

She didn't know whether she wanted to duck or wave him in her direction.

The decision was taken out of her hands when he was shepherded in the opposite direction, never having seen her.

Figures. It was typical of the type of day she was having.

She turned her attention to the menu, knowing good and well that she wasn't hungry and feeling more by the minute that this little jaunt was a mistake.

She shut the menu, silently cursing the invisible waitress, then gave herself a short counseling session. *Everything takes time, Ms. Lane,* the voice in her head was saying. *No one can expect progress overnight. Take one step at a time. This is the first one. The hardest. You should feel good about that. The next step will be easier. If your colleagues don't reach out to you, you make the effort.*

She looked around, again seeing a continuing stream of familiar faces. Whom could she approach and strike up a conversation and not feel like the total party crasher?

"Hi."

She turned to her left, and Tre was standing there looking down at her.

She smiled in the hope that he'd forgiven her for the sorry way she'd behaved. "How are you?"

"Is that a clinical or a rhetorical question?" he teased. She noticed again the appealing way his eyes crinkled at the corners when he smiled.

"A bit of both."

He chuckled. "Fair enough. In that case, on both counts, I'd say I was fine, Doc."

You certainly are.

"However, I'm sure there are many who'd question my assessment." He smiled again, and she saw the fine lines that bracketed his mouth. It gave him character, instead of aging him as it did with women.

"Are you meeting anyone?"

She wished she could say yes, so that she wouldn't appear as the lonely waif—but of course that would be a lie that would unravel in a matter of minutes.

"No. I'm not. Would you like to join me—if you're not here with anyone?"

"Yes, I would. And no, I'm not."

He pulled out a chair and sat. "Did you order?"

"No." She frowned. "This section seems to be off limits to the waitress."

Tre chuckled. "You just have to get used to Misty's. They have the greatest food to be such a dive, but the wait could turn you gray. Most of us try to fill up on beer, peanuts, and conversation until we can get some service. Can I get you something from the bar?"

"Well, now that I know the rules of the game, maybe I can play." She pressed lips together in thought. "I'd like a pineapple daiquiri."

"Oh, one of those fruity drinks that flatten you when you're not looking." He stood. "Be right back."

Maybe this adventure would turn out all right after all, Summer thought. But her nerves were like Rice Krispies in milk. He made her nervous, undid her usual calm demeanor. Maybe it was his casual attitude, or maybe the way he looked at her, or the scent of his cologne that made her want to move a little closer. Whatever it was, it was getting stronger every time she was in his presence. The feeling was totally foreign to her. She was accustomed to being in control of situations and her emotions. These feelings were a little scary—the extra beats of her heart, the warm flush that heated her skin when he smiled. Suppose Tre Holland was someone she could really care about? Then what? How would a relationship between them affect their working relationship?

Stop analyzing, girl, and just go for it, she could almost hear Kia whisper.

Tre stood at the bar and ordered their drinks. While he waited, he thought about how the rest of his day would play out. She didn't seem averse to him joining her, so maybe he'd just blown her turning him down out of proportion. Maybe she'd just been having a bad day. It could have been a number of things, and he'd let his fractured ego take charge of his head. Pangs of guilt grabbed him in the gut. He took a deep breath and pushed it aside. Maybe this was the point of starting over. He'd give it and her another try.

He collected and paid for their drinks and returned to the table, bringing a waitress with him.

"Here you go." He placed the frothy yellow liquid in front of her and, when she smiled her thanks, his heart did a little tap dance.

They placed their orders and the waitress walked away, and the moment of uncertain silence took her place.

Tre took a sip of his drink, using the time to get himself together. "What brings you to Misty's? I don't think I've ever seen you here before."

"I'm not sure really. I was walking and then it was right in front of me. I'd heard a lot of the radio crowd came here, so I thought I'd see what it was like."

He grinned. "Now you can see how our tastes run. To be honest, this doesn't seem like the kind of place for you."

"What do you mean?"

He shrugged slightly. "You don't seem to be the type of woman who would enjoy herself in a dingy little dive like Misty's. I see you more as the glitz and glamour type, hanging out in restaurants with chandeliers, soft music coming from some unseen source, and drinking wine that was imported."

He stared at her until she averted her gaze. Is that how she came across? Was that why the staff didn't go out of their way to include her because she seemed above it all?

"I didn't realize that was the impression I was giving," she said softly, and the almost hurt tone of her voice knotted Tre's insides. "I—enjoy a lot of things. I guess people have preconceived notions about others when they don't know them."

"You have to admit, you don't make it easy for anyone to really get to know you, so they stay away."

She rolled his observation around in her head. She knew he was right. It had always been difficult for her to form relationships. The only reason why she and Kia remained friends was because Kia was determined to be her friend. She'd made a bet with some of the other girls in their sixth-grade class that she could be Summer Lane's friend. And she never gave up until she was. However, not everyone had Kia's determination.

"It's not intentional," she finally said. "Just easier."

"Easier?"

"Keeps you from expecting too much. Can't get disappointed."

Tre leaned a bit closer. "Is that what you tell your patients?"

"I tell my patients to be honest about their feelings, to give life and people a chance. But don't rest your hopes and expectations on anyone else."

"So why wouldn't you give us a chance?" He gave her a long look. "Be honest."

Summer twisted her lips to bite back a smile. She blew out a breath. "It's a lot more complicated than that."

"Let's hear it."

The waitress returned with their food and conversation momentarily ceased, giving Summer the few minutes of breathing room she needed. She knew she was about to tread across deep waters. She didn't want to go under in her efforts to get to the other side.

"Can I get you folks anything else?" the waitress asked.

Summer shook her head.

"No. Thanks, Stella," Tre said.

He turned his attention to Summer, and she felt riveted by his steady gaze. There was no way that Tre Holland was the type of man you could tiptoe around when he wanted answers.

She cleared her throat. "When you first asked me out . . . Tre, I was intrigued by the possibilities and"—she smiled shyly—"kind of excited."

"Only kind of?" He grinned.

"Yes. Only kind of."

He turned on an upside-down smile, and Summer laughed. "And?"

Her face grew serious. "I guess if we're going to be honest"—she wrapped her hand around her glass—"what's happening to me now at the studio, the harassment, accusations. It's not the first time. About three years ago . . ."

Summer told him about the male patient of hers who'd become obsessed by her. She hadn't seen the signs, and by the time she realized what happened her career was crumbling. He'd gone to another psychologist and began telling her that Summer had tried to come on to him, had attempted to seduce him on several occasions, and that was the reason why he stopped seeing her as a patient. Rumors started circulating, and someone—she never found out who—decided to report the alleged incident to the medical board.

"I was devastated," she said, shaking off the ugly feelings that had snuck out of the place she'd stored them. "I had to go to appear in front of the medical ethics committee. It all boiled down to my word against his. I started losing my patients because I couldn't concentrate." She took a long swallow of her drink, staring off into space.

He felt sick. "How did you get out of it?"

"I had to do something, as a doctor, I was sworn never to do: break doctor-patient privilege. I always taped every session. When it looked as though my career was about to be flushed down the toilet, I called my former patient and told him I'd be forced to reveal the contents of our sessions if he continued to pursue the accusations. He finally backed off and withdrew the charges."

"Would you have used the tapes?"

Slowly she shook her head. "I don't know, Tre. Sometimes I think I would. Other times I'm just not sure. I don't ever want to have to make that decision again."

"Wow. How did you pull your practice back together?"

"It took time. But it was never really the same. Although the case never went to trial, I was tainted. There was always the question in many of my colleagues' heads, 'What if?' They never came out and said anything, but the atmosphere in my circle had gotten chilly."

"So now you're here. How does all of that affect you and me?"

"I had every intention of going out with you. As a matter of fact, the same evening you brought it up in the hallway, I'd just received a solid dose of déjà vu."

He pulled back his head in confusion.

"Jordan Michaels approached me, and to make a long story short, he said there were stories circulating about me. He insinuated that was the reason why I wouldn't go out with him. All I could think about was *not again*. All I'd need is for everyone to start thinking that the only reason my show is at the top is because I'm fooling around with the boss. That's a headache I don't need." She shook her head and pushed her salad around her plate with her fork.

"Why don't you give me the chance to make my decisions for myself? Both of us know that your status at the station has nothing to do with a relationship between you and me. To be quite frank, I didn't want your show on the air."

"I know." She grinned.

"Oh."

"I've gotten past that. Actually, I think it made me work harder to prove you wrong." Her eyes held his in challenge.

"That you did, Dr. Lane. Without a doubt."

"So, now what?"

"You're the doctor. What's your remedy for this situation?"

"Let's see, I'd say take one date and talk about it in the morning."

His stomach clenched at the provocative look that had suddenly darkened her eyes.

"When do you think you'll be ready to fill out that prescription?"

"How about Sunday?"

"Whatever the doctor orders. Just be prepared to write out a whole pad of refills."

She laughed. Maybe Tre Holland was what the doctor should have ordered a long time ago.

Chapter Five

That first Sunday was just the beginning of many long, lazy afternoons, excursions to museums, tours of the White House—something neither of them had seen even though they'd lived in D.C. all their lives—local jazz concerts, brunches, plenty of awful movies, which they debated furiously about after each one. And before either of them realized what was happening, they'd begun building their lives and activities around each other, around their schedules, adjusting to quirky behaviors like Tre's habit of mumbling to himself when he had things on his mind. At first Summer thought she was losing her hearing, until she realized that he wasn't talking to her. Or Summer's penchant for constantly making verbal observations and assessments about everyone and everything. In the beginning Tre thought it would drive him mad, but then he started getting into it himself, and they'd have hour-long conversations about what they thought so-'n-so's problem was. Often Tre was right on target with his basic street sense and keen eye for people. But Summer would never give in and tell him so.

They'd been seeing each other for about six weeks, and so far no one at the office had made any comments on the unusual amount of time Tre was spending at the station on his designated days off. He'd even broken down and became a regular listener of her show and had to admit, Summer Lane was something else.

To make life even sweeter, the harassing phone calls from James had slowed then stopped altogether. Her ratings were rising, and Stan was sure that by Christmas she would have regained her audience and recaptured the crown as number one. Most of all she was happy, happier than she'd ever been, and she knew Tre was at the center of her happiness. He went out of his way to make special plans for them. He'd pick her up after her set at 2:00 A.M. and take her home, even though he had to drag himself out of bed to do it. "I never liked the idea of your driving home alone at that time of night, even when I wasn't sure if I liked you," he'd said. He'd buy her funny little cards, just to remind her that he was thinking of her. She'd find a single piece of chocolate on her chair when she came in to work, or he'd give her a yellow rose when they met for lunch. Whenever he got her alone, he'd kiss her until she was nearly senseless, stirring up the tide of emotions she hadn't put into action in longer than she cared to remember. His touch fired her skin, his voice soothed her soul, his laughter brightened her day. He was attentive, affectionate, protective, funny. She was falling in love.

"I told you all you needed was to give yourself a chance, Summer," Kia said, twisting her hair into a French roll.

Summer curled up on Kia's lounge chair in the bedroom, a soft smile framing her mouth. "You know I hate to admit it when you're right. But you were."

"Of course I was right. You may have all that book sense, but I've got it up here"—she tapped her temple—"when it comes to affairs of the heart."

Summer grinned. "Okay, don't rub it in."

"So you two are going away for Thanksgiving, huh?"

"We're leaving after we have dinner with his sister and her family."

"Ooh, meeting the family. That's a big move, girl-friend."

"I know. I'm kind of nervous. He talks about his sister all the time. They seem to be really close. I want her to like me."

"Why wouldn't she?"

"Well, you know. She's been like a mother to him since their parents died. She may feel threatened by our relation-ship. Maybe think I was taking him away from her."

Kia turned around and put her hand on her hip, looking at Summer from a forty-five-degree angle. "Girl, you need to stop. You don't even know the woman, and already you're busy analyzing. Give her a chance."

Summer blew out a breath. "You're right."

"A-gain. Just enjoy yourself."

Diane Holland-Pratt was everything Tre had described. She was funny, protective, and loved her brother to distrac-tion and had no qualms about telling him and anyone else who would listen just what was on her mind. Her husband, Jeff, was a doll—and their two little girls made her think about her own ticking biological clock.

"I'm glad things are working out with you and Tre," Diane confided when she and Summer were cleaning up the kitchen after their Thanksgiving feast. "He needs someone positive in his life so he can settle down ... again."

Summer frowned. "Again?"

"Ooops. I guess he never told you about Desiree."

"Desiree?" The hairs on the back of her neck began to tingle.

"Yes. His high school sweetheart. Married her right out

of college and well . . . let's just say Ms. Girl hadn't finished running around.'' She rinsed a dish and stuck it in the dishwasher. Slowly she shook her head. ''Really messed Tre up. It took him a long time to get over what she did to him. He hasn't been serious about anyone since.'' She turned and looked at Summer. ''Until he met you. Every other thing he talks about has your name in it since the two of you got together. I think you're good for him. Matter of fact, I told him that months ago.''

''You did?''

''Oh, yeah. I could tell he was interested because he acted like he wasn't. I told him he needed to ask you out, or at least ask you what a guy like him needed to do to find a woman like you.''

Summer laughed. ''You're kidding.''

''Not hardly.'' She paused a moment, then leaned against the sink. ''Summer, Tre may come across as a man who has it all together. He may seem tough on the outside, but underneath, he has a heart of gold. All he needs is someone to nurture it, take care of him. Don't hurt him, Summer. I don't think he'll recover from it next time.''

''I won't. I promise.''

''You have a wonderful family, Tre. Thanks for inviting me.''

He leaned across the gearshift of the car and kissed her lightly on the lips. ''I wanted them to see how happy you've made me, Summer, and I wanted you to be a part of my life that is really special to me.''

Her throat tightened. She stroked his cheek. ''You don't know how much that means to me. My family and me, well . . . we're not close. Holidays are usually a lonely time for me.''

He leaned closer, cupped her face in his hands, and looked into her eyes. ''If I have anything to say about it, all those lonely holidays, lonely nights and mornings will be a thing of the past. Starting tonight."

He lowered his head to meet her lips, tentatively in the beginning, as if they were sharing their first kiss, then with more pressure until her lips softened, separated, opened for him. Their tongues met, retreated, taunted, danced a slow dance while their hearts played a disco beat.

Slowly Tre pulled back. "Guess we'd better get moving," he said in a rough whisper.

Summer swallowed then nodded her head. Her heart was stampeding in her chest.

Tre pulled the car into traffic and headed for the cabin in Virginia. He'd been planning this getaway for weeks. He wanted everything to be perfect.

A soft sprinkling of snow began to fall. They looked at each other and smiled.

The drive from D.C. to Comptons Store, Virginia, was a leisurely two hours filled with easy conversation, breathtaking scenery slowly being covered with the first dusting of snow, and the sight of the residents walking along the shore of Bull Run River.

When they pulled up in front of the cabin, Summer let out a breath of awe. Like a little kid, she jumped out of the car and stood in front of the sprawling ranch-style cabin, less than a mile away from the lake, shrouded by weeping willows and gentle slopes. It looked like something right off of a postcard. She spun around and stared openmouthed at Tre.

He stood by the car, grinning, filled with a deep sense of happiness just watching her joy.

"Tre, it's beautiful," she cried and ran into his arms.

He swung her around. "You're not hard to please. You haven't even seen the inside yet." She giggled and he pecked her on the lips, then set her on her feet. He took her hand. "Come on. I'm dying to see how you treat me when you see the rest."

Hand-in-hand they took the tour of the expansive abode. Every room offered a spectacular view of the Virginia landscape or views of the rolling river.

The kitchen was fully stocked and loaded with all the kitchen gadgets to keep Summer in a state of eternal euphoria. The living room boasted a real wood-burning fireplace, a wall-to-wall glass window, with low-hanging ceiling rafters of gleaming oak and a thirty-two-inch television. There were two bedrooms. The master bedroom should have been photographed for *House Beautiful* magazine. A huge brass bed, adorned with a mint-green down comforter, contrasted perfectly with the green and wine colored paisley drapes and pale green carpet, so thick it could tickle your ankles. A six-drawer dresser in black lacquer trimmed in brass to match the bed and a six-foot armoire as its companion took up the space in perfect balance. The bath, tucked away to the left of the bedroom rivaled any major spa, with its Jacuzzi, his and her sinks, and a stall shower big enough for a small dinner party.

"This place is fabulous," Summer enthused when they'd returned to the living room. "How long have you had it?"

He supposed now was as good a time as any to tell her about Desiree. "Can I fix you a drink?"

"White wine if you have it." She watched his body language as he took two champagne flutes from an overhead rack and filled them with chilled wine, then joined her on the modular couch, and knew he was struggling with whatever he needed to tell her.

"Thanks." She took a sip.

"I was married," he began slowly. "I purchased this place after the divorce, sort of a cleansing, I suppose." He took her through his high school infatuation, the crazy college years, and his graduation marriage, pausing intermittently to take a sip of his wine or stare out through the window, as if the retelling of the story were too painful to reveal.

"We were married for about two years when things really started coming apart." He leaned forward, bracing his arms on his thighs, his thick cable-knit sweater seeming to ripple along his broad back. "I guess I saw it long before then and just didn't want to believe it. We grew apart, and one day I walked in and someone had taken my place—literally. It took me a long time to get over that, Summer. Sometimes I still don't know if I have." He chuckled mirthlessly. "I guess you could say my trust level is really low. I've spent the past five years in relationship limbo, dealing with women I didn't expect much from. That's exactly what I got, and I gave the same in return: next to nothing."

"What about now?"

He turned to look at her. Her gaze was steady, probing. "I'm not sure. All I do know is that I don't want to keep going through life the way I've been going. I want more than to wake up next to a warm body only to discover I don't remember her name."

"What is the *more* that you want, Tre?" She knew the psychologist in her was coming out, but it was important to her to hear him say the words, she reasoned, and more important for him to hear himself say them.

He reached out and gently stroked her cheek, his eyes skipping across her face. "I want to try with you, Summer. Since you came into my life, I've started to feel like I wanted to live it again, share it and make it grow. But you've got to want it too." He paused. "Do you?"

She moved closer to him, took his chin in her hand, and pulled him toward her. "That's the best offer I've had in a long time," she whispered a moment before her lips joined his.

That kiss was the bond, the part that sealed the unspoken promise between them, which erupted from a small burning ember to an engulfing blaze, spreading through their limbs, escaping through the heat of their touch, fanned by hushed words and muffled moans.

Somehow they found their way to the bedroom, leaving a trail of discarded clothing in their wake. That first instant of contact, bare flesh against bare flesh, was as startling as a bolt of lightning.

Summer moaned when the shudders rippled through her. Tre pulled her closer, longing to make her body one with his, but he took his time, exploring, exciting, memorizing the way her body responded when he touched her like . . . that—*oooh*—or when he kissed her. . . right there—*yessss*.

But nothing could have prepared him for the rush of sensations that wreaked havoc with his body when he found himself buried within her. He nearly cried.

And she did. Tears of bliss slid unbidden from her eyes as the ebb and flow of their union lifted her from that earthly place and held her captive, suspended on the precipice of release. She wanted to jump, succumb to the giddy, exhilarating ride but would Tre be there to catch her, soothe her fears?

She couldn't wait any longer, the tide kept pounding against the shore, she moved closer to the edge, could almost see forever when she stepped off, hurtling through a kaleidoscope of spiraling sensations, brilliant lights, and finally sublime ecstasy that rocked her body leaving her weak and powerful at the same time—and yes, Tre was there to catch her.

"I don't know how much of that I can take," Tre groaned in her ear as they spooned around each other. "I'm not a kid anymore."

Summer giggled. "Had me fooled."

"It's all done with smoke and mirrors," he teased. He caressed her breasts, still swollen from their loving.

"Oh, yeah, well you could certainly take your show on the road," she purred.

He pulled her even closer against his body. "This is the

end of the road for me, Summer. I found where I want to go."

She shut her eyes and smiled.

The days seemed to rush by and the excitement of the Christmas holidays and the station's preparations for the New Year's program had everyone at WKQR on supercharge.

And Summer was happy. Happier than she'd been in years. She and Tre spent all of their free time together, talking, exploring the city, taking long drives on snow-filled nights, making love until they were both wobbling with exhaustion.

She stayed so busy at the station, finding room in her life for this wonderful relationship, that when she stopped to take a breath it was only three weeks before Christmas, and she hadn't picked up a present for Tre. She wanted it to be special, so she pulled a few strings, used her radio connections, and was able to order a collection of all of John Coltrane's work—some never before released, only played live and put on cassettes—and she was having them all pressed onto a CD. She knew he loved music as much as she did and was sure he would enjoy the gift.

She got up early, dressed in several layers since the weather report said the temperature had dropped below freezing, and the wind chill made it feel like minus ten degrees.

Just as she was putting on her ankle-length, black shearling coat, her phone rang. She started to ignore it, but on the third ring changed her mind.

"Hello?"

"Hey, baby. It's me."

A big grin stretched her mouth. "It better be. I don't want just any old strange man with a sexy voice calling me baby."

He'd been debating with his conscience for weeks. The guilt of what he'd done had weighed down his spirit. Summer had been open, loving, and totally giving once she'd gotten beyond her reservations. And he couldn't live with himself any longer if he didn't do the same. If they were going to work at and maintain their relationship, it had to be from a foundation of honesty. He couldn't walk into the new year with this on his conscience.

"Are you busy?"

"Well, I was on my way out of the door."

"We need to talk."

"Tre, what is it? You don't sound like yourself." Her heart started beating a little faster. She unbuttoned her coat.

"I can be there in about fifteen minutes. Please wait for me. It's important."

Well, the longest fifteen minutes known to man did the slow drag, just like those long, seemingly endless love songs that played in the blue-light basement parties where you bent over backward and just prayed the song would end so you could stand up straight and get the kink out of your back.

In other words, she wanted to scream. She paced. She turned on the stereo, turned it off and put on the television. When that didn't work, she paced some more.

What could it be? Another woman? A disease? He was gay?

When the doorbell ding-donged, her whole body snapped like a piece of dry wood. Taking a breath of calm, she crossed the living room to the foyer and opened the door. The tortured look on Tre's face in no way eased her anxiety.

"Hi." She stepped aside to let him pass and wondered what happened to his usual kiss of greeting.

He walked straight into the living room, hands jammed into the pockets of his pea coat, and took up where she left off with the pacing.

"I can't stand this another minute," she blurted, crossing her arms beneath her breasts.

Tre stopped, looked at her, then ran a hand across his face. "I don't even know how to tell you this, Summer. I thought I had it all worked out in my head."

"Just tell me." Her heart was totally out of control.

He took a breath and cleared his throat. "Remember when you were getting those harassing phone calls at the station?"

She frowned. That was certainly a time in her career she wanted to forget. "Yes."

He swallowed. "It was . . . me."

She looked at him for several minutes as if she couldn't quite make out what he was talking about, then asked a really stupid question, because it was the only thing that came to mind. "What do you mean it was you?"

"It was me making the calls. Getting past Leslie. Causing problems with your listeners, with Stan, with your ratings. It was me."

He would have done better if he'd just slapped her—that was tangible—because this other feeling, this sinking, sick feeling in the pit of her stomach she couldn't handle. "Why?" she whispered, the word catching in her throat.

"I wanted to . . . put you in your place. But that was before—"

"Please leave."

He stepped toward her and she moved back. "Summer, please."

"Out. Now. Don't come back." Her voice was totally emotionless, and that frightened him more than if she'd started screaming and throwing things.

He reached out to her.

"Don't touch me. And I don't want to have to tell you again to leave. Don't call." She laughed a nasty, pained laugh. "Don't write, and don't stop by."

"If that's the way you want it," he said, barely above a strangled whisper.

"No, it's the way you made it."

He blew out a breath of defeat and walked out the door.

"It's a lucky thing I like that Christmas gift, huh?" she whispered in concert with the closing door.

A single tear slid down her cheek.

Chapter Six

The days all seemed to blend together. The nights were a hazy blur of unanswered questions, restless sleep, and more of the same nothingness when the sun rose.

At least once an hour, Summer asked herself *why*? Why had he done something so despicable, and what had she done to him to evoke such cruelty? His single-mindedness in "putting her in her place" nearly cost her job. In the final moments before exhaustion overtook her, she'd always arrive at the same place she started: Tre Holland was not the kind of man she could trust with her heart.

"You did what?" Diane couldn't have been more stunned by her brother's confession if she'd opened the door to find Dick Clark and Ed McMahon telling her she'd won the American Family Publishers Sweepstakes.

Tre couldn't even look at Diane. For that matter he could barely look at himself. His own stupidity and over-wrought male ego had cost him the one woman who'd finally made a difference in his life.

"I was the one making the phone calls," he mumbled.

"What in heaven's name was on your mind?"

Diane took a seat on the couch, staring at her brother as if he were a complete stranger. "So what are you going to do to fix it, Tre?"

"There's nothing I can do. She won't talk to me. She won't let me explain."

"I suppose you're just going to leave it like that. Summer was the first woman I've seen you with in years that made any sense to have in your life. Of course she told you to get lost. I would have done the same thing."

"Diane, I really don't need a lecture."

"You need something!" She folded her arms defiantly, but more to keep from knocking him in the head.

"I screwed up. I admit it, and yes, that's all there is to it. I'm going to respect her wishes, Di, and leave her alone." He took a breath and laid his next tidbit of news on her. "I'm leaving the station, Di. I'm going to New York for a while."

There was no longer anything he could say that would surprise her. "If you think that's the answer," she said, "then run, 'cause that's just what you're doing." She stood. "I have things to do." She walked out, leaving him alone with his conscience.

"You need to give him a chance to explain, Summer," Kia said as they sat together in their favorite Mexican restaurant in Georgetown.

Summer dipped a taco into the guacamole dip and put it in her mouth, chewing slowly. She washed it down with a short swallow of Corona before replying. "There's nothing to explain."

"Of course there is. What he did was stupid. But he could have gone along and never said a word. He didn't.

I think if nothing else it shows you the kind of man he is."

"Yes, a man who thought very little of me. That's not the kind of man I want to be with."

"I'm going to say this, then shut my mouth about the whole thing. He may have had some infantile notion, some bizarre reason that escapes logic to do what he did, but that was before he got to know you. And quite frankly, I've considered playing some nasty trick on you to get you to come down off that high horse you're always riding."

"What's that supposed to mean?"

"Let's face it, Summer, you're not the easiest person to get to know. Whether you do it intentionally or not, you give out this hands-off attitude that's as potent as that expensive perfume you wear. It's intimidating and not very endearing. But that's for those people who don't know you," she qualified. "But you don't make it easy. You've spent so much of your life trying to solve other people's problems, you've never taken time out to discover who you are. You've shielded yourself behind your degrees, your drop-dead wardrobe, flashy foreign car, and Einstein intellect. It's not an easy wall to climb over or knock down."

Summer raised her eyes from her half-eaten plate of food and looked at her friend. Her friend who seemed to have always been there. The one who always stood up for her in the schoolyard when the other girls taunted her about being too smart or thinking she was too good. The one who listened to her cry when she talked about the horrible arguments her parents had and how lonely she felt. The one who always tried to include her in her life, even while she struggled against it. Kia knew her like no other and still she remained her friend.

"What do I do, Kia?"

"Do you love him?"

"Yes."

"Then you'll figure it out. But only if you really want to."

For days Summer wrestled with her conscience, which battled valiantly against her heart. A part of her wanted to hear what he had to say, forgive him, and pick up where they left off. Another part of her, the scared little girl, was afraid that to forgive would open the door to more betrayal. How could she ever hope to trust him? What would he do the next time she did something that offended his machismo?

She never had the chance to get the answers to her questions. When she went to work, three days before Christmas, there was a staff memo announcing the resignation of Tre Holland. Effective immediately. Until a new program director was hired, the memo stated, Leslie Evans would step in during the transition. Stan was in quite a state and could be seen periodically walking through the halls, talking to himself.

She took the memo, balled it up, and tossed it into the circular file. *So much for that.*

Tre sat on the edge of his hotel bed in New York, staring at the phone. It was Christmas Eve. He wanted to call Summer, tell her how sorry he was, and beg her forgiveness. But he didn't think he could stand it if she hung up on him. The closest he'd come to her was hearing her voice on the radio since he'd become a devout listener. He'd done everything in his power to stay out of her way and had arranged his schedule so that they wouldn't run into each other before he left D.C. It had been pure torture.

He'd lain awake at nights, chastising himself for his stupidity. What was more than stupid was the deceit. He knew that's what hurt Summer the most. In an inane attempt to keep it from appearing too obvious that it was him making the calls, he'd still made several more even after they started seeing each other.

But when he found himself falling head over heels in love with her, he knew he couldn't keep from her what he'd done. Looking at it now, he almost wished he had. At least they'd still be together, and he wouldn't be sitting alone in some strange hotel room on Christmas Eve.

Diane had asked him, he thought reluctantly, to join them for Christmas dinner. But the spirit wasn't with him.

To say the station was in a bit of a turmoil after Tre's sudden departure was not to say enough. Leslie had her hands full trying to fill Tre's shoes and still put together the New Year's program at Blues Alley. Fortunately the DJs had done as Tre had instructed months earlier and had prepared their playlists.

However, Summer didn't care one way or the other. All she wanted was to get from one day to the next without either screaming at her walls or crying into her pillow.

With Leslie as the new, temporary program director, one of the other engineers, Charles, someone Summer hadn't worked with much, had taken Leslie's place.

He gave her the five-second countdown to her show. She adjusted her headphones and leaned toward the microphone.

"Welcome to my world," she crooned into the mike. "You're tuned into 'Round Midnight. I'm Summer Lane, offering up some late-night talk with a dash of soul. Tonight's topic, folks, is deceit. Why does it happen, and what to do about it when it does. I'll start taking your calls right after a solid favorite from Vesta Williams, 'Congratulations.' Listen to the words."

While Vesta belted out her signature song of pain and betrayal at the altar, Summer wondered if Tre was out there listening. As much as she'd tried to put their brief but passionate affair behind her, she couldn't. She missed him. Terribly.

Being a rational, educated woman with a doctorate in psychology, she could understand the outlandish reasons why people behaved in an inappropriate manner. She could put a clinical tag on just about any behavior someone exhibited. Her rational, educated doctor-self knew that Tre's behavior was a result of ego, insecurity, and a need to challenge her on a level that worked or was comfortable to him. Did that make him a bad person? No. It made him human.

But it was the irrational, emotional, nonclinical side of her that was affected. Summer Lane, the woman. That was the part she was struggling with.

"That was Vesta singing about deceit by someone she loved and thought loved her. Let me take tonight's first caller." She listened to Charles give her the name of the caller through the headset. "Karen, you're on the line. Talk to us."

"I've been betrayed before," Karen began. "And it was the worst thing that ever happened to me."

"Do you want to tell us about it?" Summer gently coaxed.

"The man I was engaged to for two years broke it off two weeks before our wedding because he was in love with his office manager."

"What did you do?"

"Cried for about a month." She laughed. "Didn't go out, except to work."

"What turned you around? You don't sound as if it's still affecting you."

"It does, sometimes. But then I started thinking, what if I'd married this man and found out later? He could have said anything and kept going on with me like nothing was happening. Now after I got over the hurt, I was glad he told me. I'm happily married, have two beautiful kids, and I can't even remember what had me interested in him in the first place."

Summer chuckled. "I'm glad things worked out for you, Karen. Take care. That's some sound advice from someone who's been there. But sometimes it's not that easy to let go of the hurt, especially if it's been inflicted by someone you love and trust. It takes time to rebuild trust again." *Do you hear me, Tre? Are you out there listening? I need time.*

"Our next caller is Gloria. Hey, Gloria, welcome."

"Hi," she said in a low voice.

"What do you want to share with us tonight?"

"That other caller made it sound easy to get over being deceived. It's not. Not for me—and I don't know what to do. A part of me just wants to kick him to the curb. Another part wants to take him back and work things out."

Was this woman telling her story, or what? "Forgiveness is a process, Gloria. It's not something that can happen overnight. Now, not trying to get into all the details, but has he tried to apologize, explain . . . ?"

"Yes, but I didn't want to hear it."

A pang knocked inside Summer's chest. "Before too much time passes, you need to give yourself a chance to hear what he has to say. It may help and it may not. But at least you'll know what you're dealing with. Right now you're operating on hurt and anger." *Don't I know it.* "I'm sorry, but that's all the time I have, Gloria. I hope everything works out for you."

"Thanks."

"Next up, we're going to hear from Nick and Val with 'Ain't No Mountain High Enough,' because if love is meant to be, you'll find a way over any obstacle."

The rest of the show went smoothly, the balance of the callers had their usual complaints about their significant others. But Summer's thoughts kept drifting back to Gloria and how similar their situations were. She needed to follow her own advice. Or at least she should have. Now it was too late.

Tre turned off the radio when Summer's show ended. How come it was so easy for her to give advice, but not take it, he wondered, just as the phone rang. He frowned. Unless the call was from another time zone, it was 2:00 A.M. in his neck of the woods.

"Hello?"

"Hi, it's me. Diane."

"Diane—" He listened to his sister's outlandish story, first with his mouth open in disbelief, and then he roared with laughter.

Chapter Seven

"**D**on't you want to come over, Summer? I'm having a few friends stopping by for some holiday cheer," Kia said, while pouring a cupful of rum into the bowl of eggnog.

"Believe me, I'm not in the mood for holiday or any other cheer, Kia. But thanks."

"So what are you going to do for Christmas, sit in your condo and feel sorry for yourself?"

"Yep. Anyway, I'm on the air tonight. I need to get my act together for that."

"Don't you ever take a break? You need a life outside of work."

"Keeps me busy."

"And your mind off Tre," Kia added.

Summer sighed. "Yes, that too."

"Haven't heard from him, huh?"

"No."

"Have you tried calling?"

"His number is disconnected. When he took that job he totally closed up shop in D.C."

"If you really wanted to talk to him, you'd find him. What about his sister? You said she was pretty cool."

"Yes, but I couldn't drop my troubles in her lap. I don't know her that well."

"All's fair in love and war, my sister. What you need to do is drop your pride and talk to his sister."

"Thank you, Dr. Ruth." She chuckled. "Who's the psychologist here, me or you?"

"Hey, I don't need a degree to figure out that you blew it sister-friend. And you're either too stubborn or too insecure to do anything about it."

As usual Kia was right. "Listen, I have to go, and I know you have things to do."

"If you change your mind, the shindig starts at six. Have a good show if I don't talk to you."

"Thanks."

"And Summer—"

"Yes?"

"Merry Christmas, girl."

"Same to you." Slowly she hung up the phone. "Yeah, Merry Christmas."

Gloria called the station again that night and every night into the week. Each time Gloria called, Summer tried to talk her through the heartbreak of her lost love and offer sage advice on how she could restore her self-confidence enough to bridge the communications gap that separated them.

And the more she talked with Gloria and saw the tiny steps toward progress that she was making, it made her think more and more of Tre: how much she missed him in her life, how if any relationship is ever going to work there needs to be room for forgiveness and a willingness to listen. Some space to accept honesty and find a way to deal with it. Something she had not allowed.

It was two days before New Year's Eve when Gloria called again.

"We have one of our regulars on the line tonight, who's been making a lot of progress in dealing with her feelings about her relationship. Hi, Gloria. Talk to us."

"Hi, Dr. Lane. I just wanted to say thanks for talking with me. It's been a great help. We're going to spend New Year's Eve together."

"That's wonderful, Gloria. I'm glad things are working out."

"It took talking to you to realize that he's really a good man who made a mistake. I could have lost him for good if I'd held on to the hurt any longer."

Like I did. The icy finger of regret poked her in the heart. "I'm glad for you, and I know our audience, who've been rooting for you, are happy too."

"Thanks. I just hope everyone can find that special someone in the new year."

So do I. "Good luck to you, Gloria. Here's a song for all of you out there who have struggled through breakups, and rejoiced in finding each other again, and ask the question, 'Is It Still Good To You?'"

As Summer listened to the words of the song, she realized she didn't want to wait any longer to find out. She needed to talk with Tre. She needed to hear his explanation. As soon as the holidays were over, she was going to stop by his sister Diane's house and beg her to tell her where Tre was. Maybe even intercede on her behalf if it came to that. She wouldn't intrude on Diane and her family now, but come January second, Summer was going to be the first face Diane saw darken her doorway.

On New Year's Eve morning, there was a brief staff meeting to go over the final details of their live broadcast.

"Leslie and Charles will be behind the scenes, setting

up, beginning this afternoon," Stan said. "I know this is going to be one of our best programming events ever. From what I understand and from the manager of Blues Alley, the place is sold out."

A cheer went up from the staff.

"Don't do any drinking before your spot." They groaned. Stan ignored them. "And be sure to get there at least an hour before your start time. Any questions?" Stan looked at each face. "Okay then." He clapped his palms together. "Good luck, and see you all tonight."

Everyone filed out, talking among themselves about the upcoming evening, who was going to wear what, and after-party hangout spots.

Summer lagged behind, the feeling of melancholia seeming to slow her step. She didn't want to walk into the new year alone. Not this time. Not again. She passed the receptionist's desk just as the phone rang.

"Dr. Lane—"

Summer turned and stopped.

"There's a call for you on line one."

"Thanks, Christine."

She crossed the short space to a small, circular table and the well worn fabric chair that served as the reception area and picked up the phone.

"Dr. Lane."

"Hello, Summer. It's Tre."

A rush of heat infused her body, and her heart began to palpitate. She swallowed. "Tre . . . hello."

"Please, before you hang up or cut me off, I'm coming into D.C. tonight. I was hoping we could meet, talk after your show . . . before, during. You tell me. Just don't say no, Summer."

Briefly she shut her eyes. For weeks she'd longed to hear these words, have this chance. Now was her moment.

"I've missed you, Summer. More than I can put into words," he said in a rush when she didn't respond. "And

I'm sorry. Sorry for hurting you, for deceiving you. I want to see you, if you're willing."

All the lectures she'd endured from Kia, the realizations she'd come to about herself in dealing with and counseling Gloria, stood in front of her, daring her to, for once, take her own advice.

"I'd like that," she whispered.

Tre released a silent sigh of relief. "I'll see you tonight. And, Summer—"

"Yes?"

"I'll tell you later . . . 'round midnight. Have a good show." He hung up before she could change her mind.

Summer held the phone for just a moment longer, savoring the fleeting remnants of their conversations, memorizing the intonations in his voice, the underlying laughter, and her spirit felt light as a breeze for the first time in weeks.

She'd see him tonight. *Tonight.* Joy bubbled through her veins. She hung up the phone. Hmmm, now she'd have to run out and buy something really special to wear. Her step was light as she strutted out the door, waving, smiling and even making short comments to the WKQR crew whom she passed. She was so filled with her own happiness, she didn't even notice the curious looks she received from the staff, who thought of her as "the reserved Dr. Lane."

Her thoughts scattered in a dozen directions at once— how would she feel when she saw him again, what would they say to each other, did he want her as much as she wanted him—then halted on Tre's vague statement, "I'll tell you later, 'round midnight." *Tell me what?*

Summer was a nervous wreck. She'd been in such a state she'd purchased three outfits, which all lay on the bed, staring up at her. She took a deep breath.

"This is ridiculous. You're acting like you're going out on your first date or something," she chastised herself.

She paced back and forth in front of the bed, eyeing the creations. Finally, she decided on the red velvet ankle skirt and matching waist-length jacket.

She hung the silver spaghetti-strap dress and the black cocktail dress in the closet just as the phone rang. Her heart thumped, and her first thought was that it was Tre, calling to say he'd changed his mind. Why was she so nervous? He was the one who had the explaining to do.

She crossed the room and picked up the phone on the bedside table. "Hello?"

"Hey, girl, it's Kia."

"Hi. You'll never guess what happened." Quickly she launched into the story of the surprise phone call, filling in all the details up to and including what she was wearing.

"Told you, you needed to give that brother a break." Kia chuckled.

Summer reclined against the pillows on her bed, crossing her legs Indian style. "You know something, Kia, I guess it took a major upset in my life for me to take a good look at it. I didn't realize until very recently just how difficult I'd made it for people to get close to me. All these years I've been so busy solving other people's troubles, I didn't want to look at mine. I've been afraid of commitment, of giving a part of myself to anyone, because of my parents. I never wanted to be in a relationship like theirs, so I made sure it never happened by not having *any*. Until I met Tre. I know he has a lot of explaining to do, but you know, Kia, it doesn't even matter."

"Well, I'll be damned. It must be a new year right around the corner, 'cause my girl has finally seen the light. Can I get an amen from the congregation!"

They cracked up laughing.

By degrees Summer sobered. "He said he had something to tell me, but he wouldn't say what it was. What do you think?"

"I think you need to stop worrying about it and enjoy every minute with your man tonight."

Summer blew out a breath and smiled. "You're right. And I intend to. Are you still coming tonight?"

"I wouldn't miss this for all the money in the world. See you tonight."

" 'Bye."

Chapter Eight

Summer arrived at Blues Alley at ten on the dot. Even at that hour the joint was jumping.

The management of the club had done a fabulous job of making the cozy nightspot festive. Mistletoe, poinsettias, and gold and silver garlands abounded. White candles set in crystal containers adorned each red-topped table. The dimmed overhead lighting gave the space an intimate feel.

Waiters scurried around filling food and drink requests, and Jordan Michaels was already onstage in the makeshift booth doing his thing with Toni Braxton's "Let Me Count the Ways."

Summer slowly wound her way around the circular tables, her eyes scanning all the faces, hoping to catch a glimpse of Tre. By the time she'd made a complete assessment of the main room and the two small ones beyond, she was sure he wasn't there.

"Dr. Lane."

She turned, peering over heads in the direction of Stan's voice. He began moving between the montage of sequined and tuxedoed bodies.

"You look . . . stunning," he said, looking up into her eyes.

She smiled down at him. "Thank you. You look nice too. I hardly recognized you."

He chuckled. "I know what you mean. Half the people here are my staff, and I don't recognize them. But you—you were always classy. That's what I liked about you from the beginning: brains, beauty, and a sense of style."

She smiled, slightly taken aback by his statement. "Thank you, Stan."

"Listen, Dr. Lane."

"Summer," she offered.

"Summer, I know I was pretty hard on you about that phone call business. I didn't give you enough credit to be able to handle it. Threatening your job wasn't the answer, and I apologize for that." He shrugged slightly. "I guess I panicked when I envisioned my number-one show going down the drain. I didn't think about you as a person, just a way to get ratings."

"Stan"—she reached out and touched his shoulder—"I understand. You're running a business."

Slowly he nodded. "I intend to start running my business with more of a human touch. Maybe if I had, Tre wouldn't have bailed out on me. I'd give anything to have him back. Best program director I've ever had."

She wanted to tell him that wasn't the reason Tre left, ease his mind. But she knew she couldn't, and the injustice of what Tre had done, not only to her, but to the people who depended on him, rekindled anew.

"That's not the reason why I left, Stan."

Summer looked over Stan's head and right into Tre's eyes. Stan turned and appeared as if he wanted to hug Tre. He made a move to, but didn't. Instead he stuck out his hand and heartily shook Tre's, his face beaming.

Summer's gaze stayed riveted on Tre's face. Suddenly

she couldn't remember why she was almost angry only moments ago.

"We'll talk about it later," Tre added, "and I may take you up on that offer."

"You don't even need to ask." He stepped closer, his business mind in full gear, wanting to close this deal on the spot. "There's nothing to discuss. If you want it, you got it." He put his arm around Tre's shoulder.

Tre nodded. "Glad to hear that, Stan, and I'd love to discuss it with you, but now I need to talk with this lady right here."

Stan looked from one to the other, nearly singed by the heat that bounced back and forth between the two of them. For a moment he frowned, perplexed. Then realization dawned.

"Well I'll be damned." He chuckled, shook his head in wonder, and walked away.

"How have you been, Tre?"

He stepped closer, wanting to touch her, afraid that if he did, he wouldn't be able to let go. "Better ... now." His eyes skipped across her face. "There's so much I need to tell you, Summer."

She reached out and took his hand, and he suddenly felt as if he'd been tossed a lifeline. "I promise to listen, if you promise to talk—really slow." A smile eased across her face as she stepped into his arms, just as Jordan Michaels played "Been Gone Too Long" by Anita Baker.

Ain't that the truth? Summer thought, resting her head against Tre's shoulder, closing her eyes as they swayed to the music.

"I was wrong, Summer," he whispered in her ear, almost as gentle as a love song. "I let my ego get the best of me because I couldn't stand the idea that you weren't paying me any attention."

She bit back a smile. "You certainly have a way of getting a girl's attention." She arched her neck and looked into his dark, searching eyes. "I had a lot of time to think, too, Tre. To take a look at myself—my life."

"What did you see?" His lips brushed her ear, and a shiver ran up her back.

"A woman who was too busy tending to other people's lives and not her own."

"But that's what makes you special, Summer—who you are. Don't change that."

"I won't change everything, just the parts that need work." She grinned.

He stepped back and gave her a long up and down look. "From what I remember and from everything I can see, everything's in working order."

She gave him a slow, steamy smile.

He took her back in his arms. "There's something else I need to tell you." He immediately felt her body stiffen in his arms.

"What is it?" she mumbled against his chest.

"The calls you were getting from Gloria—"

She stopped in midstep.

"It was Diane."

"Diane? Your sister Diane?"

"Yes. She came up with this brilliant idea. She figured it was a way to get us back together, maybe let you see my side. Believe me, I didn't put her up to it. I had nothing to do with it."

Summer tossed her head back and laughed. "Does this phone thing run in the family, like a damaged chromosome, or something?"

"I don't know from chromosomes," he said with a grin, "but I do know we have a unique way of getting our point across. Are you upset?"

"I should be, but I'm not. It worked. For all my book sense, I fell right into it. Thank Diane for me."

"What matters is that we're together. We took the long route to get here, but I think we have arrived, Dr. Lane."

"I do believe you're right." She touched her lips to his.

The music came to a close, but they still held each other, gliding to their own beat.

"You said you had something to tell me. Was that it— about Diane?"

"No. Be patient just a little while longer, babe."

She angled her neck and looked at him through squinted eyes. "You're up to something."

"Maybe." He took her hand and led her to a vacant table, and they sat down. He took her hands in his. "Summer, there was no other job. I left because I didn't want to deal with facing you, running into you and not being able to touch you, talk to you, make love to you. I thought moving away, leaving the station, would make things easier for both of us. I figured if I made a new start, I could put you behind me. I couldn't. You're the best thing that has happened to me."

"And I almost lost you, Tre. I wasn't ready for honesty with you or myself."

"And now?"

"I am."

"Then I'm going to be more honest with you than I've ever been." He took a breath. "I love you, Summer. From the bottom of my heart. I love you and—"

"Hey, girl."

Tre and Summer looked up to see Kia standing over them, a big grin plastered on her face. It was the first time Summer could ever remember not being happy to see her friend.

"Kia. Hi."

Kia's gaze remained fixed on Tre. "You must be Tre Holland." She stuck out her hand. "Glad we finally had a chance to meet. The crazy schedules you two keep are impossible to arrange a get-together. But Summer has told me so much about you, I feel like I already know you."

"Has she?" He looked at Summer, who shrugged slightly.

Kia pulled out a chair, inviting herself to sit down. "This place is packed," she said, ignoring the fact that she was interrupting.

"Didn't you bring a date, or a date bring you?" Summer asked, praying that tonight wouldn't be that one in a million time when Kia came out unescorted.

Kia adjusted the strap on her black crepe dress. "Of course. He's getting us drinks at the bar. But when I spotted you, I had to stop by and say hello, let you know I was here." She bobbed her head to the music, a reggae song selected by Danny D, who'd taken over the mike.

Summer checked her watch. She had about fifteen minutes before she went on, and she was jumping out of her skin wanting to know what Tre was in the middle of saying before they were so rudely interrupted. It looked as if Kia had no intention of leaving. She could kick Kia, but she'd save it for later. She pushed away from the table and stood. "I have to get ready for my set."

Tre stood up. "We'll finish this later. Promise."

She smiled and tried not to roll her eyes at Kia, who grinned innocently up at her.

"I'll see you both later." She turned and headed for the studio.

"Whew. I thought she'd never leave."

Tre frowned. "Excuse me?"

"I wanted to talk to you." She pulled her chair closer to the table. "Listen, Tre, I'll get right to the point. I know you don't know me, but since I feel like I know you and Summer is my best friend, I figure I have some rights."

Tre's eyebrows shot up in an arch. *She was a real character.*

"I'm going to tell you something about Summer, and then I'm gonna shut my mouth." She leaned closer. "Summer really cares about you. Maybe cares isn't the best choice of words, but I'll let her tell you."

"Thanks," he interjected.

"Anyway, she may seem like she has it all together, but underneath that perfect-looking exterior is someone with a heart of gold. She doesn't give many people the opportunity to see it, but it's there."

"I know."

"In other words, don't hurt her—again. It took a lot of talking and soul searching on her part for her to even consider being with you again."

The corner of his mouth curved up in a wry smile. "I have no intention of being the same fool twice."

Kia grinned. "Glad to hear it." She stood. So did he. "I'd better find my date. Happy New Year, Tre."

"Thanks. Same to you."

Kia was quickly swallowed up in the crowd, and Tre decided to wander around the room—see who he could see. If there was the remotest possibility that he would return to WKQR, he wanted to get a sense of what the general attitude was about his return. If he did take up Stan's offer, he promised himself he'd work twice as hard at building the station to number one.

"Ready in thirty seconds," Leslie said into Summer's headset.

Summer nodded and took a quick look at her playlist, but her thoughts kept shifting to Tre—and Kia. She knew her friend like a good recipe. Kia was over there bending Tre's ear. Telling him who knows what. Because she was good for that. She just hoped Kia didn't spill the beans about how she felt about Tre. She wanted to do that herself, and would have if Kia hadn't turned up like a bad penny. But, of course, whatever she was rattling on about she'd swear it was in her best interests.

Her theme song began to play, and the audience roared with pleasure.

"In five, four, three, two, one." Leslie gave Summer her cue.

"Welcome to my world, D.C. This is Summer Lane and it's just 'Round Midnight. We're coming to you live from the famous Blues Alley, and the house is packed tonight. As we get ready to move into the new year, a lot of us make resolutions, promises to ourselves and to others, which we hope to keep, but most of the time we don't. I want to hear from you tonight, as we approach the midnight hour. What are some of your hopes, goals, and desires. And tell our listening audience how you intend to make them come to pass and keep them. While you're out there thinking it over, we're going to hear from R. Kelly with his anthem for us all, 'I Believe I Can Fly'."

Summer slipped off the headphones and tried to spot Tre amid the glitz and glamour. He was nowhere to be seen. She sighed and settled back in her seat.

The engineering team had set up a six-line phone, and all the lights were flashing.

You'd think everyone would be out on the town tonight, she mused as Leslie cued her for her first caller.

"Who is it?" Summer asked.

"Didn't want to give their name."

Summer's stomach began to flutter. "You're on the air, live at Blues Alley. What resolution are you going to make, and how are you going to keep it?"

"First I need to tell the woman in my life something I should have told her a long time ago."

Summer's heart began to thunder and her body suddenly flushed with heat. Her eyes darted around the room. *Tre*.

She swallowed. "I hope it's not R-rated," she said, battling to calm her nerves, trying to sound light and unaffected by what was transpiring.

"I can't imagine saying I love you to someone who means the world to you could be R-rated. Because I do love you, Summer Lane. And my resolution for this year and every year that I breathe is to love you more every day and keep you happy."

The air stuck in her throat. She could barely swallow, and the crowd at Blues Alley was going wild, cheering and jumping up and down. She turned to Leslie, who was grinning like a fool.

"Don't you want to know how I'm going to make that happen, Dr. Lane?"

Leslie was nodding her head frantically. And the crowd was screaming, "Yes!"

Summer swallowed. "Yes," she said in a voice she didn't recognize.

"I'm making a commitment here and now to you and to everyone who's listening, that I'm going to work on us, each and every day. Nothing will be more important than me and you. I promise you that, Summer."

She fought back tears and lost the battle.

Leslie was cueing her to cut to the next song.

Shaking off her shock, Summer spoke with a choked voice into the mike. "There's something I need to say to this very special caller, folks, with an oldie but goodie from Marvin and Tammi, 'Ain't Nothing like the Real Thing.' And that's going to take us into the New Year."

With trembling fingers she snatched up the phone, cutting off the conversation from the listening audience.

"Tre?" Her voice shook.

"Why don't you meet me on the dance floor. You have about two minutes to midnight."

She took a breath, trying to still her heart, and looked at Leslie then the flashing lights on the phone. She picked up her headset. "Les, I—just keep playing the music."

"You go, girl." Leslie gave her a thumb's-up.

Summer pulled off the headset and rushed out of the booth. Squeezing by revelers who all wanted to stop and congratulate her, she smiled her thanks, tried not to be rude, and pressed on, winding her way around bodies, tables, and rearranged chairs. She peered over heads, try-ing to spot Tre before the stroke of midnight. And all of a sudden there he was, almost as if the waters had parted.

His smile greeted her, leading her to him like a beacon in the night. Then she was in his arms again, dancing to the closing notes of "Through the Fire" by Chaka Khan.

"I meant everything I said on the radio, Summer."

"I know," she whispered, looking into his eyes. "I feel the same way."

"I'm going to talk to Stan about coming back to the station."

She grinned. "He won't be able to get you back fast enough."

His expression grew serious as the noise level escalated with the twenty-second countdown to the new year.

"You think he'd have a problem with a married couple working at the station?"

She froze. Her mouth opened, then closed.

"Tre?"

"Five, four, three . . ."

"Marry me, Summer."

"Two, one . . ."

"Yes!"

"Happy New Year!" The room seemed to explode with light, horns, uncorked champagne, and screaming and stomping partiers.

Tre beamed, grabbed her around the waist, and spun her around. "Tell me again," he shouted.

"Yes, Tre Holland, I'll marry you!" She tossed her head back and laughed, and she'd swear all the clapping and shouting was in celebration of her and Tre.

"Happy New Year, baby."

"And to many more," she whispered a moment before his lips touched down on hers.

As she gave herself up to the pleasure of his kiss, a

fleeting thought passed through her head. *Absolutely no phones in the house.*

Tick-tock!

That pesky biological clock was going to get slowed down after all.

ABOUT THE AUTHORS

FRANCIS RAY, the bestselling author of FOR-EVER YOURS and UNDENIABLE, is a frequent speaker at writing workshops and a member of Women Writers of Color and Romance Writers of America. A native Texan, she lives with her husband and daughter in Dallas.

SHIRLEY HAILSTOCK, a bestselling, award-winning novelist, has been writing for more than ten years. She is on the board of Romance Writers of America and is a member of Women Writers of Color. She lives in New Jersey with her family.

DONNA HILL is a multipublished author of African-American romance novels which have garnered her rave reviews and legions of devoted fans. She has readings and book sign-ings at sites across the country and lives in New York with her family.

More Arabesque Romances by
Donna Hill

SIZZLING ROMANCE BY
Rochelle Alers

__HIDEAWAY	1-58314-179-0	**$5.99**US/**$7.99**CAN
__PRIVATE PASSIONS	1-58314-151-0	**$5.99**US/**$7.99**CAN
__JUST BEFORE DAWN	1-58314-103-0	**$5.99**US/**$7.99**CAN
__HARVEST MOON	1-58314-056-5	**$4.99**US/**$6.99**CAN
__SUMMER MAGIC	1-58314-012-3	**$4.99**US/**$6.50**CAN
__HAPPILY EVER AFTER	0-7860-0064-3	**$4.99**US/**$6.99**CAN
__HEAVEN SENT	0-7860-0530-0	**$4.99**US/**$6.50**CAN
__HOMECOMING	1-58314-271-1	**$6.99**US/**$9.99**CAN
__RENEGADE	1-58314-272-X	**$6.99**US/**$9.99**CAN
__NO COMPROMISE	1-58314-270-3	**$6.99**US/**$9.99**CAN
__VOWS	0-7860-0463-0	**$4.99**US/**$6.50**CAN

Available Wherever Books Are Sold!

Visit our website at **www.arabesque.com.**

Put a Little Romance in Your Life With
Louré Bussey

The Arabesque At Your Service Series

Four superb romances with engaging characters and dynamic story lines featuring heroes whose destiny is intertwined with women of equal courage who confront their passionate—and unpredictable—futures.